The Perspectives

Sonny Gast

Published by Sonny Gast, 2022.

Dedicated to those that have become memory; that have supported me and betrayed me.

I hope you can sense the sarcasm.

S.G.

I traveled thro' a Land of Men.
A Land of Men and Women too,
And heard & saw such dreadful things
As cold Earth wanderers never knew.

. . . .

William Blake, "The Mental Traveller"

Part 1

1.

CLOSE TO THE DOWNTOWN centre of homely nightlife, rows of bright ethnic restaurants, and the rising towers of a casino that has attracted in its shadows high-priced hotels and international gamblers, the Detroit River flows between two borders.

Near the river, between a simple art museum and college campus, sits a bus station with a long arching roof, blue and metallic, and with tall windowed sides mirroring the parked silver busses.

Throughout the road across the station are potholes of water dimpling to the rain and a shine reflects the streetlights in long beams of red and green. As the cars pass, I hear their wet tires flap against the asphalt, the puddles swelling out in rippling wings over the curb.

A woman walks by a wall of panelled glass within which can be seen the dark forms of water slides. An indoor waterpark. She waits for the cars to pass. Then her feet step as if sticky to the ground, her arms locked over her chest, the black hair swinging heavy out of her sweater hoodie. Her slim figure passes the parked busses, the fixed windowpane. Under an overhang she pulls a cigarette pack from her purse. The smoke masses about her head like a warping of steel.

I imagine her pointing to clouds hanging below the skyline, the sun like a drop of white paint. Pregnant with rain, she would say. If I had a cigarette I would blow the smoke so as not to hit her. She would think, He's kind.

Sometimes there is no generic mark of a facial feature nor vocal tone. There is something like an imperceptible smell. Or some may call it an energy but the word is too mechanical. Smell captures best of what living beings do.

There are times where the physical marks are lying. The person is simply playing. But they're not playing with you because that would show interest. They are playing the scene, the context in which the interaction is taking place.

If I were smoking with her I would start with small talk which can be interesting if you're good at it. It does not have to serve as preparation for deeper discussion. There are cultures where deeper talk happens only due to tragedies or conflict or confessions.

If she continues, I will know of her interest. It's hard to continue small talk if you're not interested.

She walks through the first double doors and lifts up her hood and sweeps the beads off her arms. She shakes the collar and the beads jump and sprinkle to the mats. She walks through the second set of double doors and sits in a hard and bolted plastic chair. She looks precisely at her glossy boots. Her ringed fingers, minimalist makeup on lip and brow. She is not ugly but I will have to struggle with her attractiveness. I imagine her pale face smiling so slightly at me. That would prompt me to smile back.

Later in the window is a young man. He wears dark sunglasses which press on his skull like goggles. He walks a long time. As if scrubbing the floor with his shoes. He is bearded and thin. His oversized and rumpled windbreaker shiny with rain and his backpack unevenly hangs off his back. He stares across the seats with the ticket sticking out his hand. He stands blinking.

If he were to talk to me I would listen and ask questions to see if he truly knows what he is talking about. I know that people like answering questions concerning things that matter to them.

He shuffles to the backdoors. Then I see him shuffling wayward in the sidewalk. And then gone.

Soon families and couples and single people with suitcases and big backpacks enter the station. I see a woman wearing a soft grey dress. Her breasts jiggle like two runny eggs as she walks.

I grab my backpack by the arm straps and walk to the line. People are on their phones or standing and watching the terminal. A security guard has his thumbs looped in the straps of his vest, walking slow and sure under the terminal screens.

A Greyhound bus winks its headlights. The airbrakes burst. The driver steps out with a clipboard. People board the bus and shove their luggage in its storage trunks. An old couple explains to the driver. The elder man's neck veins are pounding with blood, his face red. The woman holds printed copies of the ticket, staring. He tells them that their bus isn't the bus he's driving, then he steps between them. They watch the driver accept passengers.

"Excuse me," says the wife to his back.

"I told you, you are on a different bus," he says over his shoulder. "I can't help you."

"Listen. So rude. I never experienced. Bad day? I am so sorry. You make our day bad too. You need to know." The husband watches with absence, the blood depleted.

"Last time we use your bus," she says. "Never again."

I present my ticket and he searches the clipboard. "Go on up." Through the windows I see them stand behind him and chatter to each other and study the lot, peering and squinting, like birds.

There are three seats in the rear wall and I sit in the one by the window, away from the washroom. The seat is firm and polyester, an aged design. I can sense its packed dust in my nose.

The last bus trip I boarded was in Vietnam. A year ago. The bus was not a normal one. It was called a sleeper bus because the seats reclined into beds. It was a fourteen-hour trip from Hanoi to Hue in central Vietnam. There were not many people on the bus. I was alone in the back, in a low bunk. I wanted a top bunk because there was too much room in the back for the low bunks. When the bus turned, I rocked in the bunk.

For the first few hours I did not sleep. I looked out at the window to the night, the motorcycles and the crowds eating in the street. The chaotic lacings of telephone wires blended into the sky. The shop lights glowed bright and colourful and energizing, and all seemed inorganic, the slim alleyways darkly polluted and the road lethal and loud with motorbike traffic.

In a low bunk across from me was a girl who looked back curiously. She had amber-dyed hair and she wore large, round glasses. Red overalls and Nike pumps. At a rest stop she bought a block of glazed rice cake. We ate the rice cake together and she told me she was from Da Nang, which is close to Hue.

"Visit Da Nang," she said. "Please, if you do, I'll bring you the best food. I ride bike."

"You'll show me around on your motorbike?"

"Yes, on motorbike."

She was a small girl who stared into my eyes seriously. She laughed at what I said and it felt stupid because I wasn't funny. We talked in the late hours of the night when the time goes by so quick. I can't remember the conversation.

She gave me her phone number and I impulsively thanked her as if we had not broken the wall that separates two strangers. If that wall had not been broken at that time then there was never a force to break it. But that didn't matter because she didn't make it matter. She got off at a stop near Da Nang and the bus continued to Hue.

When I woke I felt hungover. Outside I saw a tall red brick wall covering the opposite side of the street. Trees speared out the top and hung bushy branches down the wall. In the other side there were suitcases laying on a wide section of concrete ridged with overgrown weeds and bending trees. There was trash clumped under bushes. Some locals stood in the hot dawning sun or searched for luggage or sat on plastic stools, smoking. It seemed only locals took sleeper buses.

One man sat at the driver's seat. I thought he was the driver. He escorted me out and asked about my luggage and I pointed to it. He lifted my hiking backpack up to his shoulders and jogged to a man sitting at a plastic table.

There was another plastic chair by the sitting man. He was fatter than normal and bald and his skin was very brown. He had a big and golden watch on his wrist and a gold-plated canine in his mouth. His name was Vin and he asked me to sit with him.

"Where you from?" asked Vin.

"Canada."

He smiled at this. The other man with my backpack nodded and smiled. He sat my backpack down.

Then I explained to Vin that Canada is in North America, not in the Netherlands, as he thought. He placed a tattered notebook in front of me and flipped through the pages. It contained testimonials of his talent as a tour guide. I told him I wasn't interested and he took out his phone and showed me pictures of smiling tourists on motorbikes. He said the tour would take two days and we would be going to Da Nang. We'd be staying at a very nice hotel for the night. He made the drinking motion with his hand and said, "Bia, huh. Beer. Drinking," and he laughed.

"How much?" I asked. I was not interested.

He told me the price which was very expensive and he said the economy was bad and tourism is different now.

"You know I just got off the bus. I'm tired. Need time to think."

He snatched the notebook and slid it into his bag. "Okay. We go now. To office. I take you. For free." He made the vroom vroom motion with his fist. "Where is your hotel?"

I told him. It was across from his office. It was hard to get out of then. I thought I'd be able to dissuade him at his office. But during the ride I considered that this was a beautiful country. I come from a great country with too many advantages and this is a jackpot for him who is disadvantaged, I told myself.

We passed rice fields, those green and furrowed hillocks. Beyond us was all rural. Shack houses and locals wearing conical leaf hats and fields of bright cat grass crooked to the sun. A broken cart like the rustic bones of some bull beast. The motorbikes passing and passing.

He told me about Hue too. "Boring," he said. "You see two museums and leave. You don't stay more two day. No party here, the people quiet. Like sleep."

We crossed a one-way bridge above a narrow stream that ran endless through forest and we turned into a high embankment road that slanted down to a grey river. We went through a massive stone gate and into the city. The roads were multilane and clear and no kin to the tight-packed disorder of Hanoi.

The street reminded me of what I imagined to be backcountry streets in Hawaii. A very tropical and hand-built look. There were motorbikes parked along the entrance and Vin gave me a lesson on their mechanics. He said he'll show me how to ride tomorrow morning. I paid for the trip and then walked out to my hostel across the street.

I slept all morning and the afternoon. In the evening I met a girl at a bar. She was under five foot and enjoyed drinking beer. She pretended to be a newswoman asking me questions like if I would secretly live in the Cu Chi tunnels or why my nose was so big. From her I learned that girls who drink beer love to drink in general. Later we went to a hostel. A worker was sleeping on a mattress in the lobby. I knocked on the glass door and he sprung up instantly. He charged me one night for a private room. He mentioned free breakfast and amenities and fees, as he was trained to do, while holding his laughter slyly.

Next morning I went to the office two hours late for my trip. There was a tiny woman at the front desk and she asked me multiple times why I hadn't shown and I told her, "I want a refund." She called Vin. He arrived on his motorbike about ten minutes after. He was afraid to look me in the eyes. "Damn," he said. "Damn." He explained the allocation of my funds and he hugged me and told me the money is un-refundable.

"It's my fault," I told him. "I'm the one that changed my mind."

The previous day I had told a hostel worker about the trip. The worker was named Troy and he'd parade a chihuahua around the lobby. I told him that my money was gone. He demanded we go to get it back. I told him I deserved to lose it. He said, "Bullshit."

"Please no trouble," I said.

There were two travellers sitting at a table and paying attention to us. Troy told them, "He lost two-hundred bucks in a fucking scam."

"Woah," said one. He was so shocked. "What happened?"

"Fucking thieves scam him for bike trip. I do the same trip for eighty bucks. I know these thieves. They always scam people. I want to destroy their business for a long time."

The travellers stared wildly. I frowned. "Sucks," another said. They were both so shocked. They were enthralled in the details of it.

"They're not giving your money back or what?"

"No, they're not. Said there's no refund."

"Come on, let's go," said Troy.

We walked back to the office and Troy and Vin and the tiny women discussed in Vietnamese about my money. No one looked each other in the eyes.

Vin withdrew dong out his pocket and counted and handed me it. They continued discussing and I counted the money several times. Troy asked me how much it was and I told him, "Not enough." I had no idea how much it was. The denominations were in the hundred-thousandths. I was nervous.

"Later I give you," said Vin. His voice was warped like on an old gramophone. "I come to you later."

"He come later," Troy told me.

Vin never came with the rest. I wanted to forget. I wanted to avoid Troy and his dog in the lobby because he'd remind me.

After two more days in Hue I visited Da Nang. I took a regular bus since the trip was not long. I stayed in a hostel with bunks bored into an expansive and dark grey stone wall. The place was quiet and cool. The bunks were spacious, set in rows, with the openings curtained and circular. Metal ladders were fixed up the sides to reach the higher bunks. It all looked like a primitive mortuary. The first day in there I texted her to pick me up.

She walked in the lobby which was high-ceilinged, cool and dark, with a square bar in the middle. There were many British tourists smoking cigarettes and drinking. They didn't seem tanned but rusted from the sun and they mostly dressed in buttoned shirts and shorts, the women in blouses and hot-pants.

She wore an open-face polycarbonate helmet and she handed me one. On the motorbike I wrapped my arms around her waist. I felt funny both in an amusing and shameful way. While driving she was unresponsive to my talking. The bike was clumsy for her to maneuver.

We visited a beach. The sand was cream coloured. Far in the blue water there were mountains that surfaced dimly out of the mist. The shore was like a country. People were walking and playing volleyball and laying on the soft sand but very few were in the water.

Then we drove to a district of fast food where I ate fishcake soup with her. I ruined my shirt with the soup.

"You eat so fast," she said. "Do you like it?"

"I do."

"Not a lot like fish soup."

"Well, I love it."

"I'm glad," she said. She was very happy.

Later we crossed a bridge festooned with rainbowed bars of light. It was mythical and bold in the night, the river below was another sky darker and wavering like a mass of living fibres. The soup was still hot in my gut and I was nauseous with the speed of the motorbike.

Vendors sold skewers of pork and chicken and stockpots of fried noodles and rice. The air was spiced, greasy with the smoke of meat. She handed me a stack of crispy pancakes dotted with tiny baked shrimp.

It was oily with little flavour other than salt. We licked ice cream from paper cups. She started giggling and I asked what's funny. She said she never rode a stranger on her motorbike before.

We went up the stairs of a bridge that was crowded with people. The bridge was blocked from traffic and people were rushing in from the street and packing themselves closer to a huge statue of a dragon. A jet of water blasted out the dragon's mouth and hit us like rain-shower. She fled to my back, burrowing, as the blast sprinkled my face and chest.

Now we depart the station.

A black woman is sat next to me. She has a farther open seat and she chose the one next to me. She has round cheeks that push into her small eyes. Her lips are lightly puckered.

I look down to the cars and the drivers inside. Rain is pouring down the window and rain is pattering on the top panels. The neighbourhoods are twins of a modest blueprint, suggesting little variation in social class, a look of respectable suburbia.

There is a pouch behind every seat and the black woman wriggles a coffee cup in its elastic band. Soon we merge on a highway.

"I'm sorry do you got a charger?" she asks.

"I do."

"I don't think there are any ports?"

I look in the floor. "There's not but I got a portable charger."

I hand her the charger.

"Oh, wow," she says. "I'm so glad to sit next to you." She laughs in two bursts. Like a squeaky toy.

"I'm surprised I can talk to you," she says. "I'm so nervous but I need a charger." It's as if someone is squeezing her.

Outside there are vast crop fields and farmhouses timeworn and rotten. Stables where horses stand like stone, some craning their necks down bundles of wheat. The polka-dotted cows look like broad canvases. The dripping tall grass bows from the rain-beads and an assembly of giant wind turbines spins slowly.

The woman smells like fresh lavender detergent. The hard nubs of her dreadlocks press into my shoulder. I ask her, "Where you going?"

"Toronto. You?"

"I'm going to Montreal."

"It's super nice. I went with friends I regret now because they're not my friends anymore and they spoiled it for me. White girls if you know the type. I don't know French too. If you know French you'll be good. I was confused lots."

"I'm learning French. Hoping to improve it there," I say. "Why were you in Windsor?"

"Work," she says. "I dance."

"You're a dancer?"

"Yep."

"There's no dancing in Toronto?"

"There is but I got scheduled in Windsor. Also got a friend to room with. No other reason to be in Windsor."

I look to the road. Borders of pale water steeped along the sides of an underpass. The tunnel sends all to a noisy dark and then back again.

"You're nervous to talk to me and you're a dancer," I say to the window.

"I know, right? Weed helps with my anxiety. I get high as fuck."

"As fuck, huh."

"As fuck."

"You smoke a lot then?"

"Unfortunately or fortunately can't work with no weed."

"Never been a fan. I'm very sensitive."

"Well, I got a lot of shit myself. Helps my depression too."

Then, "You like barn animals?"

Her shoulders jerk.

"They're great, huh?"

"Cows," she says. "I like cows."

I notice the cup which she hasn't touched.

"You ever tipped cows?"

She rolls her head to me. The dark eyes which if focused into reveal a rich burgundy. The black pupil is like discovering a secret. "Have you?"

"No. Have you ever milked cows?"

"I hate cows. I like pigs."

"Excuse me," she says. She removes her shoes. Her white socks are stained grey at the bottom. She tucks her feet under her right buttocks in a feline fashion.

"Can you tell me what kind of dancing you do?"

"The adult kind."

"What does that mean?"

"I'm an adult entertainer."

"Do you like doing it?"

"Pays me, right?"

"But do you like doing it?"

"It can be fun. Also shit." Then in a freakish voice she says, "You gotta make the men feel manly."

"Is that how you talk to them?"

"How I reel them in."

"This is interesting."

"I know, right?"

"I'm interested in the life of a stripper," I emphasize.

"You've never been to a club," she tells me. I smell cream and coffee in her breath.

"You know, huh?"

"I'm not being offensive," she says. "It's good I can tell."

The bus parks in a station in London, Ontario. She stands and elongates her lean torso and presses her palms on her mid-back, crack, and then walks away. She comes back and sits and screws earbuds into her ears. Her warmth is causing my side to sweat and there is a feeling of carbonation rising in my spine.

The diesel engine pops until reaching a steady rumble. The bus goes backward and then forward to turn into the street. Between my feet is a drawstring bag carrying a book and protein bars. I don't remember what the book is. A man walks to the back. The washroom door folds open like an accordion. The flush is very loud. Then he walks out grabbing the rails at the top to his seat.

We pass through the city streets slowly due to traffic. The stores have colours washed-out and cracked in spindly forms. The office buildings look abandoned.

I peek at her. Her neck is long and toned and flexing, the thick dreadlock settled limp and curved behind. Women have beautiful necks and her neck is a wonder of form and flesh. I ask her a question and she unscrews an earbud.

"Candy Lyons," she says.

"Candy Lyons."

"Yep."

"That shouldn't be a stage name but a regular name."

"Thank you. I'm proud of it."

"Oh, Candy Lyons, are you going to finish that coffee?"

She pulls the cup out of the band. She sips it and then flicks it back on the band. "No good when it's cold."

"What was it?"

"The coffee?"

"Yeah."

"Double double."

"Can I?"

She nods and I grab the cup. It is a sweet cream taste, not a trace of coffee.

We get on the highway and she tells me about her time in Montreal and how she has had to cut contact with many friends due to not being able to trust them. I want to tell her that if she is constantly seeking trustworthiness in people then she is living too recklessly to be worth any.

I tell her I have no plans in Montreal. I don't like making plans because it feels like I get too familiar with the place, which ruins it. I ask if Montreal has good strip clubs and she says she never went to them but they're considered to be the best in Canada.

Later on the skyscrapers stand in the distance, the highway bends up to be elevated among ramps that curve in and out and loop under columns and wind along smooth and glassed complexes. The street we drive into is narrow and busy. We pass a long alleyway where thick and white smoke lingers out of airshafts and the ground is buckled through the centre yet level with pools like finely placed mirrors. There are people walking or waiting at the intersections, people under a raised building which seems balanced on a square peg. Soon we enter the parking area of a station.

I type my number into her phone.

"Also, my real name is Melody," she says.

"I'm Sonny."

"Sonny like the sun?"

"Yes, like the sun."

Then I wait in the bus for a long time. I finish her cold coffee and then walk to the front to throw it in the bin. I count five people in the bus.

Several enter along with a new driver. A man sits one seat away from me. He has tattooed arms and tiny discs in his earlobes. Next to me sits a tall and blond young man wearing a denim jacket stitched with the logo of thrash bands. "Hey," he says. "Where you guys going?"

The tattooed man says, "Airport."

I say, "Montreal."

"Why're you going there?"

"For fun."

"That's all the reason you need." Then he turns to the tattooed man. "I'm going to Pearson." Then he faces forward, confident. "Got an acting gig in BC. Found out like five hours ago."

"You're acting in a movie?" the man asks.

"A Netflix show. The wild part is that I've been auditioning for two weeks." He tells us about him attending an acting school. He says he never thought anything would happen. He claims it's a once in a lifetime opportunity.

"So, you're really into film?" I ask him.

"Hell yeah, I'm a film lover."

"But do you like movies?" the tattooed one asks.

"Hell yeah."

"What's your favourite flick?"

"The Deer Hunter. Robert DeNiro."

"Now The Deer Hunter is a good film but a bad movie and an even worser flick."

"Is DeNiro your favourite?" I ask him.

"I'd say so for the male actors," he says. "Don't start me on the female actors."

Then he asks me, "Do you want a chocolate bar?"

"No thanks."

He unzips the backpack between his legs. "Got all these chocolate bars. You sure?"

"Yeah. Thanks though."

He chews on one. "So wild," he says. He asks the other if he wants a bar. He scrunches the wrapper in his backpack.

"Bro," I say. "A girl was sitting where you're at. She told me she was a stripper. She was like this," I wave my hand a curvy shape, "I got her number."

"Things are looking up, eh?"

"Yeah, they are."

Then he asks, "Wanna listen to music?" He fingers for earbuds. The tattooed man already has headphones on.

"Okay." I put the earbud in my right ear. He plays rap music and some hard rock.

"You like it?"

"Yeah."

"Not a very enthusiastic *yeah*." He switches playlists.

I ask him if he wants me to play a song and he hands me his phone. I play a death metal song. "Fuck yeah, dude," he says. It sounds like pure noise. It itches the ear.

The bus parks in the airport.

"Okay dude, I'm going to need that back." I pop it out.

"Nice meeting you gents. I'll tell you a nautical joke before I head on. I've grown up on boats my whole life. There's a lot of jokes to that lifestyle and this one's stuck with me. A new deckhand asks a captain of what there's to do to pass some time. The captain says go down the cabin at midnight, there's one barrel with a hole in its side you can't miss. Just stick her in and you'll pass the time all right. The deckhand goes down and sticks it. The next day he says to the captain that was the best I ever got. The captain says it was the best he's ever got too."

We all laugh. "Good luck," I tell the young actor.

He extends his fist to me. "Take care, dude."

They leave. I sleep for a short time. The bus parks.

In this station there is a custodian propping caution signs and talking loudly on his phone. An older man asks me what time a specific bus will come and I point to a blocky television with all the times and he pats me on the shoulder enthusiastically.

When the bus comes I am the third in line. The driver talks to me in Québécois French and I nod mindlessly and then walk to the backseat.

• • • •

WE PASS DARK GREEN parks, hills and dips that form waves through the open grass. Yellow and white trees with the crowns like many orchids, dark poplars. Ferns stretch throughout the sidewalk, darkly toothed under shade, the rowed and trimmed hedges like so many prickly blocks where one can lay or stand. Gothic fences flash their twisting black iron still defined against the dark. Even more gothic the buildings, a church, the museums. The chateaus bone-white and columnated. Sharp geometries of the colonial era. Greasy-glassed lanterns are hung on chains or screwed on decorative posts. The street signs and advertisements are exclusively in French. The streets are lean and paved or cobbled in antiqued stone. Bikers whiz by the curb, their backs highlighted neon and their legs pumping in liquid speed. They are like electrized shuttles in their designated lanes.

Inside the bus station there is a long hall connected to many terminals. Across the terminals are eateries and tourist shops. I wait in the line of a Tim Hortons. In front of me is a woman with an ass like a saucer, the cellulite casting round shadows across blue spandex.

Soon the girl at the counter asks me and I say, "Uh."

She stares with eyes like billiard balls.

"Medium coffee with one cream."

"No sugar?"

"No sugar."

I go to sit with my coffee and stare at the schedules and the people walking with their luggage rolling on the linoleum. I can walk or ride to the hostel. But why ride when I can walk? I walk and enjoy both easy and hard paths, busy or empty, long or short.

When in Vietnam I walked everywhere. There were men leaning on motorbikes hollering at me to take rides with them and I learned in Vietnamese to tell them that I preferred walking.

While walking the heat and pollution made me dizzy. There was always a burn like a fragment of lighting trapped in my gut. But savagely I walked and ate. There's a higher price to pay. I'd think about higher prices as if there was a rule which necessitated them. Bad will come and you can't stop it like you can't gravity. But whatever little bad came was manageable.

In my dreams I saw the images of what I'd seen on my walks.

One image is Hoan Kiem lake in Hanoi.

The lake was guarded by tall oak trees that shaded a path running along the entire perimeter. During the day the water was green and smooth, at night, black yet yellow crested with the surrounding lights of shops and restaurants. In the open vastness of it, in a corner cupped by the giant trees, there was a small tower resting on a plot of bushy grass. It had four levels. The bottom two had arched entries opening to the other side. The top was roofed and adorned with what looked like fish tails wriggling out the four corners. Far across from this tower was a red bridge between the path and a little island hidden by round and green canopies.

Around the lake, before the shaded path, was a large road that at times was blocked for events and festivals. Motorbikes entered and scattered and sped across the road's wide-ranging land and then slow and cluster into the congested vein of some district.

I walk out the station.

The buildings are muted to be more ancient, the sinewy clouds morphing to colours of bluing milk. The reticent moon lodged in the backdrop like a cut stone.

I can smell the beer being drank in the patios. Two people sit cross-legged against a stained wall. They are filthy and smoking and talking in Québécois. I see backpackers, a man wearing a shirt saying *Tabarnak!* A church with metal spires salient in the starred dark.

I wait and cross an intersection.

The city releases into narrow corridors, the clogged backstreets of an other-Europe. Cats sidling the corners and on steps with orange eyes watching the European night, these tourists and few locals. Groups well-dressed smoke cigarettes outside pubs, talking drunk, nightly dramas, French and English. These people will largely have formulaic behaviours and decision-making afforded to them by a strong and proud culture like this. And it's good and assuring and useful for a traveler to have available a heuristic, which a culture provides, on how to deal with the people. Surely a traveler can reveal to them the best aspects of their culture.

My phone directs me to a narrow four-story apartment. There is a scrawny attendant at the desk facing a living room of couches.

"J'ai reservation," I tell him, politely.

"Yes. Name?"

I tell him my name and details. "Okay, okay," he says. He types in a laptop. It's the only thing on the desk. I look at the couches and a coffee table with magazines and a paperback. A shoe rack by the entrance doors, stinking with shoes. He asks for my ID.

"Yes," he says. "Two weeks?"

"Two, yeah."

"Vacation?"

"Yeah, enjoying myself."

"Sounds great." He smiles with a mouth full of very tiny teeth.

"I'd like to learn French here too."

"Super easy to pick up."

He tells me that I have to buy a lock.

"Do I have to buy a lock?"

"I'd advise you do for the locker or you can't use the locker."

"I can't use the locker?"

"Without the lock."

"You sell the lock?"

"Yes. We sell the lock for five dollars."

"Okay, I'll buy one lock."

Later he hands me a strip of paper with the key-code of the actual hostel.

"What's this?" I point to the ground.

"This is the reception, dining hall, storage, and rec room. Free breakfast everyday. The sleeping rooms is in another building. Do you require the storage?"

"No."

We walk out. We pass an underground restaurant. The windows show people dining as if in a cavern. The hostel is next to the restaurant. He enters the code in the keypad and then we go up the stairs to the third floor.

The room has three two-bed bunkbeds on each sidewall. It's dark even with the two ceiling lights turned on.

"Wait," I say. "Is that the locker?" In the middle there are metal panels screwed together in a box shape.

"Yes, that's the locker."

"Okay. Thank you."

"You're very welcome."

I look into a standing mirror, my wanderer's body. I do not check but I know no one else is in the room.

The mattress is firm and thin. A lamp and fan. Each bunk totally visible. I prop the blanket on the rails to make a curtain.

· · · ·

ON THE SAINT LAURENT boulevard is a bridge leading to the arched and medieval gates of Chinatown.

In the night the lights trail a magma of spectral colour through the street. The knife-cut logograms of Mandarin so bold as to brand an afterimage. The spice-shops are compacted among pharmacies and appliance stores. In their closed darkness the nightmare contours of ribbed sea cucumber and mushrooms all dried and cockled.

There are Asian men watching the road and smoking, middle-aged and shop-worn men, young and absent men, some chatting outside hot-pots and dumpling houses, they enter and drink and eat combo meals and leave.

Some of the women drink bubble tea and sit on painted picnic tables, their phones in their powdered faces. They're mostly in a crowd where they walk uncaring or on guard, dressed in skirts or jeans or tight pants. They always have dark eyes that gift no glance.

The Japanese transform themselves with coloured powders. So do Koreans. All their cultures idolize the pale and smooth. Some of them fashion by whatever method Caucasian eyes, subverting their Asian aspect. Vietnamese women mostly borrow standards from an idealized West. The dark-skinned, Filipinas and pure Thai, so dissimilar but same same the stock of sun-lovers and outdoor labourers, flash their almond eyes eternally.

I walk through an outdoor gallery of cartooned or picturesque faces, pastoral landscapes mixing into an industrial earth, wolves and bears and birds posing in ancestral fantasy, the spray can brands of local gangs and artists. Gallons of paint are spread across one-inch plywood, high boards, that craft a passage into a plaza of food and drink. Advertisements for dances and local movies and exhibitions glued to the boards and wrapped around street poles.

There are small medical-looking shops with just a counter serving take-out and upstairs restaurants that have balconies where patrons rest elbows on the railing and look out like spectators to some arena or show. A grand fixation to observe in these top floor onlookers.

Maple trees are planted in carved squares throughout the concrete pedestrian road. Tied to their branches are the strings which hold paper lanterns swinging like lambent balls of helium. Some lanterns are detached and roll dim yet with direction like a sensing spider egg.

Above a studded double door is the lit lettering of the word, Phở. A paper is taped on the door. In purple marker it reads *Please try other door. Sorry.* It's a heavy door, the cold metal handle shaped like that on a teacup. Inside are cushioned booth seats and brown tables, the beige walls hold Chinese paintings, ships and beaches, a rim of flowery wallpaper below the textured ceiling.

I run a finger through the items of the menu. Vietnamese or English, hi-res coloured pictures of meat dishes and desserts. The waiter pours hot rice tea in an aluminum cup. A mild, velvety smell. The taste is near water yet satisfyingly ricey.

"I'm ready," I tell him. "Beef pho." I tap the picture of it.

"Yes."

"J'ai beef pho," I say.

"Got you," he says turning back to me, smirking.

Then the tray is supported on the waiter's shoulder, his palm flat on the centre, his arm like two snapped sticks. A white tail steams out the bowl. The tray spins in an arc until landing on the table. He pinches fingertips around the lip drawn in blue lacings. It smells oniony. He sets down a small plate with bean sprouts and mint sprigs.

I tell him, "Cam on," which is *thank you* in Vietnamese.

"Cảm ơn anh," he says. "You know Vietnamese?" A delicate rise to his voice.

"I've traveled there."

"Very nice. How was that?"

"Incredible. I want to go again."

He grins.

"I'm traveling here too," I tell him.

"Wow. How's that?"

"I'm enjoying it. Thanks."

"You're a big traveler?"

"Not really. I'm new."

"Oh. You look like an expert. But that's the funnest time. When you're new."

"Right."

"Let me know if you need anything else or you need suggestions. Where to go, what to see, whatever."

"Okay. Thanks."

I pick a clump of bean sprouts and sink them into the soup using the chopsticks. I tear and chew some of the sprigs. The mint radiates to my nose, my breathing infused with frost. I squeeze drops of chili paste and stir.

I remember the first time I ate this. It was with a woman who was severely English Second Language. Our conversations could never have the emotive force to be neurotic. She said that on one of her dates the guy had excused himself to the bathroom and left. She said this concretely, lightheartedly, a poverty of words which seemed judicious.

She had jagged teeth and in down angles her features became those of the fat Buddha. Puggy nose and fat lips, a look of forever happy. Her nestled black eyes watched stealthy out the plump hills of her flesh. She told me she was mistaken for Chinese. I told her this was not as bad as she had thought. But I never told her I preferred her ugly face over the pretty ones. To love an ugly face is a personal pleasure like knowing a secret fact of the world. Every pretty face is pretty in the same way. It is cheap to love a pretty face. The ugly face is a goal and a reward.

She had a beautiful singing voice which she did not believe was beautiful. One night in a live music bar she whispered a song by the Fugees. Her hot and tremulous breath in my ear. She stared at me in the dark of the bar, pouting. She loved to be kissed.

After the soup the waiter asks in his feminine voice, "Was it as good or near as what you're used to?"

"Honestly," I say. "The same."

"Glad to hear. That's a huge compliment. Room for dessert?"

His eyes are locked into me. "I'm full," I say. "Bill, please."

"Got you."

I pay.

"Any plans for the night?" he asks.

"I'm going to walk about, introduce myself to the place. I love walking." I want to tell him that I can walk anywhere for a long time. In pain and struggle.

"Oh, me too. Sounds fun."

"Thank you. See you around."

"If you're free, I can show you around."

"That's all right. Bye bye now."

I go outside and walk out the gates and continue to the St. Lawrence River.

A trail runs along the river and turns into museums and piers. The river is black with every wave a wink of pale light. In the distance there are ships like mounds of tubular earth.

I want to smoke. The risk and reward of it all depend on position like in a poker game. You'll play different hands in different positions and each of these differences compound to offer distinct risks and rewards.

I'd go out on the hotel balconies or on rooftop terraces and watch the sunrise and smoke. Quickly the streets swarmed with motorbikes, their engines swelled to a long drone in my ears. If I was in a terrace the foreigners would come out with hot plates of fried rice and eggs and fruit juice. We'd smoke and talk about where we came from and what we were going to do. A traveller from Holland told me he never smoked back home but he started when traveling to SE Asia. I told him I started so as to be social. We agreed that cigarettes are tremendous for building friendships.

"Non-smokers will never understand us," he said. "They look at us simply as stupid people. But we have a unique benefit out of our stupidity."

The more I walk the more the architecture impresses me as holier, the ornamental lights wrapping a golden film on the stone and marble. The quiet emptiness is like passing through an art gallery, so still and solemn and ancient.

I find a convenience store.

"Bonjour," the cashier says.

"Bonjour. Phillip Morris."

He watches me. His eyes clogged with fleshy lids. "ID?"

I present my ID.

"Hmm. King size?"

"Sure."

He flips open a panel.

"What is French for lighter?" I ask.

"Briq." He grabs a lighter. "Briq."

"I am traveling here," I tell him.

"Voyager." He gestures a stubby thumb.

I light a cigarette. It is harsh like sucking air until at the last inch of lung-space an air hose shoots dust in your throat.

· · · ·

ACROSS A CLASSICAL church is a walkway of grey brick planted on a slope, a thick stone pillar rising at the top with the statue of a colonial man looking to the Champ de Mars Park.

In the walkway there are garden boxes of tulips, lavender, feather grass, bonded between tan oak benches. Along the sides are the many and slanted tourist shops and cafés. Every dozen feet the thin trunk of a hedge maple, a leafy globe, and the larger maples stalk the levelled top, their heavy and green foliage banking the façade of a seventeenth-century city hall, a giant clock above its metal-plated entrance displays the time in roman.

Before and above the park, between the government buildings, is an open area with long and winding benches and a fountain. A dramatic statue of a soldier reflects in the blue-grey water. The Canadian flag spreading and folding high on a pole, the blue and white Québec flag, le fleurdelisé.

A woman articulates the Québécois with the consonants not caring for the laws of French vowels. I recognize only *rue*. She weaves a wilted finger through an imagined street layout. I tell her, "Je ne sais pas."

"Oh," she says. She walks away muttering *je ne sais pas*.

I smoke a cigarette on a bench and look to the fountain. Two children around it, looking into the bottom. What do they see but corroded coin. One begs a guardian for something to throw. This young guardian hands a quarter or fiver and the child plops it with no hesitation, no sign of wish made.

The day is bright and warm and easy to breath in. There are people walking the sidewalks and in the park you can hear them. You can see some inside the diners eating breakfast or outside accepting the pre-noon sun. They are older but they add a relevancy to the place regardless. See some of the younger people with their families, the teenagers follow along snapping pictures. Parents with baby strollers that block the babies from the sun and streetwalkers. People walk small dogs that look at you woodenly and sniff and bob like floating apples with each step.

I pass the Quebec Court of Appeal. People in suits talk to each other on the steps though not seriously. Coffee breaks and five-minute smokes all over these steps. A statue of a peasant woman attempting to hold a child's hand, a striking scene.

I see a bum panhandle in the street corner. His cap shaking to the passerbys, rustling the small change to the slow cars. He is tanned brown, his jeans dirt-stained, raggedy man with rodlike clavicle bones sticking out a shirt too large. His pale eyes flirt between his oily locks.

I enter.

The air-con is chilling. A line of few people. It is a dark place with dark walls and furniture and darker the floor. Cool, funky jazz.

"Tall. Blond. Noir," I tell her.

I sit down on a hard wood chair. A man in a tracksuit is parallel to me and his coffee is unlidded and steaming. He listens to something on his bulky headphones and stares at the door.

I finally answer Melody's text. *What's up?*

I'll wait a few hours after she replies. I don't like tailoring my mood to the schedule of text messaging. I notice how easy it is for my mood to sync with my phone use. People are irritated when you leave them unread for hours.

When I was in Vietnam I texted one woman all in emojis. It did not prevent her from nonstop texting me. She texted late at night. I felt the vibrations and it prevented me from sleeping.

I had met her at a club. She was with her friend and her friend's boyfriend. She gave me her number and then told me, "Wait here, we come back." They left me with the boyfriend who offered me cigarettes. I left the club because it bothered me to wait.

She texted me that night, *You go to sleep?* I replied the next evening that I did.

She was very short with muscular runner-legs. So lean the muscle threads popped like coiled springs when my fingers pressed them. The back of her head was flat and I told her a level ruler would measure it perfect. She said her mother did not turn her over as a baby. She was good with humour because she was secure.

I remember looking at her naked in the room as the lights were on. I closed the lights and the room hardened in a silver gloss. She looked far better under the moonlight. People always do.

Randomly she told me, "I don't care you take three hours to text back." I knew she wanted me to know how much she cared in a way that was reasonable for her. She accepted that I didn't like being on my phone though her frustration didn't stop. If there is something that clashes between people, the only way to stop the clashing is for them to separate or to expose it. We left it hidden and the clashing got so strong it separated us.

Now my phone pulses. I feel instantly a sensation as when sugar touches the tongue after a fast. I walk outside and trash the cup in a bin and light a cigarette. That bum sits on the ground with the cap set before him. His head looks ready to fall off his neck.

I wait for the lights and then cross.

Bakeries and cafés passing me. So many people on the sidewalk. A man talks to himself in Québécois but he is not crazy. In his ear is a device which you assume exists the voice of another.

I wait and cross and wait and cross.

Ahead a convenience store there is an open lot. It's not a park and it's not reserved for some future store. There are leafless trees bordering it, a column of marble for sitting.

There is a man in a wheelchair, his fleshy stomach squeezing on leg stumps. He smokes with a group of skaters. His bearded cheeks seem stuffed with bread. There is a great drama about him. His hairy forearms pump like pistons as he wheels. The flesh of his leg stumps is polished and hacked even.

A skateboard drops in a hard clack, the skater stomping on the ground to speed in the lot, jumping and kicking and twirling the board mid-air and stomping again.

Her hand is rattling in a large purse she peers into enormously.

"Do you have fifty cents?" she asks. "Only need fifty." Her skin is wrinkly and honey coloured. Two hollows out of which she looks out darkly.

"I don't have fifty," I say handing a loonie.

"Thanks a million."

She walks in the store. I smoke and watch the skaters. They take turns doing tricks in the centre and the wheelchair man watches and yells at them as someone who's known them a long time might.

I walk on.

The cars and delivery trucks are creeping in the street as if all linked by slow-acting chains. Yellow leaves in the trees like flickering coins of foil.

I have interests in the varied Asiatic languages, the stores loaded with giant sacs of herbs and dried seafood, and the elderly Asians handing out flyers for yoga classes. I take one and they thank me and I read it and they watch me. I fold it and shove it in my back pocket and continue on.

The fishy reek of this street. The young Asians walking as a group in whispers. A casual red temple. Stone tables with seats like urns. I smoke a cigarette. Interests in all of this. In the back alleys and the stories in those alleys. The local keeping of accounts and never-resolving feuds. The love and hatred between people of different location and mindset, the trials and triumphs and failures that define a person, a community.

I take a picture of a bubble tea shop, the windows fitted in laminated menus. I send the picture to a woman I met in Vietnam. She loves bubble tea or as she calls it: *boba*. Her name is Tracy. At the time I met her I had been in Vietnam for nearly 4 weeks and was scheduled to be in Saigon for three more days. Her dating profile had an emoji of the Canadian flag and I messaged her that I was from Canada. She was planning to attend a school in Ontario.

Saigon had a large business culture and there were many selections and unique services. It was Westernized more than the North where I was treated best. It felt like Asian cities nested inside each other. Worlds within worlds. Like in Hanoi, the nightlife was concentrated in a few districts dedicated to it. Each district was like a city itself and not from size but from activity.

We met at a restaurant she picked, far from the tourist areas. The area was old but not decayed. She said it was scary how much I was eating. She was quiet but she answered questions until exhausting her knowledge and communicative ability. It was unexpectedly charming, her determined searching.

We walked after the meal.

"You walk fast," I told her. It was like she was jogging. She slowed. She apologized.

"Don't apologize. If you want to run, we can run."

"Race?"

"Yeah. Let's go."

We ran for under thirty seconds. It was raw and free running. We stopped before a cross section. "You're fun," I told her. The inside of my chest felt like it was holding a sharp rock.

Then we continued, heading closer to tourist streets. The silence between us was part of the family of indecision. Who would talk, what could they say. It was warm and assuring silence. If I talked she'd look at me with what was like her dopamine eyes, limitless and terrible romance, so rich as to waste and ruin and hollow.

It was my first time buying boba and I told her this. She told me not to worry and that I'll get obsessed. The girl at the counter asked about pearls. I said, "Yes." She pointed to the menu taped on the plexiglass. Percentages of pearls from zero to fifty in twenty-five percent increments. I told her fifty. Then the pearls were packing in my mouth. It was gooey and malty. It channeled through a creamy chocolate milk like a syrup that poured in me with a burn.

Under the hanging roof of the temple is a dark grey bust of a man. An elderly group are doing yoga in front of it.

Melody texted, *Bored. Met anyone?*

I text, *How about you come here?* That should whirl her good.

The cigarette is a glowing nub. I crush it and light another and watch the fluid exercise of the elders. The melodious strings of a guzheng evoking resonant drops of liquid metal.

Melody texts, *I want to but I be working.*

I imagine her dancing, dancing. On a thin reflective pole dancing. In a neon pink bikini which contrasts on her skin a lusty chiaroscuro. Weighty dreadlocks inertial to her dancing. I am in the audience which for her is covered black behind the stage lights. I am watching that dancer, her feline-body opening and closing as nature's greatest construct.

Later I text, *Quit.* That should give her a good whirling.

2

FACING ME IS A YOUNG traveller with black hair and freckled forearms. He drinks orange juice. His neck juts forward to cave his chest as if he is to insert himself in his glass.

"Good morning," I tell him.

"Hey, good morning."

"Where you from?"

"Winnipeg. Ontario?"

"You got it."

"God, I hate Toronto. No offence. Was there a week ago."

"What's wrong with it?"

"Too big and dirty."

"You're a country guy."

"Not even."

I only taste the margarine the eggs were cooked with. The bacon is dry and salty.

He says, "I've never been to a place with so many homeless coming up to you like quest givers."

"Toronto ships the homeless to Kitchener," I tell him.

"Kitchener, eh? Then why were so many unshipped?"

"What I heard. I don't know. So, what you doing here?"

"Seeing what's in Canada."

"Alone?"

"I'm waiting for my fucking friends right now."

"Been in the clubs yet?"

"Oh, yeah," he says. "There's one right there. Hey, buddy." A man tongs the eggs and looks over and says, "Morning."

"I haven't been out yet," I say.

"Morning," the freckled guy says.

"Good morning," the man says. He sits down. His plate is loaded with eggs and the bacon is snapped so as to fit on the plate.

"This guy's never been out," he tells him.

"Really," he says. It's not a question. "The hell have you been doing?"

"Walking around," I say.

"Well, come out with us tonight."

"I'm down," I say.

"My names Lyndon." He twists his torso to give me his lean right hand. His face reminds me of a hawk.

"Sonny," I tell him.

"Sonny day."

"Yeah," I say. "Nice to meet you. By the way, what's your name?"

"Eric."

I peel a peanut butter packet and lodge a spoon into it and scoop a glob and spread it on the bagel that feels like cardboard. The inside is doughy. Another guy sits down by Eric. His plate has a purple muffin and eggs.

"Hey," Lyndon says. "Junior's green as shit."

"I'm Gabriel. Top of the morning." Gabriel looks to be on anxiety medication. He nods vigorously at nothing. "Enjoying Montreal?" he asks.

"I am. Are you?"

"For sure, man. I used to actually work in the east side as a barista. Here's a gem. You'll find whatever you're into here."

"The people though," says Lyndon, blinking. "Can be assholes."

"Sure but you get people like that wherever," Gabriel tells me.

"Was there a problem?" I ask.

"Some dickheads the last night," says Lyndon.

"Close to banging em out," says Eric.

"So, are all you exploring Canada like Eric?"

Gabriel says he's visiting Montreal because his girlfriend lives here. Lyndon is traveling in from New York.

"I'd like to do a whole trip through Canada," I tell them.

"PEI if you've never been gots the best nature by none. I'm from BC. Trust me," says Gabriel.

"Awesome," I say. "BC is top on my list."

"Do a lot of travelling, Sonny?" asks Lyndon.

"No," I say. "I've only really explored Southeast Asia."

"How was that?"

"Unreal."

"I heard it's dirt cheap," says Eric.

"Like how much is beer?" asks Lyndon.

"Two to three bucks," I say.

"Damn." Then he asks, "Canadian or US?"

"US."

He shakes his head sadly.

"The tourism is huge there though," says Eric.

"It's big of course but you can get out it easy."

"I don't like rice," says Eric. "I like bread."

"It has a huge underground for drugs," claims Lyndon.

"Thailand has a big market for amphetamine," adds Eric. "Like the type world war two bomber pilots'll take."

"Fuck," says Lyndon. His plate is empty.

"But one thing that's everywhere is nitrous oxide filled in balloons," I say. "Bars and clubs sell them. Pump the balloons from the big dentist office canisters."

"I hear there's snake-shit that happens all the time like a hooker'll make a guy fall in love and extort the living shit out of him," asserts Eric.

"I don't think it's usual," I tell him.

"I saw videos of poor guys jumping off balconies. Blam."

"One thing I didn't like was motorcyclers riding up trying to sell me weed or girls. Likely police informants."

"Bro, when I was in Mexico on the beach there's cartel dealing in plain daylight," announces Eric. "They'd protect and treat the tourists like baby lambs."

He continues, "Mexico is thought as a dangerous country but it's not for tourism. The bad stuff is done to locals or gang members. That's where the reputation comes from. Bro, you should go to Mexico as a tourist and not anything else. And the women? Oh, baby."

"How's the girls in Asia?" asks curious Lyndon.

"They're adorable," I affirm.

"How sexually?"

"Depends."

"See," rebuts Eric, "in Mexico none of them depend, bro. No depends in South America. I've seen it. But don't go to Brazil. I don't advise Brazil. There's whole favelas being shot up by gangs and cops don't give a fuck. Fucking cops'll shoot up neighbourhoods too. The luxury hotels filled with bullet holes even. Helicopters shooting down in the streets. I'm not lying."

"Man, you guys got me hungry," say Gabriel. He stands and grabs a muffin and sits down.

I imagine continuing on with the sharing of late nights and unlikely circumstance. But my motivation inverts, the topic reaches a cliff and jumps.

"You're here all alone?" asks Lyndon.

"Yeah."

"You prefer it that way?"

"I do."

"All right. You decide what to do. No one to answer to," he says to himself.

"Exactly," I say. "Any of you been to the strip clubs?"

They say they haven't.

"Me neither but I heard they're the best in Canada. Cheap too."

"It's already in the itinerary," says Eric. "Thank you."

"Welcome, sir," I tell him.

"Indeed."

"More orange juice, sir?" asks Lyndon. Eric has stood. "Indeed, sir," he says.

He sits down with a fresh glass. "Love OJ, sir."

"Indeed," says Lyndon.

Eric gulps the juice. It's audible.

"Righty oh," says Gabriel.

"You're a fiend for those fucking muffins, eh pal?" asks Eric.

"Legit fiend," says Gabriel.

"Indeed."

"Indeed, sir," says Lyndon.

We make a plan to meet in the later evening. Then Gabriel and I go smoke.

"What's your plan before we go out?" I ask.

"Hanging with the girl." Then he says quietly, "Banging."

"Doesn't she have her own place?"

"Parents, ahaha."

"When are you hanging?"

"She gets off work at two."

"Do you drink coffee?"

"Oh, I wish," he says. "Doesn't work with me."

"Why? Do you take some kind of medication?"

"Yeah but I don't like coffee."

Then I ask, "You speak French?"

"A little. Not needed."

"J'ai apprendu le français pendant trois mois."

"Sympa, sympa," he says nodding robustly. "C'est bien et facile."

"Oui."

"Ouais," he says. "The Quebec *yes* is ouais."

"Ouais, ouais." There's a careless whang to it like a whipping towel.

"Almost forgot," he says. "You smoke weed?"

"No, I'm all right."

"Damn, okay."

It does not feel like morning but evening. I'm usually fasted in the morning. Hunger gives me precision. More goal-orientated with hunger. Now a flattening heaviness in my core, a sympathetic lethargy. Like a laminar flow of wind-energy which has grown turbulent and curling to flow backwards.

· · · ·

THEY ARE LEADING ME to where we will do battle. That is what a night out drinking feels like. There are challenges and rewards, a spirit which animates and a spiritualization of the experience. We share the heights and depths of ourselves.

Watch them instead, the battlers, I imagine telling the drivers as we cross the streets. See how the night welcomes them. They are like animals. The animal is superior because it does not argue with its desires. And therefore it crafts no idols to worship nor enemies to conquer.

We stop at a club where a large crowd lines at the entrance. They are a young and fashionable crowd. Every male aggressive, prepared and planning, every female a salving agent, laughing and presentable and ignorant.

A large metal panel with the club name is traced from a weld-torch. The brick walls are painted in a fresh black. By the double doors is a podium with three very fit women dressed in black. A wedge-shaped bodyguard in black suit. As people enter he says, "Turn up, turn up."

The corridor is dim and cool and pungent. The booming audio-system jiggles my organs. There are blue lights fixed to the rafters. They are cleaving into the mobbed dance-floor. They shift to blurs of magenta and cobalt. A mass of fog like a funeral fantasy circles the crowd.

As the Jager bomb drops in my gut my pulse accelerates.

"One more," yells Eric. He flicks Lyndon on the chest. "One more," says Lyndon twirling his finger.

The next round comes. Rancid. Electricity flares up my scalp.

Gabriel yells at them. Like a scream in a bathtub. We follow him to a metal disc fastened on a wooden pole. They order beers. Gabriel and I go smoke. When Gabriel sucks his cigarette I notice a tattoo of barbwire peeking out his sleeve.

He looks to me smiling with the glowing cigarette in his lips. "Expect a fire on Friday nights," he says.

Then the corridor passes.

I imagine and somewhat feel in me a set of gears clinking to a new orientation. I don't remember my beer. I order a tequila and gulp it and bite into the lime faintly tarty. The crowd on the dance-floor is not ready. I watch that crowd. The music playing is good only in this context.

Another tequila shot comes and I pluck the lime wedge off the glass. My teeth clinch and tear off the lime-flesh.

The club is excellent.

And the people I am with are excellent and in case of danger we will protect one another. People like belonging and feeling safe because of it. People deserve to be part of a group that shares the same goals as them.

An individual can borrow goals from the group to belong with them. But borrowing is different than having. An individual by themselves has practical goals. Abstract goals are group goals. They require and offer membership to a group.

Abstract goals are meaningful goals. An individual can have meaningful goals. But it is a constant mark of their selfhood that they will struggle for meaning precisely because that meaning is not shared. They can forgo membership and be a lone master of themselves. But of what point is an alienated master?

Tonight I don't have to borrow the goal from Eric and Lyndon and Gabriel. The goal is rather borrowing me.

And I watch the crowd.

But I have a head like a despot.

I'd gather the blueberries while Eric and Lyndon and Gabriel hunt the large predators.

I'd have to beg Eric and Lyndon and Gabriel for a woman since it was only a few elite men who had the majority of women in polygamous societies. They'd make me do tasks of humiliation. And then reward me with their ugliest woman. No, not ugliest. Rather, their most uninspired and domesticated. I'd be forced to love her for she'd be my one and only. I'd reason her plainness as edifying so as to feel good about it.

The crowd allows me to enter.

I rock my head and hips. Seesaw motions with my eyes closed. A short girl in a low-hanging white shirt. Her face is texture-less. She turns her bony ass to me. The hard denim of her jeans. Her pelvic bone. I press harder. Her hair is fruity scented and tickling my nose. My hands slide from waist to stomach and pull in. Her elbows dig in my forearms and my fingers graze her belly ring. Her arms rise laterally and then she vanishes.

I move through all the people, quick and unrefined. I light a cigarette. The gears in me. I don't like this metaphor because I'm not a robot. I'm flesh and blood.

There is no one in the trail and the starlit and stinking river is chilling me. The head despot sucks cancer fumes and I hope it be poisoned in its bloody bone-cell.

• • • •

WHERE? Tracy texted.

I text, *Montreal. Wanna come?*

I remember drinking with her for two nights. We went to a street dedicated to bars. It was busy and bright and as you walked you felt it like a tunnel with tight and iron-hot walls that kept you centred.

The girls paraded the bar fronts with the same booty shorts and heels. They hollered at you for drinks and if they were brave they'd stop you and mouth the generics of their trade. You'd look down to see the lust-laced gloss of her eyes and the scant flesh of her body. You'd walk and she'd block you and you'd smell the young sweat and fruit perfume and you'd feel the bone of her shoulders. "No," you'd say. She'd scatter back to her bar like a sheltering villager. If you said it with eye contact then she wouldn't do that. She'd stay with you, following, for she sensed interest. She'd have that developed sense.

We went to a quieter bar that had a lawn of plastic grass rolled out the front. We sat outside and judged the other tourists. We held hands and kissed. I told her I didn't want the older Vietnamese men to see us.

"Stupid," she said. "You worried?"

"They judge harshly."

"Judge what?"

"What we are."

"What is?"

"Lovers."

"Kiss me," she said.

"They're looking."

"Kiss me so we kill them in heart attack."

She had a large face but it was not fat. She was taller than normal. Her black hair was always done in a knot, long and bundled like a tail. Her lips were big yet lacking definition like two half-cut circles. I never told her that I loved her lips.

Later we went inside the bar to a pool table. It was dark and we could not see the numbers on the balls. There were few people in the bar and two waiters at the counter. We were drinking Saigon beer and playing a haphazard game of pool and laughing.

You travel now?

Yeah.

See me.

When I can.

Say when so I prepare.

One time we went to a market. I didn't want to buy anything. She was getting bored following me. The market was a chaos of wares and food, noise and people. I ate a meal at a stall but I wasn't hungry. She was texting on her phone and then she covered her mouth to dampen the sound. I asked her what's wrong. "Nothing," she said. Then after we left she told me her mother had seen us.

"Should I be worried?" I asked.

"The worry is mine."

I don't remember what we did after the market. I think she either went back to her place or we spent more time walking. I remember that when she told me about her mother I didn't want to see her anymore. But that feeling died easy.

Then a ruinous feeling enters the brain but first you felt it in the gut. Then there is a sick vertigo, nausea, an upward acceleration. The blood shakes with it.

If Eric or Lyndon or Gabriel were with me they'd help me draw it out. Their knowing may not be declarative but procedural so they would not be able to explain the letting method. They'd know the ingrained practice of execution.

I wipe myself with the thin napkins which soak and break on my skin. I walk to the front desk. The girl handling it is cute and precious. She stares at me and smiles. "Co khoe khong?"

"Excuse me?"

"Co khoe khong?"

"Are you talking Vietnamese?"

"Yes. I've traveled there."

"Cool. I'm actually half-Cambodian. I don't know Vietnamese or at least not good."

"It's okay. I only know the very basics."

"It's a really hard language." She giggles.

I tap my credit card on the machine while she holds it.

"I'd love to go to Cambodia too. I've only been to Vietnam. Asia is very interesting to me."

"A one-up on me."

"You were born here?"

"Yes."

"Well, yeah. You have zero accent."

"Thanks," she says. "Wouldn't be good for me having an accent being born here."

"That's true."

"How was the food?"

"Delicious," I say. "Have a good day and enjoy yourself."

"Have a good day too. Enjoy Cambodia when you ever go."

"Merci." My feet are moving to the stairs.

"Merci," she says in a singsong way.

3.

THE FIRST THOUGHT OF traveling to SE Asia was not serious but the possibility caused me restlessness. I'd be in the school library researching for the trip and looking up travel videos imagining myself as the people filming. I remember walking the nature trails around my neighbourhood listening to Peter Murphy's All Night Long and having fantasies of myself in Asia.

I had the initial thought while in my mother's room. Two suitcases were on her bed, rolled clothes, plastic bags of toiletries and phone chargers, the packing cubes bulging with undergarments. My mother was going to Cuba with her friends that same summer. I could go somewhere too.

Years ago I knew of someone online who lived there. He exited the United States because of his dislike with the politics and society. He'd post pictures and stories of himself and how-to videos on how to live out there successfully. It seemed he was in a great adventure.

Canada was too familiar to be exciting. Asia was exotic and cheap and I love Asian food too. It was very natural for me to pick SE Asia. The choice reduced to Thailand or Vietnam. I chose the latter because the former seemed more westernized.

"But why can't you go to Niagara or Chicago? Remember you wanted to go to Chicago? Or New York, the Midwest? Why so far?" my mother asked me.

"None of those places interest me."

"What's in Asia?"

"I've no idea. That's part of it."

"Please think about it. We'll both think and weigh options."

Soon I booked my ticket and she began to reason it to herself so as to accept it. She said it was good for me.

I had a friend in the university who was half-Vietnamese. Her name was Ming and she called herself Mi-mi. She had a boyish face and she was short and blocky in a way a farm woman is. She had a grandmother that was raised in the wilderness with a misfit family. Her grandmother suicided at the age of seventy-seven.

We explored regularly the bars and cafés around campus. She would take pictures of me in abandoned buildings for she was studying photography. We shared a similar humour and the conversations were easy which led me to wanting to be lovers. But she was failing classes and stressed from work. She rarely saw me.

I told her about me going to Vietnam and she was excited. We scheduled a meeting at a ramen restaurant. It had been three months since I had last seen her.

She looked beautiful and lean, her robust white teeth showing constantly. Her new haircut looked like a dark coconut on her head.

"You have anything to tell me?" I asked her.

"Absolutely nothing. What the fuck do I know?"

"Right."

"I'm just excited. How is you?"

"Good," I told her. Though all my thoughts concerned my trip which made me anxious. "How are you?"

"Meh. I'm me."

"That's okay. You're good."

"Only you could say that about me."

Seeing her in the sunlight as it pooled in her big eyes, her face bright and smiling, I felt again the feelings that I had for her.

"You look good," I said.

"Gross."

"What?"

"Stop being gross."

The ramen came and we ate and talked as if we had entered the early days of our friendship. I tried to meet her again after but she was busy. First it was due to schoolwork and then it was mental illness.

I had another friend at the university, Andrew, a communications student who read a lot of books. But he had met me at a time when books no longer weighed as important on me. It was sad for me to feel this way about books. He would meet me over coffee. He'd talk about topics like film theory and techno-humanism. One time he told me he was in love with a girl in his class. He used the word *love* emphatically and it had a profound significance for him. He said, "Love is like, is like, is like a death in the family. No one should be actively seeking it. If they do they're naive. They haven't matured enough to realize what it is. You know. It's forever. It's like really fucking serious. I can't do the things I enjoyed. There's a gap in everything I do and feel. When she's there, the gap is gone. But she can't be there all the time. I'm forced to take in the gap, like even if she's there, I know the gap is coming. Mentally, I'm ruined."

I told him that I was going to Vietnam. He forever had this look of disbelief, my friend.

"Why?"

"I got drafted."

"Drafted?"

"I'm joking. It's for travel."

"Oh. Interesting."

"Interesting."

I wanted to tell him someone should kidnap him and transport him to somewhere foreign where he'd have to fend for himself. I imagined him being terrified and it felt good to imagine. When I was in Vietnam I sent him pictures and I imagined he looked at them with longing.

I worked a landscaping job part-time to finance some of the trip. One of the contract workers was a Vietnamese man of twenty-nine named Bruce, very short and stocky. He was frequently in squatting positions that looked comfortable for him. He accepted tasks with enthusiasm but his actual work was slow and needlessly complicated. I told him I was visiting soon. "Spread the perm," he said. He was hard to understand but that didn't make you stop wanting to talk to him.

"What?" I moved my ear close to his small mouth.

"Spread the perm," he whispered. He stroked an imaginary cock with his hand. His laugh sounded like it was coming out of a barrel.

"You are favourite in Hanoi. Not in Saigon. Saigon is rich. Hanoi is poor. They love handsome white. In Saigon, huh, there so many."

"I see."

"In Hanoi," he continued, "oh, Sonny come save us. Thank you lord for Sonny." He rose his hands and the rake dropped, he looked to the sky, flaring his fingers.

"Everywhere the whole country you are spreading the perm."

"I know," I told him.

"So much fun. The funnest summer. Point of no return."

"Bruce if they made a movie on your life it would be called Point of No Return."

He had come to Canada eight years ago with his wife. He had never been to Asia since.

"You know sweet?" he asked me.

"Sweet?"

He made an explosive motion with his hand.

"When girl sweet," he said.

"I don't know what you're saying."

"Sweet. Sweet."

I thought about it. "Are you saying squirt?"

"Yeah. Sqweet. You ever make girl pussy sqweet?"

I told him I hadn't.

"All girl there can sqweet really good. But they do not have the mentality to know they can. Their mind close. Small mind. They need education to know they can."

Bruce shoveled mulch into a wheelbarrow and dumped it in the dry soil. Watching him work made me feel positive and lighthearted.

I asked him where I should go and what I should see. But he said these were not questions for him to answer. He said Vietnam, while I'm there, will reveal to me what I should do. Then he told me about there being many rich Vietnamese families that you'd never know are rich. He was obsessed with this topic. He said the Vietnamese keep their wealth secret. He was winking.

"Pumping," he said. "All the time. Then dumping."

"Pump and dump. That's what the movie should be called."

"The best summer."

"Yes, Bruce."

"I'm happy."

"You're happy about me?"

"Happy you will spread the perm in my country."

Later in middle May I took the train to the Toronto airport. In the morning my mother drove me to the station. We were both silent. When I got out she hugged me for a long time.

While waiting for the train I listened to Peter Murphy but music was too saturated with meaning for me to enjoy.

In the train I sat in the first-class because my mother paid for it. The ride was quick and pleasant and I felt like a traveler.

In the airport I was exhausted with excitement. I sat at the terminal watching people. We all seemed members of the same community. But I carried a cheap hiking backpack along with a drawstring bag. There were other backpackers in the terminal and their gear looked better than mine.

In the plane I sat with a man who was going to Thailand. He ordered a shot of vodka with ginger ale and I copied him. The alcohol hit beautifully on the plane.

Arriving in the Vietnamese airport, it was past midnight and barren. After getting my one-month visa stamped I needed to exchange money and then to buy a SIM card. The currency vendor was the only one open. I could not use my phone and I was nervous about getting a taxi since I had read about scams.

I walked outside and there was a man with his hands grabbing air as if reeling me with rope. He wore a stained polo shirt and shorts and sandals. The shirt was wrinkled and dark in the middle from where he had rolled it to expose his gut. Men do this in Asia to air themselves when it is hot. I made sure to avoid eye contact but he followed me. I asked him the price, repeating it until he repeated it himself.

Then he led me to a shuttle-bus that had one man in the back and a woman in passenger side. I said, "Hello" to them. The man said he was from Russia. The woman said Lebanon.

I looked at the road. Trash was packed along the highway blockades. Shoddy houses with corrugated iron roofs and glassless windows. The traffic lights dangled from bundled wires and un-helmeted motorbikers passed us with their shirts long and flowing like capes.

"How long are you staying?" I asked the Russian. He was dressed in all black and he was like a floating head in the shuttle-bus.

"I don't know. I'm getting a bike to go up north. I'll figure then."

After a few minutes he asked me the same and I told him two weeks.

"No, no, no, no," he said in the serious way Russians say things. "My journey is three months and it's still not long."

The road narrowed into a strip of pavement. There were small stores loaded with clothes or jewellery or tools as if all were dumped garbage. A language riddled in accents, like curly branches with leaves. There were locals gathered on plastic chairs smoking long wooden pipes. The shuttle-bus seemed close to crash but it went by faultless.

My hostel looked like a glass-panelled cart in a row of boxcars. When I got out the driver demanded more money than we agreed.

The hostel was safari themed and hotter than the outside. A worker took my passport and put it in a locked drawer. He stared at me, waiting for my response, and then said, "All hostels hold passports. Standard rule."

Then he gave me a card to enter the room.

I said, "Cam on."

Another man sitting at the desk yelled, "Oh."

He guided me on how to say it and he was drunk and excited.

The room was cavernous. My bunk was next to the door and I climbed a ladder and slid the curtain.

I woke up early in the morning because I had scheduled a tour. The staff at the reception desk greeted me. They all looked like good friends running their own business, conversing hushed with one another, eyeing the tourists. On a bench by the glass doors I watched people passing and the constant activity in the street. It was entertaining to sit and watch.

Then the tour guide arrived. She was a girl from a local university. "Hello, hello," she said.

"Hi."

"You are lucky."

"Lucky?"

"Yes, you. The only booking for today."

"Oh? Is that unusual."

"Yes."

"How many go on these tours?"

"A group. Four to six, let's say."

Outside the heat pressed on my skin as if I had put on a coat. The shops were unraveled and filling portions of the street with merchandise. People dawdled on their motorbikes to pass through the congestion of the road. They weaved around tourists and stalls and parked bikes and merged into a hot and noisy mass.

When walking past the open kitchens the heat from the grills caused an instant sweat. The smell of lemon grass and fish sauce and broth mixed with gas and pollution.

In a kitchen stall I ate chicken and rice and the tour guide talked about local history. I could not pay attention but I was asking questions regardless.

She talked Vietnamese with the lady that served me. When we left I said that she talked so long she gave the lady a headache.

"Ohhh," she said. "She's my good friend!"

"I know. I'm joking."

"Oh my God."

Then we visited Hoan Kiem lake, St. Joseph's Cathedral, the Temple of Literature, and a lush garden and park. I asked her questions about her life. She told me she had six siblings, her mother and father wanted her to study in the States. She didn't like the conservatism of her parents and she wanted an American lifestyle. Being a tour guide allowed her the opportunity to improve her English. "It's very good," I told her. I was not lying. She responded to much of what I said with a theatrical, "Ohhh."

She studied for one week on the history of Hanoi and the landmarks because she knew nothing. She carried a leather backpack and a notebook of facts. She had been a track and field athlete for eight years, played regularly in a volleyball team, danced since she was ten, double majoring in economics and finance, a student representative managing the tour guide and volleyball club at her school. I very much wanted to be her friend. I told her this and she said I already was.

Then we drank egg coffee in a semi-hidden café overlooking the lake. The egg coffee was foamy and sweet with a delicious hint of coffee. The interior of the café was cool from the concrete walls which trapped an aroma of roasted coffee and fruit. There were miniature chairs one had to squat down to.

At a table I saw a group of tourists with a tour guide. They had expensive cameras hanging off their necks. The tour guide explained to them and they listened like it was a lecture. They took pictures of the coffee. I thought I was not like them. As tourists we belonged in separate categories.

"What do you want to do in the United States of America?" I asked her.

"I want to study law."

"Have you applied?"

"Not yet I haven't."

"You know what you have to do to apply?"

"Yes," she said. The conversation was professional now. "I tested already the LSAT."

"Great. You know where in the States you'd go?"

"Denver, Colorado."

"It's cold there," I said. "Is it because of the snow?"

"Yes. And the mountains."

"Where else?"

"New York?"

"Are you asking me?"

"Have you been?"

"No. I've been to Chicago. It's kind of the same. I think New York is better. In New York if someone sneezes every other state catches a cold."

She skewed her head like a dog in confusion. "What does it mean?"

"Means big things happen in New York. That's where you should go."

"Ohhh. I understand."

She sipped softly the egg coffee. The leaf design in the foam was undisturbed.

"You drink alcohol?" I asked.

"On occasion. I can't drink all the time. I'm allergic actually."

"Allergic how?"

"I develop hives."

"That's awful."

"I took pictures."

She showed me them.

The tour guide showed the tourists the coffee plants on a ledge under the open window. He twirled a few beans in his fingertips and sniffed them and recommended the tourists to do the same. One man put his palms on his knees and bent and gawked at the plant.

There was a cabinet table and by it, sitting in an armchair, was a woman. She seemed like only a shrunken head sticking out of the gown she wore. Some random and wrinkled hands and feet suspended from the seat edge. She watched out from a world hazed in glaucoma. A face struck by permanent sunset. Preparing the coffee at the table, cracking and stirring eggs, was a woman who I assumed to be her daughter. Outmoded portraits of the family behind her.

I asked my guide and she said that the woman was the original owner of the café. That was not her daughter but a family relation who now runs the café with her husband. The old woman worked here during the war, she had never left. But she was not solely serving coffee then.

Maybe her father was a Viet Cong, her brothers. Maybe she was. If she could speak what could she tell me? Do her secrets matter to her or do they only concern others? Has she killed, has she witnessed, has she considered its terrifying simplicity and complex consequences? If age continued forever who with passion and sane mind would still speak the words of good and evil?

The tour guide moved to the table and picked up utensils and a ceramic bowl and made moves to demonstrate the making of egg coffee. The family relation looked on pleasantly and the tourists regarded her. The tourists were amazed how easy it was. How delicious it turned out.

When I said goodbye to my guide, we had spent nearly five hours together. I gave her a large tip.

"Take my contact," she said.

"Like you want to hang out?"

"When I get time."

"Awesome. Like this weekend?"

"We can. Text me."

Two days after, still in Hanoi, I met a traveler named Danny. It was late evening and the hostel terrace was busy. There was a small outside patio enclosed by a high chain-link fence. Smoking was allowed indoors though no one smoked indoors.

In the patio I sat by myself drinking a beer. Danny talked to a man from France who looked over forty. I overheard him say he was from Arizona and that he was on a mission to explore some main parts of the world in six months. He was a half-ginger with curly hair and eyes which shone green only in the light. Pale freckles on his cheeks and nose, the nostrils where blood vessels had burst pink and crawling. I told him that I was from Canada and he said he was jealous. The French man seemed annoyed by me, then a group of women passed us, he whispered, "Dutch," and followed them inside.

A man from Australia rolled a joint and told Danny that he lived in Vietnam teaching English. Danny was enamoured. They shared the joint and offered me a hit. It made me feel sleepy and unfocused.

At another table was a German who regularly inhaled nitrous oxide balloons. He had a bruise over his eye from fainting and hitting a chair. We watched him huffing, his heel tapping the ground, and the woman he was with looked ready to cry.

"I've been trying," said Danny watching the German.

"The Spanish girl?" asked the Australian.

"Yeah. I'll marry her."

"Are they dating?"

"Probably by now."

"I guarantee they're dating."

"She texts some wild things."

"If that's her type she's not worth the trouble."

"Probably."

The woman had a beaky nose and she was fridge-shaped. I could tell the Australian did not understand why Danny liked her. "What you doing?" he asked. Danny was standing.

"What I am born to do."

"Does he know about you?"

But Danny was gone.

"Well, it don't matter. He's pissed."

We watched Danny talk to her. They seemed like new friends. The German didn't care. She and Danny walked inside. Then she came out clinging a balloon and Danny followed her like a child. He walked back to us.

"Close?" asked the Aussie.

"Could be."

The next day Danny and I were drinking beers at six. They were free from six till eight. They were watery beers so tiresome to drink. Soon Danny introduced me to two British tourists.

They had been traveling Vietnam for one week and before that they were in Cambodia for two. Greg's face seemed smushed in his broad skull. Todd had acne scars and sleepy eyes and he was an amateur boxer. Both muscular, dressed in soccer shirts. Greg talked routinely about his family. He said his great grandfather was a mobster who financed movies in Hollywood.

Greg had gotten a tattoo in a local parlour. It was two red coy fish courting each other on his calf. Plastic was wrapped around it and the skin was red and oily. He said that he was scared. It was impossible to tell if he was serious. "The lymph nodes swell," he said. He touched the lymph nodes on my neck and then touched his.

"You think a craftsman doing a tattoo like that one is going to cock up not changing the needole? All the years he has and what the persons he's tatted?" asked Todd.

"Forget the needle then. In the climate it's an open wound. Things come to contact. Yeah, it's why I got joggers to prevent the sick getting in."

"Ain't you been feeling a little wonky though bruv?"

"Yeah, the weird bit of it. Like stomach's gone tattered."

"Shit," said Danny. "Me too."

"What about that crumpet you're up in. Ever worry about catching sick from her?"

"Clean as they come. Don't get nebby."

"Aye, clean as your tat."

"Where'd you catch her?" Danny asked.

"Club. She's this body," Greg traced a figure in the air, "like this...right like this."

"Hell."

"Bloody loves me too. Why not?"

"A love like theirs comes but once a lifetime," said Todd to everyone, "and you better treat her right."

"We got a spiritual connection, me and her."

"I'm saying treat her right. Ain't I?"

"Are you?"

"What you getting at?"

"Me? Nothing."

"You just have a history, mate."

When Greg was talking about visiting Thailand for the ladyboys Danny discontinued eye contact with him.

"Genetic girls take their womanhood for granted," he said. "Ladyboys work for what they are. Take the best stereotype of a girl you can think of and you'll see it presented every way on ladyboy street."

"Can you quit?" asked Danny.

"No problem," said Greg.

Todd was sipping his beer in intervals like a machine. Then Greg asked, "If you got nothing to say mate then why're you stopping the conversation?"

"I think you're more likely to get AIDS from ladyboys than a tattoo."

"Every man thinks its repulsive and that's exactly how it hooks you in," he said theoretically. "The shock of seeing a cute girl, breasts and a fit body, the most innocent and adorable girliest creature you've ever seen. Then she pops the bilk." He gestured it with his finger.

"It's the shock that gets at him," said Todd.

"I'm not commercial," said Greg. "That's what you got to know." Then he leaned closer. He smelled like cheap beer and outside air. "I got lot of problems Tommy but being commercial isn't one." I learned later that Greg changed people's names for the comedy of it.

When Todd handed Greg a cigarette Greg told Danny, "You should try it. You'll freak out rightly at first. But it'll hook like heroin. Oh, Danny boy. Like heroin." He was singing.

Danny lit a cigarette. He looked professional when lighting cigarettes as if he was advertising them.

"Take one of those tubby putrid pig faced cunts and I mean repulsive sewage-cunts and then take the primmest cleanest girly loveliest ladyboy on ladyboy street and you can only choose one for one night. You must choose."

"Mind you the ladyboy will be hung like Mandingo," said Todd.

"Mind that."

"Mind she's a rabid top," emphasized Todd.

Danny was rubbing his forearm slowly. The hair on them looked like sunburnt cotton. He said he'd take the pussy.

"Bet," said Greg. He slapped the table. Todd wrenched Greg's collar and pulled down. Greg stood and shoved his shoulders into his chest. "Fucking all right. All right," said Greg and Todd let go.

Later we played a card game called *shithead* which was very popular in the hostels. The German sat in a stool far from us. I could hear him ask an Italian woman if she had Ritalin. He said Italy has a lot of it. Then Danny's crush approached the German. They talked for a long time. Then she came to us.

"How are you doing?" Danny asked her.

I didn't hear what she said.

Danny introduced me to her.

"Where you from?" she asked me.

"Canada."

"Oh, Canada. I never. I from Colombia."

"Nice."

She stood over us as we were playing the card game. She was like a teacher watching us.

"How is in Canada?" she asked.

"Not as good as here. How about in Colombia?"

"You love Colombia."

Danny agreed.

Todd yelled, "Shithead."

"What are you up to tonight?" Danny asked her.

She rolled her eyes to the German. He was looking at her sickly.

"We're going out for food and drinks," Danny explained to her. "Come."

"I go to stay."

"But why?"

She rolled her brown eyes again. "Need me."

"He's a big boy."

"He really struggle."

"What's he struggling with?" asked Todd.

She explained to Todd about the balloons.

The German walked to us and pulled her hand to his stomach as if he wanted her to feel inside. He whispered in her ear.

"No, I can no," she said to him.

He whispered to her with his eyes closed.

She looked to Danny and rose her eyebrows and walked away. Danny called her a bitch. But then he said he would marry her.

Later we went out for banh mi sandwiches and Danny continued about the marrying and the having of children with her. The night passed with us drinking more beers and walking the Old Quarter, being offered *boom boom* from motorbikers, which means sex.

The next morning Danny told me he was ready to leave Vietnam. I asked him where he was going and he said Amsterdam. He told me that he was planning a new career after these six months but he was on his fifth month and wanting to travel for longer. "I change my mind every morning," he said.

Danny was thirty-one and he had spent his twenties doing nothing and wasting what money he had. He said he regretted not focusing on the long-term, prioritizing the short-term. This was his first time traveling overseas. I asked if he'd look back at these five months as a waste and he said, "It was good for what it was."

We were in the patio and there was a man sitting in the floor eating a plate of fried rice. He stood and walked to our table. He had come to Vietnam after staying one month in India where after he was inspired to wander. His name was Charlie. He had a long and sunned beard and he wore a bead necklace that hung past his belly button. His forehead was flaking badly. He started a conversation on psychedelics and social perceptions. It was interesting but he liked to dominate the conversation. He had answers to questions that Danny and I didn't have.

"Do you know Bruce Chatwin?" he asked me. I said no.

"He was a travel writer who was obsessed with the question of why we travel. He posited that human beings evolved to be nomadic or semi-nomadic. Meaning we're not meant to stay locked in one place," he said frowning at his food.

"We need movement. Life is about movement. I wasted a long time limiting myself. Unmoving. But I think it was the thesis needed in order to reveal to me the truth. The antithesis was India. The product of the synthesis is now."

The last time I saw Charlie was at night in the terrace. He was very drunk. There were two woman with us. One was from Italy and the other was the Colombian woman. Soon Charlie left like a thief with the Italian. Hearing Danny flirt with the Colombian was depressing.

Then Danny and I went out to the clubs by ourselves. Danny didn't care for Asian women but he needed to be there. Danny clipped two large balloons in each hand. I sucked a few hits and it made my body feel like a vibrator. A deflated balloon hung on Danny's lips as he swayed his arm.

After the club we walked the street and Danny bought four packs of Marlboro reds and stuffed them in his shorts. We went to an expat bar where prostitutes wandered restlessly. An older prostitute with dead doll eyes stroked my cheek. She was touchy and I held a conversation with her. She told me her price and I negotiated from fifty to twenty USD. Danny said it was cruel.

The next morning Danny was drinking black coffee in the recreation area and watching Spiderman 2. I pressured him to come out for a smoke.

The sunlight was twinkling in the panelled roofs, the sharp antennas, and when I looked away I saw how intensely it burned in my vision. Clouds of grill smoke rose to the patio. Before noon Danny had almost finished a pack which he then offered to me. We ate fried rice and hotdog slices. I asked him about the Colombian woman.

"I'll see her again in Colombia," he said. "I'll see her wherever."

"Do you think the German will be there too?" I was very comfortable with Danny.

He inhaled. Short exhale. A laugh. "I don't know, buddy," he said.

I carried one of his backpacks to the taxi. "See you around," he said. As the taxi disappeared amid the motorbikes, I wished for the mobility to kick myself in the head because I had not gotten his number. After the day he left there were like iron grids between me and the other tourists.

I changed my plane ticket to depart in four weeks instead of two. I called my mother and she was glad. Then I left for Sapa and then central Vietnam, to Hue and Da Nang and Hoi An, and then to Saigon where I had booked my departure.

When I came back to Canada I felt good and everything was irrelevant. For weeks I felt that I was still in Asia. This faulty coupling of my actual location to my mental state was the ultimate sensation of surreal. I was finally inspired when thinking about traveling Canada which seemed more intimidating for at least in Asia mistakes were forgiven. When I told friends about my trip I felt embarrassed. Inside of me it was hard and perfected and when expressed it degraded into such fragility as to perish.

4.

ON THE SMOOTH SIDE of a multiplexed building is a portrait of Leonard Cohen, bright and warming in the afternoon sun, a soft gaze with a hand over his heart, his sedated thankfulness and low-vibrating charm. Near the building is the Musée des beaux arts. I buy a ticket and enter.

In a room with renaissance paintings a woman is giving a lecture on a small statue of The Thinker by Auguste Rodin. She wears a striking red dress suit. She asks what the furrowed brows could mean. Someone says, "He's perplexed."

"Exactly. See here," she points at the feet.

I walk down to the bottom floors where there are colourful paintings of paint splatter. Thick globs, ballish lumps that look still-wet. Tendrils of red and blue and yellow as if they are the nerves of some animal plucked and dyed. A background of hot blue swirled ghostly with white. Among these abstracts are metal sculptures that look forged by the blind.

In university I volunteered three hours each week to working the front desk of an art gallery. The supervisor instructed me on how to welcome visitors. She said it was important since for many it was the first time they visited an art gallery. I followed her elaborate greeting for two weeks and then abandoned it. I don't know how to inspire interest in someone without that interest already existing in some capacity. The art gallery was contemporary and most people looked for a few minutes and left.

There was one man who spent nearly one hour in the gallery. It was not a large place. He walked slowly, reading the brochure. He inched closer and squinted to examine the grain of paint. He asked what type of paint was used.

I do not have a reasonable answer to why I visit art galleries. They are not entertaining or amusing. I considered that ultimately it is a secret which if revealed would destroy my engagement with the art. Others that do not care for the art have no secret and therefore the art is dead to them. I considered that the man had a secret he'd been maintaining for years.

I thought about how unsuited the modern mind is to things like paintings and poetry. These things are not entertainment. At least not for me. They reveal some other deeper yet higher and descriptively elusive domain of experience.

During the six months of volunteering I wanted to have ahistorical tastes, to not be tied to the sentiments of my culture or time. I used my three hours reading books and I finished thirteen.

One book which I had taken out of the university library was by Goethe, titled, *The Sorrows of Young Werther*. Goethe was considered an eighteenth-century renaissance man who was very scientific and rich and successful. He inspired many suicides in Europe from his book. In it, a sensitive young man named Werner falls in love with Charlotte who gets married to another man. Werner likes walking in nature and fantasizing about his sensory perceptions. He savours the intensity of his manic emotions and he hates working. He writes long letters of either joy or anguish to his friend, Wilhelm, who tries to stabilize him by finding him a job. But Werner hates normal life, would most likely hate a healthy relationship with Charlotte, and his hatred becomes an undeniable logic that kills him.

When I left the volunteering the supervisor allowed me one free book since most volunteers stayed three months and I stayed six. I choose a photography catalogue which had black and white pictures of hands in varying angles and environments.

I said goodbye to the gallery workers. "We should do something," said one of the workers named Denise. I'm just a volunteer, I imagined saying.

A man named Jackson said, "Celebrate?"

"Well, no," said Denise, lengthening the *no*. "Not to celebrate. But you know."

We went out that night to a bar.

Jackson had seen me many times reading books and he asked me about them. I told him that I was on a mission to have ahistorical tastes and he said that it was good for me.

"What did you learn?" asked Denise.

I thought about it. "I learned I can't help liking what's relevant to me."

Jackson laughed. "Who does?"

"Maybe someone would if they wanted to escape what's relevant," said Denise. "Were you hoping to escape?"

"No," I told her. "Not at all." Then I said, "I wanted to be oceanic." I waited for Jackson's response but he made none. "You know," I continued, "with experience."

"Oh, very nice," said Denise. "I like that."

We ordered a pitcher of beer and they talked about their boring tasks and new exhibitions. We looked through artwork on our phones and they suggested artists for me. We ordered chicken wings except for Denise who had a chicken wrap. We finished the pitcher and ordered a new one. We passed what must have been three hours drinking the next pitcher. We entered a mock-debate on whether or not a bar should replace a pitcher when the beer had gotten warm.

Then we exchanged numbers and finally Denise gave me hers. She had eyes like anodized discs. Blue specked in the rim and growing greenish to the pupil. She was born in South Africa yet having no accent. She used to talk to me routinely during her lunch breaks.

I just came out the best art museum I've seen.

Stop telling me.

Montreal is the best it's ever been and you're being a loser.

You'll make me lose my job.

Good. You can make more online.

Somehow performing to a camera is more nerve wrecking. Less fun too.

I walk further into the downtown. "Cigarette," a man says. He is short and fat and unwashed. "Cigarette." He points to my cigarette. "No cigarette," I say and walk on.

A bookstore which is small and disordered like a cave with books. Tall and wide shelves bearing tarnished spines, the pages a piss-yellow, multilingual shelves and huge hardcovers settling heavy on top shelves which need the old sliding ladder to reach. A tremendous reek of dust, elderly wood.

There is a Quebec section and I pick a book with a melancholic painting of a cat on the cover. I open it. The mind's calculus softly clicks these alien pieces to known pattern. My understanding is indistinguishable from imagination.

I find Camus' *The Myth of Sisyphus* essay collection in the original French. I'd like to use it as a means to improve my French.

There's a man moving boxes in the backroom. "Comment?" I say. He protrudes his bleached head.

"Comment?" I poke the book cover.

"Front flap."

I bend the cover and the price is there in airy pencil. Twelve dollars.

A woman with a long neck sits behind the desk. She has thrifted herself into the dead clothes of an old-time librarian. It seems she is burrowed in the floor. "Found everything okay?" she asks. She lifts herself up.

"Everything's okay," I tell her. "I want to improve my French."

She eyes the books as if I ruined them. "Good choices."

"I read Le Petit Prince so many times."

She laughs a wide-berthed laughter. I see the dark fillings in her molars. "That's cute," she says. "I haven't read it in maybe twenty years."

"It gets tiring."

"Oh, but you think you're ready for these expert choices?"

"I think ultimately it depends how interested I am."

"Hmm. Certainly important."

"J'ai apprendu le français pendant trois mois."

"D'accord."

"Tu compris?"

"Oui."

She presses the total into a calculator.

"So, I've been traveling here for a week enjoying how unique this place is."

She puts the two books in a plastic bag. "Visited the big art museum?"

"I was just there."

"There's several you should check out. Interested?"

I stare at her. "What?"

"Are you interested to know which?"

"What?"

"Galleries. Art galleries."

"Yes," I say. "I'd love to know."

She folds a sheet of paper and tears it. She writes four names in sloppy cursive. She tells me of the best ways to reach them.

"And you should check out the library. It's fantastic."

"Where is that?" I ask though I know. She answers with speech and hands.

"Merci," I say.

"Merci. À bientôt."

As I grab my bag of books I try to remember. I stare at first edition prints in the glass as if the answer is there.

Then I stuff the bag in the inside pocket of my jacket. I light a cigarette in front of the store window. She is sitting with her back to the window. Her head teases out of a stack of folded draft paper. Then she lifts herself up. The cigarette breaks in a long glowing ash when I walk in the street.

I continue on for a long time. My stomach sucks inward. The sensation of hunger is fixed to an idea. Uncouple the idea and the sensation is aimless. I stop walking and grow dizzy. The sense of passing out enlivens me.

Soon I stand outside the large library. There are a few people smoking cigarettes. A man hacks and spits. Ahead of me are scaffolds blocking a church. The pointed cross is emerald and rising high. The sidewalk stretches widely to the road where there is a line of parked cars sparkling in the sun. The cigarette has excited a barbed pain in the centre-point of my skull.

I pass a security guard and metal detectors. There are stairs winding around an elevator shaft. The ground floor is open enough to be like a gymnasium. There are shelves for new arrivals and beyond is a coffee shop that looks like a bar. Leather couches with worn creases like the brands of lightning bolts. My body meshes to the soft shape. On another couch is a youngster with a beanie, a suitcase lying flat by his feet. He is charging his phone in an outlet. He unplugs it and talks Québécois and points to the suitcase. I nod.

The suitcase is black, a red stripe with a white logo that reads *Canada*, following a maple leaf. The contents press on the fabric causing the square shape to be round and lumpy. The two wheels are scratched as if by saws.

A man says, "Maricon, oh maricon. Fuck. Fuck." He stands over a table and possibly watches his reflection in the large window that looks to an underground garden with a big tree in the middle.

I walk to the café and tell the barista, "Café au lait." I pass the man. It only seems like no one else is paying attention. "Anybody fuck with me, fucking maricon."

I imagine punching him in the head and throttling his neck and banging his head on the table. He slashes the air with his finger side to side. I feel the blood like a cool gas releasing in my chest. He grimaces and jostles his head. I can tackle him and kick him in the gut and stomp his head. I imagine the brain and blood and a kind of yolk which as a child I considered to be inside the eyeball.

I open a page in *The Myth of Sisyphus*.

Take Camus seriously for Camus helped me realize that I would not throw my mother in a canal if she died. I would give her a worthy funeral.

There is like an octopus curling inside my belly. The café au lait is the exact taste of pale.

"You fuck. Fuck maricon."

I imagine kicking in his right knee, thrusting his head in the table edge, the teeth carving the wood until stopping when the jaw cracks out of the socket. In the final kick I can feel the hard edge pound my heel.

I finally check my phone. No message. Depression.

I remember waiting outside of her house. It seemed she lived above a hair salon in a backstreet. A Chinese couple approached me. The husband put my arm over his wife's shoulders. The tip of my cigarette grazed his palm. But he didn't react. He took a picture of us. She was smiling large and he laughed at us. They thanked me and then left in a shuttle-bus.

Tracy came out shortly after. We went to our favourite bar. The tourists were crowded in the first floor with the pool tables and the jukebox. There were wood pillars throughout the floor, wrapped with fake green leaves. Thick and strawy ropes interwove the ceiling. Large and insinuating pictures of apes.

We got two beers and watched a fat woman in a silky yellow dress playing pool with two men and they were drunk and the game was not serious. The men wore Hawaiian shirts of bananas. Tracy said most of the British tourists wore either banana or pineapple.

We went upstairs to sit on a deck overlooking the street. It was before midnight and there were a lot of people walking. Across from us were other bars and restaurants which all looked like a stage set, the night like a black pastel smeared over cardboard.

There was a two-wheeled pushcart fitted with an umbrella which had a radio strapped to its base playing some Vietnamese speech. It was being pushed by a small women in sandals. On top the cart was a portable grill cooking thin strips of beef and chicken. Underneath were two ice boxes, one with cold drinks and the other with vegetables. She'd stop and pull bread buns out from a plastic bag tied to the handle and slice them with a thin knife and grill them. A man followed her about, watching her prepare the sandwiches and talking to the tourists who bought them.

"Are you excited about going back to school?" I asked Tracey.

"Yeah. Scared too."

"I know it's scary too."

I saw the redness across her chest. She was allergic to alcohol.

"You're crazy for drinking," I told her.

"What can I do when I'm with you?"

"I'm a bad guy."

"It's not your fault."

"It is," I said. "You're killing yourself cause of me."

"So dramatic." She tossed her eyes to the sky and back. It irritated me.

"When I'm with you I am."

"What else are you?"

"Stupid."

"Shut up."

We went downstairs to the outside where there was a verandah with matted bench seats. We ordered another beer and watched more of the night passing.

The man that followed the pushcart hollered at us. "Cute," he said. He did kissy faces. I realized then that I rarely saw other young tourists with local women.

He spoke in Vietnamese and Tracy giggled.

"What did he say?"

She kept giggling. He continued with the Vietnamese.

"He's asking when is the marriage." He grinned at me when she said this. He was a big Vietnamese man, loud and smoking.

I was hungry and feeling good from the beers and I asked the woman for one sandwich. Then I remembered I should ask Tracy if she was hungry too. She said the sandwiches didn't look clean.

"Where you from?" the man asked me. He was still shouting.

"Canada," I shouted.

"How much in Canada?"

"A sandwich like this?" I held it up so he could see. "Ten bucks."

"Wah, wah. Expensive. No good."

The sandwich was small and tasted very plain. We walked on and the man said nothing to us. Then from behind us he shouted, "Oy, goodnight Canada."

Tracy said, "I like him. Funny guy."

I go out to smoke.

I see the beanie-headed youth talking to a girl who's crying. There is another young girl who looks to be on the team of the crying one.

A stranger walks about them. He asks the crier if she needs emergency help and she says, "Fuck off."

· · · ·

I HEAR PEOPLE WHISPERING, the zipper-trill of backpacks. The blanket-curtain is hung and my nude legs are airing. The little muscles in my feet are raw and hugging the bone.

Soon the people leave.

I'm alone and relaxed. But with my phone it's not true loneliness. And the worst loneliness is this artificial kind. To be absolutely alone is like a drug which the body does not tolerate at first. The more one does it the more it becomes tolerable until it integrates into the organism. It must be therapeutic to experience loneliness, here and there, once it's integrated.

Of course I use dating apps when I want to be social. Especially when traveling since people get excited about showing foreigners around their town.

My interactions on dating apps have always been worthwhile. I know people who have had bad encounters. Every woman I've been with has texted me back after the first date. People appreciate the relaxed nature of my texting, the lack of demand. For me the date is experienced in the moment, there is no goal, just two people sharing themselves. Some dates are experienced as a future event. One or both parties are not truly in the present. They have abstracted the moment. They're strategizing in the abstract model they've created. My friend Cal did this. He moved to another city and we communicated solely through texts, nearly everyday. I texted Cal to forget himself as a man and the woman as a woman. Packaged in those roles are too many goals that confuse and frustrate the present moment.

Cal texted me that on a recent date he kept asking the girl, "What else do you want to do?" She said she was tired which means she's not interested in him. He kept asking. "What else?" She finally told him that they could do something the next weekend. She never replied to his texts. Then he texted me that before her there was a woman with *Dinner or netflix and chill* in her profile description. This gave Cal the idea to ask her, "So, you've had the dinner, now do you want the Netflix and chill?" She said, "Not tonight, I'm tired."

Cal was not ugly. He was tall and athletic with a masculine face and grey eyes and he had a speech tick that caused his words to undulate. I told him to be confident with his tick and confident in his nervousness. I told him that hooking up is rare and really only happens when people are drunk. Or there is some special circumstance that has brought them together, that the date is not some outing they've fitted into their schedules. It happens when you're not expecting it. It comes quickly and it settles slowly. You don't know what it is or what it wants. The brain you use to figure it is not the one needed for it. There is a part covered by all that new matter and it has been there since the start of you and the things like you. Its function is not for you to control, like the heartbeat is not, and if it presses on you as a mystery then you are still within its grace.

Cal called me a *Casanova*. And I felt a goodness one feels over another that is unequal to them, a silent power roused in the underworld of what you are.

My profile description reads *Traveling in Montreal. Show me around?*

A good profile description doesn't matter. Ultimately pictures decide. But something is better than nothing. Something helps clear whatever imagining is in the viewer's head, which is typically negative without a description. Funny is always best. For a long time my description was simply *I'm good at making bios*. Cal texted that it was a funny description but he didn't show it. His was *Not sure what I want here. Help me figure it out?* Then he listed his hobbies. He included a picture of his dog. He said it was a huge help.

A huge help in attracting matches with mono?

Listen, not only is this city built on a literal swamp but the women look and act like they're out of a swamp too. And not everyone can go to Asia and fuck desperate poor bitches like you do.

I asked him if he thought that's what I did.

He texted, *Yeah, it's called sex tourism. Fucko.*

I don't care enough about sex to do that.

Sure. You culturally enriched yourself plenty.

I've known Cal since high school. When members of that school died he made sure to text me about it. It seemed the deaths were part of a curse inherent in the school. I told him that if he was selected by the curse his gravestone would read *Here lies an asshole. Want to give it a try?*

I match with a woman who is pale with black hair and blue eyes, the nose sharp and roman. Wide face, the skeletal frame of marble statues. She has no description. I text her *Bonjour, I'm traveling here and looking for someone fun to show me around, maybe help in my French.*

From my locker I get a fresh pair of jeans. I go down the stairs and grab my smelly shoes from the rack.

Outside the cigarette stokes bright. The sky is a velvet-blue dark. Above me are flowerpots hanging on chains, the petals curling over the pots like many tongues. People, very mature, converse in the dark tunnel leading to the parking lot. I see their glowing red cigarettes, the white smoke. A talking man in an open dress shirt moves his fingers with delicate dexterity. The others watch him.

The buildings seem dusted in fine powder and lamplights are fashioning a series of soft-glow discs through the stoned road. Above the river the clouds are swelled and grey and the dark water has with each movement a thorny texture. The path is busy with people, bikers, dogs, every so often brightened by the few lamps and then gone again to bolded shadow. A pier leads to some museum and a Ferris wheel rests in a starless backdrop.

The dark forested borders of St. Helen's Island out there bound to the river. Throughout its black branches bleed whatever lights. Towards the sky is the crawl of its dark tree crowns. The naked moon, a large and bright fugitive, reels free and high above it.

I pass under a bridge, wood planks throughout its underside, the lacework of its steel supports like some giant cobweb trap. I walk along a fence above a yard with so many cargo containers, stacked or solitary, all closed. Weeds coil high on the fence and cushion a knotty bed through the base. Weeds squeeze out the cracks of the pavement, tangled and dead. The near-hit whoosh of high-speed vehicles by me.

I get on a sidewalk that soon declines to an underpass. Black graffiti, shattered glass and blankets and trash in the sides, an atmospheric stench of organic spoil and exhaust. I walk on and see cubed apartments facing the river, unlit and austere. In the distance the city is muted and uncanny, a picture of artful and glowing structures.

Two men are walking to me. They are young and casual. "Ça va?" one asks. He stops and waits. I say, "Good," and walk on.

I pass the old neighbourhoods with empty houses that look squished together. An archaic iron railing shields the small lawns bearing amorphous plants.

I light a cigarette in a parkette. There are rows of arched trellises and crawling them are vines crested with flower-bulbs. The perimeter is hedged by bushes trimmed an egg-shape, many plank benches. Squirrels are skittering up and down the trees. They are thuggish squirrels that run to you and stand and sniff the air, their furry chests trembling with craze. I rub my fingers and they sprawl and spin and stand and suck wildly into their pinhole nostrils. I walk and they follow close, scurrying in the dusty path. Soon they dart back into the dropped foliage rustling to their claws.

Now be lonely a while and enjoy this wilderness. Maybe find yourself in a hovel as a neutral hermit. There is a pilgrim here also. Help him find the light of your burning hovel. Pray he does not crawl into a cave and grow strange.

I continue walking past the blinking traffic lights and construction zones where portions of street rest pulverized and dusty. Boarded rental homes cordoned with red tape, couches and cabinets and refrigerators piled in the balconies.

There is a crowd outside the McDonalds. Crumpled figures, smoking. It seems like something is always happening whether inside of them or outside.

It's deep night and there is no marked path for wanderers here. We must confront the many heads and fangs of the world. Be our own cartographers.

I need courage to be my own cartographer. The maps people use are used for a reason. But not using them is not a disrespect. It's just that they're not my maps.

I stand outside an open bar playing pop rock and light a cigarette. I feel adventurous and the cigarette is hitting fine with no taste, no sense of hunger in my gut. The night is warm with a wetness to the air.

I enter the restaurant and say, "Pour moi."

With the chopstick I stab the pinkish beef into the bowl's hot recess. I squeeze the juice out of a lime wedge and drop the sprouts and leaves of mint and squirt chili paste and with the ladle spoon skim the soupy surface and sip. The sauce accompanying the spring rolls is peanuty and near acidic with sweetness. I use the chopsticks to grope into the bowl and lift a flap of grey beef, rubbery and spicy. I lace the noodles around the chopsticks. It looks like a dripping mound of wet silk. My teeth clank on the snappy wood and the noodles tear easy. They are squishy with salty broth and bottomless in satiation.

Outside it rains but slight and aesthetically somber. Few colours, ruby and pink, cling to trails of rain in the window.

BY THE METRO STATION is a woman in a tan corduroy overcoat, smoking a cigarette. Her skin is brightly white. She nods and I nod. "Bonjour." Her lips project to my cheek and she throws the cigarette behind her. The other cheek. The lightest lip smacking. "I am French," she tells me. We walk like automatons.

"Sorry for being late," she says.

"I don't mind."

"My shoe broke."

"You possess a great accent."

"I am from France."

"Incroyable."

"I am not lying."

It is impossible to know who is leading.

I ask, "Are you hungry?"

"Did you want to go to the gallery first?"

"Oh, yes."

"The seam of my shoe broke in the train. I needed to grab a new pair. Sorry."

"You had heels?"

"Not full."

We wait at an intersection.

"It's so difficult for me to understand spoken French."

"They do not pronounce right here."

"Ouais," I say.

"You like living here?" she asks.

"I don't. I'm traveling here."

"Oh, you're right," she says professionally.

"Do you like living here?"

"Montréal is nice actually. The only city I lived was Paris."

"They are proud people here."

"As they are in Paris and as they should be."

"I like hearing you talk," I say.

"My accent?"

"A dream."

"Merci." She laughs maturely.

"Do you drink?" I ask.

"I love beer and wine."

"We'll drink some later."

"Do you smoke weed?"

"I do not know how."

"You do not know how to smoke weed?"

"I never learned how."

"I can smoke a joint and teach you."

My thumb slips on the button of the lighter and then grips and sparks. She asks for one. Then her red lips purse on the filter waiting, her eyes switching from me to the cigarette. Like shuffling discs of blue china. I hand her the lighter and she lights it.

I ask, "Do you like the city or country? I know France has beautiful country."

"My dream is to live in the country. The city is nice now but I will hate it when I'm older."

"You ever lived in the countryside?"

"During childhood my family moved in and out of the countryside."

"You milked the cows?"

"Like you with weed I do not know how."

"I have milked."

"Fun?"

"For me, not the cows." A twang down my sternum as if a cord was yanked.

Then, "I love to live in the country and do nothing," she says. "I am upset you mentioned it."

I can see the board sign of the gallery. The lane is tight enough so as to feel like your shoulders might brush the walls.

"Let's smoke before we go?" I ask.

"We smoked did we not?"

"I'm an awful chain-smoker."

"I will wait for you to finish."

"You don't want one?"

"Okay," she says.

We light the cigarettes.

"Nice night, huh?"

"Yes, perfect weather for an art gallery."

"So, you like art?"

"I do and I celebrate new ways people express their lives in whatever medium."

"Exploration is necessary. I tend to explore and experiment."

"I can sense that energy in you."

"Energy?"

"I am sensitive to people's energy. Do not worry, yours is good. Playful."

"I don't know if I can sense people's energy."

"You can but you do not think of it."

"Do you think I'll have good energy in Paris?"

"How can your energy be bad in Paris?"

"Want me to be honest?"

"Let me say first that there is a difference between honesty and openness."

"Paris looks too touristy."

"Touristy is not equal with bad," she says. "If this city suits you then Paris will too. Do you think Montréal is not touristy? Do you know how many tourists arrive from New York? The city is catered to tourists. But do not confuse me. The tourist is not the old and retired. They are most like you."

"I hate thinking of myself as a tourist."

"Nevermind then. I don't wish to ruin your idealisms."

A narrow hall leads to a front desk where Alex speaks French beautifully. We pay separate and then go up two flights of stairs.

In the exhibition floor each piece is separated by hospital-like curtains hanging on hooks. Alex sits in a beanbag and a worker adjusts a visor on her head. Her jeans are tight and show her legs fatter than they are.

The worker straps a visor on my head.

I'm in a jungle. A shaman wearing a crown of feathers, a colourful shawl, inserts a wooden pipe into my mouth. The visuals are hazy and spirals form and interlock with the vines. I'm transported to a shifting place where the geometry is not bound by physical laws. The shaman vanishes amid chaos spirals. I'm passing in a tunnel. Snakes and birds appear as I move into them. Centipedes and spiders. All being atomized and relinquishing hidden geometrical blueprints.

I unlatch the visor. I walk into a dark room. There are three pieces separated by black cloth curtains. A worker talks to me in Québécois and points to each piece. I stare at him and nod. His tone heightens, he looks serious. "Which do you want to try?" he asks.

"I can look around."

"Do you need assistance?"

"I can put the thing on."

I'm a giant stomping through a desert, the other is in a decrepit gymnasium with basketballs bouncing around me, and in the last I'm standing on panels in space where featureless bipeds dance in front of me.

I walk out to light a cigarette.

In the opening of the lane I watch the dark paved road. At the right it bows like in the cusp of a dome. The two road markers are bold like highlighter bands. It is smooth and flush and in the side which lines the lane is a granular skirting of the newly cooled asphalt.

Alex comes out. Her lips twists to my coming footsteps.

"Are you hungry?" I ask.

"Starving. The art augmented my appetite."

We find a pizza shop like a kitchenette. We get two slices of pepperoni pizza. The slices cover fully the soggy paper plate.

"I don't want to eat too much before drinking," I tell her.

"Ah, I forgot about drinking. L'alcool feels best with empty stomach."

"The consideration for l'estomac is so European."

"I am European."

"Okay, European," I say. "Why don't we trash this and go to a bar?"

Her chewing is like someone walking in mud-puddles. "Such pizza needs to be washed out," she says. Then we trash it.

She tells me she has never traveled alone before. I tell her it is preferable and not as frightening as she thinks. She tells me a story about her friend who was in a hotel in India and the desk workers tried to access her room when she was alone.

"The boyfriend showed. They called the police but what are the police for?"

She waits for my answer.

"How was India?" I ask her.

"Genghis Khan rated it too hot and the water filthy. I agree."

"So, you hated it."

"Not necessarily hated. India is a harsh country."

"I kind of like harsh."

She laughs wickedly. "Touts would love you there."

There is a bar with a picket-fenced dining area. We wait for a long time and then get escorted to a table. She orders beers and a shareable pizza. I order two shots of whiskey.

The whiskey comes first. We toast.

"When did you learn you could sense energy?" I ask.

"Last year."

"When you were fresh off the boat?"

"I did not know before then that what I was doing my entire life was sensing energy."

"Who was the first person's energy you sensed?"

"My father"

"Here I mean."

"Not remarkable enough to remember."

"You can sense it anywhere though?"

"It terrifies me how I can."

Our beers come.

"Listen," she says. "When I arrived I wished to be an actress. I wanted to waste my life in film. I am auditioning for theatre roles. It is so cliché."

"You can make le film with les yeux."

"You are funny."

"You have streetwalker de les yeux."

"What does it mean?"

"Do you know le prostitutes?"

"I don't."

"They look at men in the streets like you do."

"Am I doing it now?"

"Yes."

When the pizza comes I tell the waitress for two more shots. Alex makes a noise and the waitress looks at her curiously. I ask that waitress for two more. Then I tell Alex a few nights ago I was drinking tequila and feeling sick. "You're not a drinker," she tells me.

"But it's so nice being a drinker with you."

"I never drink tequila unless there is a problem."

"People always say shit like that about tequila. S'not for us Europeans."

"We are a dying animal."

"So then. Another shot for this dying animal?" The waitress comes with the shots. We both order two more beers and then we toast.

"What do you do?" asks Alex.

"What do I do?"

"For a living."

"For a living?"

"You are joking?"

"I am a student."

"How is being a student?"

"Okay but of course I want to forget it."

"You never worked?"

"I worked construction." I had only done so for one summer.

"Do you wear a white shirt and blue jeans?"

"Everyday I do. With big steel toes."

Her eyes wheel as if to stare into her brain. She laughs lubricatedly.

"I get very filthy," I tell her. I want her eyes to whirl.

"Your mother must scrub hard."

"Why do you mention my mother?"

"From fear because you look sixteen."

"I'm twenty-two."

The beers come. The pizza is decked with bacon and peppers and tomato and ham and a tangy sauce with rosemary bits. The cheese is a warm shell. In my mouth the bread is like a moist tortilla chip.

"What do you want to be?" she asks.

"I want to be a French poet."

"Why French?"

"They do poetry the best. Know Rimbaud? He's my favourite. An interesting psychology on him. He was a poetic prodigy and he abandoned it at the age of twenty-one."

"I suppose you have a theory."

"Of course. I have theories on all my favourite artists. Arthur Rimbaud wanted to kill himself but was not able to and so he killed poetry. Now you might think poetry lived on regardless of Rimbaud. It did but poetry for Rimbaud was dead. Therefore he was reborn in an afterlife which no other soul but him had access."

"He associated poetry with Paul Verlaine and so by abandoning poetry he finally broke with Paul."

"Amazing. You're a theoretician too."

"No."

"But don't you consider French poetry is the best?"

"Not when theorizing it."

"Do you think I can be a French poet?"

"I think anyone can."

I stare at her like a drunk. "Do you have to work at being a French poet or are you born into it?"

"You are made a French poet either by being born blue-blooded or by heartbreak."

"Heartbreak is such a lifestyle."

"True in one respect," she says. "But also clear it never broke for you."

"I actually got high blood pressure." I forget what I'm saying. "My mother is very proud of my levels."

"Please eat more pizza."

"Do you think I'll be a French poet in Paris where there are so many like me?"

"You will be eaten in Paris."

"Eaten?"

"You are too tender."

"Why the frick would I ever go to Paris?"

"Maybe you'll like it."

"You are a cannibal," I tell her. The beer is bloating my gut. "Do you prefer to eat tender filthy boys in white shirts and blue jeans?"

"If they are behaved of age boys."

I lurch forward and my rear shoots off the chair. My feet are waltzing to the urinal. I go into the stall because the urinal is unstable. There is a terrific smell of piss and the ground is sticky on my shoes. I can go to the hostel and masturbate and sleep. My phone reads near midnight. I squeeze the phone as if to crush it. I stand and finger the zipper on my shorts. I wash my hands and look passionately in the mirror. My brown sun-kissed hair is lying flat and wiry on my forehead. She is European and you can never understand her, I tell my anti-self in the mirror.

I glide back and sit. She thumbs her phone and stands and walks away. The strap of her small purse is hanging off the chair. Take the money and go to the hostel and masturbate.

"Finish your beer," I say.

"Okay," she says. "You too."

"I can't. Finish it for me."

"If you prefer," she says. "Are you all right?"

"What do you sense?"

"Too much l'alcool."

"I can ruin a good time if I'm not careful."

She drinks my beer in mouthfuls.

"I'm a shithead," I tell her.

"No. You are funny and your tummy hurts."

"Shut up, Cannibal."

"Change my name to something fun."

"I know either to call a body professor or boss."

"Call me Professor."

"Professor."

She finishes the beer. We do not wait for the waitress. At the counter I insist to pay. We get out the doors and the uncertain depth of night falls on me like a bucket of paint. We walk and my feet are walking two meters behind me.

"Slow down," she says and hurries.

"Sorry. I'm a quick walker."

"You walk funny too, on your tiptoes."

The man inside watches us in the street. He is perfectly bald with a big hook-nose and his arms are crossed to expose corded forearm veins. The shop is cold and bright. A collection of country flags along the top board.

Alex points to a bucket of green specked by dark chocolate. The scooper shaves sheets of it. She requests the thick-crust waffle cone shaped like a jagged crown. He dumps the round shavings into it. His moustache spreads like arms to flash a tiling of plaqued teeth. As he looks at me his baldness catches the gleam of the overheads, it sweeps across his skull like a puck. His glossy eye a marble cupped in soft clay. Lack of vital subject, a gaze both courting being and nonbeing. The vocal gears pump between the laced flesh.

Alex asks me what I want. I'm not sure at all.

"Do you want a recommendation?"

I look at her. "What?"

"Oh, sit down," she says. "Sit down."

My rear bangs in a fold-up chair and my skull bobs. From out my seat my neck stretches and my eyes peer at caramel swirl, strawberry sorbet, butter brickle and the chunky cheesecake mix, hills of vanilla plain. The frost is bulky and furrowing on the fridge walls. He watches me.

"Do you like strawberry?" he asks.

"No. No strawberry."

"Well."

"What about chocolate?" he asks.

"What's your special?"

"I'm not making soup."

"Just joking," he says. "Sorbet is our special. We serve four varieties."

I stare at Alex. "I only want ice cream."

"Okay," she says. "How about a recommendation of peanut butter?"

The scooper shoots into the bottom. Twisted creamy tails fall in the waffle cone.

"No, I insist," I tell her.

"You paid so much for me to be comfortable."

I'm angry when I say, "I insist."

Then we stand outside the shop, in the coolness, before concrete steps that go up to the sidewalk. My tongue catches the melting edges from reaching my hand. The peak whittles down and my numb tongue sculpts to flatten it fully. Montreal is so brief as to be traveling by wind.

"You are so funny, oh my," she says.

"I'm not doing funny right now," I tell her.

We sit on a bench facing a smooth pond. With a napkin from her purse she wipes her lips and fingers. She folds and sits on the napkin. From her jacket pocket she unsheathes a slender joint. Pinched in her lips it sags. A forward shift of the jaw, the bottom lip raises it nearly touching the roman nose. As the flame cooks the tip she puffs. Excites the glow so red and bright. It floats to me.

"I don't know how," I tell her.

"Are you playing me?"

"I don't know."

"Stop playing me."

"What I mean is I don't know how to enjoy it."

"Then nevermind."

I pinch the joint. I suck and my head bloats as if with lead.

"I love sitting in the park and smoking," she says.

Fingering for a cigarette and my thoughts moving like the flipping pages of drawings, each page differing in a way that does not give the impression of movement.

"Let's perform a scene, actress."

"What scene?"

"Called improvisation."

"I know what it's called. Improv. Set it."

"We are in the park." My mind trips on *park*.

"I'm a serial killer trying to lure you," I say.

"Do you watch True Crime?"

"No. Please focus on the scene."

"All right. I am a stupid young girl and you are sophisticated serial killer."

"How young?"

"Eighteen."

"Good."

"Wish me as young as you look?"

"No. Don't spoil the scene with additional meanings. I want to be a normal serial killer."

"So commanding," she says. "You should wish to be a director instead of a French poet-actor."

"I am a thirty-five year old killer."

"Perfect age."

The cigarette is unlit in my hand and I touch the tip with the lighter.

"I am so excited. When can we begin?"

"Acting cannot happen in an excited state even if the scene calls for excitement."

"My director is a lecturer too."

"And your laughter is too mature for a young girl. Infantilize your laughter."

"My multitalented director is a life coach too. When will I hear your laugh?"

"I'm nervous."

"No, you are perfect and in this entire date I am unsure you like me."

"I don't show it."

"Can I be closer?"

"Yes."

"What?"

"Yes."

"Now can we start?" she asks petulantly. "Call me Suzanne. A mature name for a young girl. Such names are flattering."

"It's a good flattering name for a young girl," I say, my dry tongue sticking and peeling off the palate. "What happens when she's old?"

"Suit her perfectly then. What's your name?"

"Name me then."

"Thomas."

"People say you should go into what you're talented in and your talent is naming."

"You are playing me. No one is making money in naming."

"Oh, Suzanne," I say. "When are we starting the fucking scene?"

"On your call, director."

"Suzanne is beautifully melodic."

She sings *Suzanne*.

"Why aren't you a singer?"

"I am crazy you know. And you inspire me with silly dreams. You don't care? Do you know I am really crazy?"

"Okay, let's be silly." Our mouths touch. Thank you for your spit. My hand goes through her arm to wrap her waist.

"Serial killer Thomas you needn't to try."

She stares at my mouth and scratches the back of my neck. Her nails feel so dull and uncertain. I peck her lips and she laughs. "So fun," she says. She lifts both legs to my lap. They are heavy and awkward legs. I do not remember extinguishing the cigarette. I rub my nose on her's. "It is so fun," she says.

She inserts a key into an apartment and we go in a stairwell like one found in a factory. In the hall the thick carpet is stained and there is a smell of expiration. In the end of the hall she opens a door and out wafts a massive weed-stench.

The wood floor is warbled like burnt plastic in the living room. In the corner is a neat queen-size bed and across from it is a fold-up couch which is in a slight dip within the floor. There is a mirrored closet in the wall between the door and the open kitchen. I see my shoes are on and I take them off.

She walks out the kitchen with a container of croissants, her jacket off and she has changed to pajama pants. She goes into the bathroom next to the kitchen. She opens the shower tap. When she comes out she is wearing a loose undershirt, no bra. I need water and she hands me a glass which my fingers stain with the croissant chocolate sauce.

"Music?" she asks.

"Something French."

She plays a song I don't like. "Play Serge Gainsbourg, dear," I tell her.

"Oh, look at you knowing Gainsbourg."

"Play Couleur Café!"

The song starts. She sits on my lap. I swoop my right arm under her right armpit and pry her off me. She lays oddly on the couch watching me as I take my shorts off. Her thumbs slide down her pajamas and I pull them off at the knee. She is wearing panties that show the faintness of what is underneath. Her legs crane over her head a welcoming.

The song changes. She rushes to replay.

In the bed she is vigorous with the wrist, her turbulent china eyes. She reaches a shaking hand under the pillow.

"What's wrong?"

"Nothing."

She runs to the kitchen.

I forget that I am not in the hostel.

I imagine myself as a local who has been living in Montreal for a couple years. As she walks back she reminds me of idyllic scenes found only in fantasy. Then why did you find one.

In a medical manner she cups the top and kneads down. The smell of latex is repulsive. Soon she is saying, "Oui oui oui." I say, "Ouais," on my knees. I try making sense of Gainsbourg's lyrics. I imagine him sitting on the fold-up couch and judging my motion, my floppy ass.

Then, "Did you come?" she asks.

"No." She holds a rebellious stare as I push her head down.

"Play another song," I say. "Play No Comment."

She types in the laptop. Her breasts hang like dollops of batter.

She crawls up to cuddle. The song has replayed two times.

"You can sleep here," she says. "I don't mind."

"My stuff's in the hostel."

Before the door she asks, "Can I see you again?"

"When?"

"Tomorrow. We can watch a movie."

"I'll see what I'm doing tomorrow."

"All right."

We kiss. She opens the door. I fear being lost in the hall. I walk into the park and light a cigarette. Hard darkness around me. I walk in the road.

In a convenience store I request a pack of Phillip Morris. He talks Hindi in an earpiece and he's very leisure with my request. He tosses the pack across the counter of lotto cards.

I open the door and wait for the chimes to stop clinking. I shout, "Oh, tabarnak!"

His middle finger is high up in the window.

6

"WAITING LONG?"

"Half hour," I tell her.

"So, so sorry. My dress." She wears a black skirt under the leather overcoat. "I bought the shoes in the morning." Heeled shoes that pop her calves.

"It's okay," I say. "I can forget it."

"Ugh. I hate how you must feel sitting around so long. I am sorry."

"No, don't be."

"The second time is worse than last. I am making you a fool."

"I've forgotten it."

"If you're upset I fix it."

"I'm okay now."

"Positive?"

"Positive."

"How have you been?" she asks.

"I'm okay. I only saw you yesterday. How are you?"

"Good."

Then she says, "You are quiet."

"Oh, it's nothing. I like to be quiet so it's not a problem."

"I am evil for being late."

"Oh, I forgot already," I say. "What are we watching?"

"Horror is the mood."

"Now you're taking the piss."

She laughs. "Who taught you Anglo expressions?"

"Got Anglo friends, love."

"They're so bloody funny, the Anglos."

"They're my favourite friends with their bloody accents and mannerisms."

"But you ought not be too friendly with them. No, no. They bloody drink like fish."

We turn a corner and I see the round overhead of the theatre.

"Shithead," she says.

"Professor," I say.

"Cigarette?"

"Of course."

You can forgive her easy. She is kind and beautiful and she smokes. Though forgiveness is easy to do intellectually. The challenge is in the body where forgiveness has to first exist like an organ.

Some do not have it and maybe they have to grow it. When they have it, it needs to be nourished and kept healthy. If it is not there then it does not matter how much the intellect forgives. But that is for an extreme case and she is not one.

She is easily forgivable because she is French and I have learned the French are stylistically late and so in her perspective it is disturbing for me to be on time and even so early. I imagine telling her that if I have plans the entirety of the time before the plans is spent thinking about them.

In the glassed booth is a young man with waxed hair, his arms tattooed in iconographies covering a spectrum of cheap urban designs. His voice is loud and static through the circular receiver carved in the glass.

"Please, no," says Alex. "I will fix being late by paying."

"No. I don't want you to. I can cover it."

"Please let me."

"Keep this on and you're going to make a big deal where exists no deal to begin with," I tell her. "You can cover it later with drinks."

At the snack bar I buy a large Coke Zero and Alex buys a bag of sour candy. I show the tickets to a woman sitting in the theatre hall. Her morbid stomach is halved by a thin belt. The chin rests plump in a fleshy cushion. "How old are you?" she asks me.

"Twenty-two."

She winks with her entire face moving. "Enjoy the show."

Alex chuckles in the hall.

"Have you watched the original 90's version?" I ask her.

"Unfortunately no."

We sit at the left side of the bottom rows.

"If you don't like the movie you'll appreciate it with these seats," she says. They are the cheapest of theatre seats.

She takes a vodka soda out from her inside pocket. It is peach flavoured though the peach is a mild aftertaste. I finish it during the trailers.

I stroke her knee, cool and soft, her leg gets warmer as my hand moves. The breath through her nostrils sounds like she is feeding.

After the movie she asks if I liked it. I say I did.

In the hall she holds my hand and whispers, "You are scary." I ask her why and she says, "You are horny all the time."

Outside we light cigarettes. "Quiet," she says. She stares curiously.

"What?"

"Quiet and cute and mysterious. What are you thinking?"

"About you."

"Talk to me instead."

"Oh, yeah?"

"Lay it on me."

"How about load it in you. How about that?"

"Now you are scary."

I suck on the cigarette. "The sour keys ruined my appetite."

"We'll find an appetite somewhere." She flips her pocket flap open and pulls out her phone. The screen light reveals mini globs of foundation clustered around her eyes.

"Suggest me where?" I finally ask her.

"Pizza?"

"Fuck pizza."

"Fried chicken?"

"Like fast food?"

"No, no. Korean fried."

"Okay," I say. "But let's drink first."

"Fine, Shithead," she says. "I need wine. Are you okay with buying wine in a store?"

"Doesn't concern me."

"We can drink in a park and smoke," she says assuredly.

"That's painfully European."

"It is adequate."

Later we find a depanneur which is a convenience store stocked with alcohol.

I watch her searching the wine bottles. She is taller than the shelves, the thick corduroy of her overcoat conceals the feminine action in her hips. Her nose is swathing the air like a paddle on her face. It is a beautifully bridged nose catching the rogue strands of hair as she bends and tilts. She is good and adapts effortlessly to your humour. Her head is beautiful with a robust jaw and her calves express the low insertion of the muscle belly, the legs meaty and built for mountain hikes. There are beautiful dints in the collar bones which cup the sweat when she is fucking. She matches you in the mysterious way that you've considered people who are suited to each other match. You cannot understand her precisely because of how much she likes you. But that is the only thing you cannot understand. The other things are understandable. More understanding will come and do not neglect that she is able to tell you explicitly. You neglect that. She is not a black box. There is electrical activity in her head. That activity must be the colour of hot pink. You can excite it with your words as a stimulus and you tend to forget that.

She walks to the door, her face lowered and shouting.

"You stared at me the whole time," she says.

"Is that disturbing?"

"Not for me but the guy asked about you."

"Who is he?"

"How do I know? He was concerned."

"What did you say?"

"I said you are my personal voyeur. He did not know what *voyeur* means."

"If you liked his energy that's all that matters."

"But not a bit," she says. "Stop smoking. On y va. He's staring now."

She holds the paper bag like it is a suitcase, her gaze to the ground. She asks if I am embarrassed and I tell her plainly that it's fading.

"I like you staring at me," she says.

I tell her I like it too.

"Need anything?" I ask.

"Just buy the cups," she says.

We go inside a gas station.

"Listen," I tell her. "Distract the cashier and I'll get what we need."

She looks at the cashier and then me. "I can buy the cups."

"No need."

In the coffee counter the dome security mirror bolted in the upper corner returns my image fast and groping and stashing cups in a back pocket, crushing them.

"He was clueless," she says.

All around the face of a hill are people sitting, people running among the trees scattered in the peak. We find shade under a thick tree growing out skewed. Huge boughs curve upward high and tunnelling through a vault of foliage, the bark buckling off the under-layer. The roots are raised and twisted in the dusty soil like they failed to pluck the tree out the earth. The grass is short and cool.

She lays her jacket in the ground. She sits cross-legged, tucking her skirt under her pale fleshy legs. Then she twists the cap of the wine bottle and pours it in a cup.

I hand her a cigarette and light it for her.

"Okay. Tell me now. What was the episode in the cinema?"

I say nothing.

"I am not supposed to ask questions?"

"It's your life."

"Come closer to me," she says.

"I don't want to burn you."

"Light me on fire."

"A very old proverb says the best thing that can happen to your enemy is for their wishes to come true."

"Why talk about enemies?"

"It's the essence of the proverb."

"Let's not talk about proverbs."

We smoke and sip the wine. She looks at me and laughs. "Don't think of me as crazy but curious. Maybe crazy and curious and silly. What is your number?"

"What do you mean exactly?"

"Mine is thirteen including you. Yes, you're the thirteenth. Scary, huh? What is yours?"

"What's your reckoning?"

"What?"

"How many do you think?"

"I think I am third or fourth. Am I being rude? Tell me if I am being rude."

"No, you're not."

"Honest?"

"Well, honesty is different than openness."

"Yes. Yes, you're right. I am silly. And I know for sure you are not a player. The last boy I dated was a player. His number is over forty. This is one year ago."

"Do you like that?"

"The high number?"

"Yeah, the number."

"Honestly." Her eyes glide up. "I think it is hot. I hate myself."

"So, it's not hot mine is not high."

"I know," she says. "I want to roll down the fucking hill."

"I'll do it myself," I tell her. I finger another cigarette.

Then she says, "But you never answered."

"About the number?"

"The number."

"I shouldn't tell you."

"Oh, wine makes me stupid."

"I don't count."

"Really?"

"I don't care to count."

"Okay. Forget it. Now I am embarrassed."

"It's a healthy number," I tell her. "I don't understand the attraction of a high number."

"Do you think I am gross for liking it high? Not like. I mean for feeling it hot."

"No, I don't. I think you have your reasons for liking it high and not healthy."

"Tell me my reasons because I hate them."

Then I say, "Thirteen is not a high number. Pathetic, actually."

"Thank goodness," she says.

Some ashes drop in my cup and I chuck it to the yellow grass. "I am dying today," she says. "The dénouement of my destiny. My life will repeat here for eternity." She does a pouting face which reveals her surprisingly ugly.

As I stand I finally feel the wine. I trudge down a few feet and lay and revolve several times and clutch the grass. She laughs. The wine bangs in my stomach. I claw to her. We finish the bottle. We walk down the hill along the sides where it's less steep.

We walk for a long time. She finds a lingerie store. She begs for me to come in. She says she needs to be saving money this month but she is compelled to buy it. She talks French to a retail worker and I try to find somewhere to sit. The mannikins are dressed scantly with profound tits.

I can't find a seat but I can leave the store and sit in the sidewalk. Alex buys a full set of white lingerie.

Then we go to a restaurant that is dark and spacious and empty.

"Can you please excuse me?" she asks.

"No, I can't."

The waiter sets down menus and ice water. We both order beers. After the waiter leaves Alex asks me, "Please, can I be excused now?"

"No, you may not."

"Why the cruelty?"

"What do the French say about cruelness. An accompaniment to love?"

"We never claimed such nonsense."

I look under the table where her thighs are banging together.

"A show for me?" I ask her.

"I really need to be excused."

"I'm not going to excuse you."

Later I ask, "Figured out what you want?"

"Fried chicken," she says.

"That'll dry you out nice."

Her shoulders squirm.

"I am in the right mood for soup," I tell her.

"You will bloat with soup."

The waiter sets the beer bottles and we order. I ask for a frosted glass.

"We don't do frosted glasses." He pronounces *frosted* like a foreign word.

"I'm sure you do," I say. "It's putting the glass in a fridge."

"No one has asked me for a frosted glass before."

"Is it weird?"

"I'm sorry?"

"Nothing. Can you do it?"

"I'll ask."

"But do you think it's possible?"

Alex stands and I tell her, "Please sit down. They have fridges. Let's not leave."

She sits. "I am just surprised," she says. "Every restaurant serves frosted glass."

"I'll ask," he says to her.

"Not a problem," he says to me.

"She's traveling from France," I tell him. "She's the one that introduced me to frosted glasses and I'd like to treat her to one of her simplest pleasures very common in France. But if it's not available at least make the beer cold. Look how this bottle is sweating. That doesn't happen with the frosted glass. I hope it's not weird."

"Be a few minutes," he says.

"Whatever it takes."

Alex kicks my foot. "I guessed it too late," she says.

"Couldn't perform in the moment?"

"Distracted with something." She flicks her eyes to her crotch.

The waiter comes with the frosted glasses and apologizes. I tell him to apologize only to her. He looks passionately at Alex and says, "Sorry about the confusion." The glasses are pint-sized and smooth and blurred by the frost. I pour my beer bottle, slow and facile, in the glass.

"Excuse yourself," I say. She runs.

It would be redemptive to go back to the hostel. She motivates the worst qualities and I do not want to drink anymore. But what can you do when you have such a force of personality? One who also seems to have hypothesized the relations of food and your digestion. This makes me feel vulnerable and inferior. It is very unexpected. But now you're discovering the greater mismatch between gut and brain.

Soon the waiter arrives with two saucer-like plates. The chicken looks like a pile of crushed rock. It crunches against my teeth, feels grainy in my molars, grease squeezing out of the cracks and pooling about my chin. The meat is pure white and tender and tastefully appropriate for the fried skin.

She snatches the bill when it hits the table.

As we near the station she says, "I feel like you need to get drunk to stand me."

I pull on her jacket sleeve so she turns to me. "When I start drinking I don't want to stop. Nothing to do with you. I'm enjoying myself when I'm around you. It's fun for me so don't think more about it."

"Okay," she says.

"Don't believe me?"

"It is me," she says. "I am disappointed in me. And drunk."

We go through the double doors of the metro and down the escalators.

"You can pay. But cross. We've no people."

I watch the turnstile.

"It is okay to cross," she says. Then she turns to scan her card. I follow her.

Within five minutes of going through a tunnel we get off the train and go straight to a set of glass doors. We enter the apartment and then up the stairs and to her room.

In the kitchen I open the fridge where inside is an egg carton, almond milk, spotty bananas, bread. I snap open the container of croissants which are stale, the chocolate filling hard and cold.

Knocking on the door.

I step out the kitchen and talk to her through the bathroom door. She opens and asks, "Who is it?"

"I don't know."

I watch her eyeing the peephole. She opens the door. I stop looking. I hear a man talking to her in French.

She passes me and says it was a neighbour wanting a screwdriver. I look into the peephole. Two men talking. I sit on the couch with the last croissant. I am fanatically hungry.

She comes out of the bathroom wearing a corset and stockings. We kiss like our tongues are gas-sprinkled flame.

"Play Serge," I tell her.

She plays Couleur Café.

She reposes on the bed. I grab both ankles and lift her up to my mouth.

She is flesh and blood like you. For sure she is precious and sweet and inside her is the predilections of the species.

I pry her torso over. I bite her ear. "So good," she breaths. I roll her to face me. I wrap fingers on her neck. It's spongey in my grip. Indeed her pupil like a spongey planet swelling in the blue ocean of her iris. I release when it rims the top lid.

Then her lips lock, her head bouncing like a shaggy ball.

I decompress on the bed.

"Up my nose," she says fingering her roman nostril. She runs to the bathroom. I dress. She comes out, face wet and flushed red. "Fun?" she asks.

"Sense it?"

"Felt all of it." She shuts the music.

We peck lips and I pull on the doorknob. She flicks the lock and I pull again.

7

HE SLEEPS IN A PARK bench. Overgrown and clumpy hair rests on his ear like a small animal. Even in this chill morning, soiled in sweat and feigning death.

Two officers talk at a distance. His eyelids tear open a bacterial crust. In his vein-burst eyeballs the sun must be shades darker, the two figures too cryptic for what little neural calorie pumps still a clear image. He wipes his swollen face with a big palm and rubs it on his shorts. The legs so startlingly clean as to look obscene. The buried voice splits heavy mucus to become audible.

He pushes himself with his big brown hands to sit up on the bench and he reaches for the wheelchair arm and pulls it in and raises himself on the seat. The officers walk back to their cruiser.

"The cops bothering you?" I ask.

"Huh," he says. "Quoi?"

"Le police."

"No. No police." He looks around.

"How are you?"

He yells, "Huh."

"Comment ça va?"

His head jerks when he says, "Ça va."

"Bien," I say. "Can I buy you anything? You want smoke?"

"Smoking'll kill me."

I point to the convenience store and he says, "Huh," like a hiccup.

"T'aide," I say. "Want a coffee?"

"Café."

"Comment?"

With his bulky elbows he presses into the armchairs, unslouching, long hair flapping like leather straps, and fashions his palm a cone on his ear. Notice under his sweat-dried beard a cord necklace of a cross.

"How do you like café?"

"Au crème. Trop sucre." He raises four fingers. The linings like nets on a ham. Across his forearm are long vertical scars. Dimpled and deep grooves.

I go into the store and pick the biggest coffee cup and pour the strongest coffee and load in four creams and four sugar and grab handfuls of each. I take another big cup and pour in water. I wiggle the cups in a cardboard tray and go to the snack aisle. I grab a box of cheese crackers and a box of donuts containing three chocolate and three glazed.

"Do you know who he is?" I ask the cashier.

"Him out there?"

"Him, yeah."

"He's always there," he says. "He sleeps outside."

"But who is he?"

"I don't know his name. I know nothing."

Then he places them in the bag. He says, "For him?"

"Yeah."

"You're a sweetheart."

He waits in the same spot by the marble, a sleeping grimace. Thoughts of slashing horizontal not being an effective method. Across the y-axis is where he found God.

He thanks me in Québécois and drinks the coffee and I tear open the donut box and then hand him a donut wrapped in a napkin and he is happy.

"Okay, man," I say. "I'll treat you when I'm in this spot." We are both happy and I forget everything.

"Do you drink?" I ask him.

"Huh?"

I make a drinking motion. He agrees.

I try to formulate what I'd tell him in French. Tu es mon favori.

Alcohol can wash you out without you knowing, I imagine him imparting on me.

The most I ever drank was in Vietnam, I imagine replying to him. I remember distinctly how easy it was to become someone I never considered myself to be. Maybe the alcohol revealed my source or bound me stronger to a social role.

That night I met a young man from Wales. He was an engineering student in his fourth year and he recently broke it with his girlfriend of three years. His face was disturbing, he'd look at you wild-eyed and mouth agape, voidful aspect like a pointed gun.

People were getting drinks at the counter. I noticed he knew no one and I asked him how long he had been there. "Three days," he said. "You?" We were sitting in a settee with a coffee table in front of us. Both of our packs were laid on it, our lighters.

"Nearly three weeks."

"Fucking all right. Just by yourself?"

"Yeah. No problems. You meet people as you go."

"That's fair."

Then he asked the question of why I came. I told him a lie that my grandfather traveled through all of Europe in his youth and this inspired me to travel. I told him he was a proud vagabond. I didn't feel anything about lying to the Welshman. I told him, "He," my grandfather, "animated for me the hard consciousness of potential." His head nodded indiscriminately to what I was saying.

"Sounds like a good guy, your gramps does."

"Yeah," I said. "We're really proud of him."

"What's he up to now?"

"He'll go to Cuba or Cancun once in a while with the old misses."

"That's fair." He nodded with that look of nightmare-shock.

"I'm only staying a week first. See how I like it," he said.

"Good. See how you like everything. How're you liking it now?"

"Bloody great."

"Met anyone else?"

"Well, this girl."

"Nice, nice." I grabbed my pack and pulled a cigarette and lit it.

"Going to ask me if I fucked her?"

"Did you?"

"Close." He showed the measurement with index and thumb.

"Why not?"

"I meet her right outside the street. The girl eats for two fucking people. Hardly an English word out her mouth. Stuffed. I ask to go back to the hotel room. Replies, for what? To be honest I thought she was a prostitute. Then she tells me she's got work later on tonight. I'm for sure thinking she's a prostitute. Says she'll come over quick and leave. Okay. You know what I'm thinking. We go in. Sits on the bed like a plank. I turn the television. Watching Discovery. All right. Parrots and what not. Giggling to herself. Ask if she wants to do anything else. She says, no. I'm like bloody fuck this."

I laugh with the cigarette in my lips. "Then what?"

He drinks his beer. "This beers fucking piss, eh?"

"I know. Then what?" It was my third beer.

"Fucking nothing. She goes out, says she's working tonight. Leaves me. I got the remote in one hand, my prick in the other. No hole. What do I do? What fucking else?"

"They'll always say no if you ask them. They've no idea what they want. They dress up and get out the house completely clueless to why they're going out. They'll stay clueless until they meet a bloke like you who'll give them a clue."

"Lesson learned," he said. "These are some streets."

"Have a cigarette," I demanded. "I hate seeing blokes not smoking."

"All right." He lights one.

Then we went to a spot where the beer was under a dollar. The area was called Beer Corner.

It was a warm night. The garbage and its smell was less salient at night and there were a lot more tourists. Bar workers were outside their bars, waiting. They ran to us and shouted, "Cheap, cheap." The street was like an overcrowded club, hot and touchy. On either side were low-sitting people. They drank and ate meals on short plastic tables that expanded far in the road which made an even narrower path for the crowds to walk through. As you walked you looked below and saw their cooled bowls of soup and water-beaded beer bottles, their chattering heads and wet napes.

An older woman sat on a stool. She was short and wide and friendly. She grabbed my elbow and sat me down. She stepped in the door and tilted out a keg of beer. She pinched the tops of two plastic cups and pressed the nozzle. The beer spouted foamy and yellow. She balanced the cups in one hand so no beer dripped. She set them and winked at me. I paid her and winked back and felt aroused.

"So, it tastes like watered piss but it's cheap," I told him.

He made a sour face. "Fucking hell." A visage before death itself.

Next to us was a table of guys from Western Europe and they were inhaling balloons. One of them, a big and tall guy wearing a soccer jersey, started shaking. He hit the table behind him. His friends apologized to the people at that table. They weren't bothered.

"Want to try a balloon?" I asked him.

"What is it?"

"Nitrous oxide. Dentistry grade."

"What's it do?"

"Lifts you up for ten seconds and after you fall back down like a feather."

I waved at the old woman. She looked pregnant on the stool. I enjoyed waving at her and her presence made me feel good. She knew what I wanted without me telling her. A boy who looked under fourteen fetched me one big balloon. He strode with it over his shoulder like a bag.

"Fifty," he said.

"Fifty?" I asked.

"Fifty."

"Last time thirty." There was no last time. I'd never seen the child before.

"Fifty now."

I drew out a fifty-thousand note. The picture on it was of a red Ho Chi Minh, the very dead patriarch, whose body I had seen in a temple one day ago. It was fresh looking and tranquil as if captured in a fairy tale, reminding me of my grandfather's funeral. That *object in nature* look.

"What a little prick, huh?" asked the Welshman.

"Who cares."

"Little cunts enjoy haggling too."

The Welshman sucked the balloon. I told him to breath it in and out. He twitched back and laughed. "Waaaweee." Then I depleted the contents and my body exploded in vibration, the street ascending, and I was extremely happy, an apex sensation of power detonating and crawling outward to discharge in the planet.

The Welshman overheard another table's accent. He yelled, "Where you from?"

"United Kingdom!" They were roaring. We sat with them. Later a local fellow stood out. He was dangerously lanky. He sat down on a plastic chair some feet away from us, his limbs settled in a peaceful method.

"Oh!" he yelled.

"Who're you?" asked one. He had a tall forehead and brown moles in his face. He wasn't drunk but he liked to act it. "What are you?"

"Bong."

"Like the *bong*, yes? for skunk, for weed."

"Bong like Bong."

"You got weed? Co maywanna khong?"

"Sweet as."

"What sweet? you selling same bunk motos are?"

"Where from?"

"Britain, Bong boy."

"I like Britain."

"I get discount? Friends get discount too?"

"Ain't taking advantage of the Queen like that," said the younger.

Bong got up from the chair, picked it up, placed it at our table. Now that he was close I saw the extent of muscles grinding in his skull. His knees looked like burnt crab joints.

"Why you like Britain?" asked the drunk pretender. "Britain treat you good?"

"Britain polite, not Australia."

"You hate Australians?" asked a man with a sportive sling bag across his chest. His legs were very hairy. It stuck wetly to his thighs. Our chairs put us in a squat so our thighs were exposed.

"I love people," said Bong. "Where live Britain."

"I'm from Norwich," said the high-rise forehead which seemed to buzz.

"I know Newcastle, what North-ehdge?"

"Norwich like porridge, orange."

"Norritsh."

"Uh huh. What you got?"

"Dance club?"

"Soon, soon."

Bong reached into his cargo shorts and took out a large plastic bag with a mix of pink and white tablets.

"Love Britain. Beatles, Stones, Who."

"Ha," said the pretender from Norwich. "You up with new music? hip-hop?"

"Classic me. Love Datcher, Diana."

"You love Margaret Thatcher and Princess Diana?"

"Love in-tweeners. Top Gear."

"You like Jeremy Clarkson? He your favorite? He's mine. Gave a producer a black eye."

"Love."

Bong dropped the bag on the table and spread out the contents under the plastic.

"By God look at the rings on you. No zircons those." He peered into the rings. "Business good?"

"Like hip-hop."

"What colour on your head?"

"Indigo."

"Looking absolutely mad."

"You ever contemplate Brexit?" asked the one whose legs looked like watered wool. "I've been holding back to ask."

"Oh," expressed Bong.

The man from Norwich asked the Welshman and me.

"I'm not thinking so," said the Welsh.

"Yeah," I said.

"How much for three good British lads and a Canadian?" he then asked.

Bong got distracted by some noise in the street.

"How much man?" The Norwichman asked. "Money. Dong. Dong for Bong."

"Five," said Bong displaying all five digits of his hand. "One million."

"Look at the cheeky smile. I trust you, Bong? Vang or khong."

"You ask," Bong said, waving horizontally, grimacing.

The Englishmen discussed with each other. They did it as if Bong was not there. As if in front of them was not a consciousness like their own.

"What he mean by five?" asked the satcheled freak.

"Five?"

"Five," said the quiet younger. Lining his lip was a moustache like a thin etching of dirt. It was the thing that made him look young. "We're five, ain't we? He'd sell us five for a mill."

"Is that fair?"

"I don't fucking know."

Bong had that indigo patch on top his fatless skull, which gave him a wild look but his personality did not seem as such. Perhaps the jewelry beautifying a deeper apathy. His skin was darker than the usual Vietnamese and it looked harder too. He seemed young but he was likely older than us. He was as erudite as he needed to be but he seemed uneasy by the matters he engaged. He stayed at the table and the Englishmen stopped paying attention to him. He left silently with his product.

I wanted to reach for him. Wait, I imagined saying, don't worry about them.

I imagined doing the drugs and the night no longer being a phase of the world but in me, unimaginable and infinitely tactile, infinitely stimulating, the variable in some unknown function of natural laws multiplying in what chamber of my brain houses happiness.

The bars closed down as police patrolled in their jeeps, driving with sirens and megaphones, demanding closures. The chairs were collected by what appeared to be random locals. The tables stashed under tarpaulins. The old woman, hands on her hips, stood and saw the tourists leave and some said goodbye and she said it too with the same excitement as when they came. She grabbed the cold keg of beer and walked in the door and shut it.

The Englishmen walked to their hostel which was viewable from where we sat. It was very busy with white people. I took the Welshman to a club. We drank two shots of tequila and smoked cigarettes in the dark away from the crowd. He liked to dance and soon he had local women around him.

The club had two floors and I stepped up to the top where there was a quieter bar. I looked out to the dance-floor, the swinging light-beams switching intermittently to epileptic pulses. The people looked like a bed of rippling pins.

I drank two beers and the music was hitting me as if my body was a gong. My stomach grew nauseous. I did not see the Welshman again. No one bothered me in the street.

I struck into my mouth and vomited in a drainage hole and walked to the hostel. My bed was a hot and spinning catacomb. My bowels squirmed like a rodent clenched in predator jaws. I woke up in the night and vomited in the shared bathroom. It was cooler in the bathroom and I wanted to be in there a long time.

The toilet was equipped with a hose called a *bum gun*. The sewage pipes in SE Asia are thinner and easier to clog. So these hoses come with most toilets. A plaque on the tiled wall read *Why treat your bum like your nose? Take better care and use the bum gun.* I took the hose and sprayed its tepid water in my face.

• • • •

A BLOND WOMAN SAYS good morning to me. She is pale and large, telling me she's from Belarus and asking if I know where it is.

"Of course, I know. Belarus is near Russia."

She smiles and says, "A lot of people don't know."

I force myself to drink more water.

"You don't talk much," she tells me.

I chew on the apples which abrade my throat. The bananas are sickly mushy. I wipe my plate with a paper towel. I stand outside with the air crisp on my skin, an orderly throng of geese overhead like a scraper polishing the sky cloudless.

I will limit my intake to five. I inhale the smoke and my throat is fine and healthy. I can go out drinking tonight and it will be good for my body because it will introduce it to productive stress and the body loves introducing itself to stress that's productive.

I pass tourist shops which I've never stepped in to, locked restaurants with windows showing stacked chairs. Slim, elevated sidewalk where I totter to balance, a delicate hike through this colonial tourist-land. Murals, decorative glass of a child's dream, colours of the fly's abdomen. These ornamental bushes have never hidden garbage.

Take in this and hold it and work it in your memory like a stored clay and do not worry, it won't harden to some premature shape, when you need it you can take it out and still work it.

There is that homeless man on the street corner, with the cap stomped on the ground and him eyeing the passers and smoking a cigarette. His hair is not gelled back, that is hard sweat on a scalp shellacked with lice turds. The pokey beard rolling to the wrinkles of his face, patchy underside, whatever lint and speck of dirt, dried millipede or friction-burnt spider. He says nothing, just looks, smokes. The pale blue eye is a billiard ball slammed in the pocket, still whirling. Is he judging or only observing. And what does his judgement consist. The world at large and all the small creatures between him and infinity.

I pull the heavy glass door. It tugs my scapulars, my hips swivel. There is that man with the steaming cup. He listens to those same boxy over-the-ear headphones. He's dressed as if he was in a marathon.

Hey friend, I'd imagine saying to him.

Hey buddy, how're you?

I'm good. What else?

Hey that's all right. It's a good morning.

I know it is. Keep yourself steady.

Always steady.

Keep yourself above ground.

Always treading it.

The bagels and breakfast wraps and globs of egg look waxy in the pane. I can't read the menu. It's on a chalk board, scrawled in bold chalk.

"Bonjour," the barista says. His hair is like pencil shavings. He wears square glasses with the wooden trimming.

"Bonjour. Bon matin."

"Bon matin."

"How's it going?"

"It's going fantastic. Thank you for asking. How about you?"

"Same. Thanks."

"What can I get you?"

"I'm thinking of something I never had before."

"Okay. I can help you out. What have you had before?" He seems excited. Did he take a class or is it natural to him.

"Coffee."

"Just normal coffee?"

"Yeah."

"Which roast?"

"Both of the standard roasts. One time I tried a clover. I liked it."

"And you're looking for more than just coffee?"

"Yeah."

"Ever had a... latté?"

"Yeah, I did."

"Cappuccino?"

"I've been around." We both laugh.

"Okay. Let me think." He looks behind him. I peer in that ear hole so clean.

"Misto?"

"Misto?"

"Yep. That's it. Steamed milk coffee. You should try that."

"Okay. Give me it in a venti."

"So confident in me."

I wait for the drink, hands in my pockets, observing the dark wood walls and shelf of thermo-cups and roast bags, the austere drawings of coffee plants. He nudges the coffee to me. "Here you are."

"Looks good," I tell him. "Thank you."

The misto tastes useless. See what happens in thirty minutes. You cannot judge a coffee after the first few sips. Your body is very tired from last night and needs more time to wake. Today I'll walk further up north to Mount Royal Park where I will smoke my second cigarette.

As I swallow I feel the dry itch in my throat. But that might be the milky coffee splashing in my throat, mixed with the dry air.

Are you going back to Windsor after? texts Melody. I'll text her in three hours when I have my third cigarette.

I go outside and feel good and the itch in my throat is nothing.

I have a slow-throbbing pain between my brows when I walk St. Laurent boulevard.

If I go to the river the air will be very healthy for me. If I go to the river with the reasoning that it will be good for my throat then I have accepted it as a fact.

I search for the wheelchair homeless man. Like an idiot I don't know his name. I smoke a cigarette. I am tired.

I walk back to the hostel.

When I wake up I know it.

I should've gone to the river, not for the air but for the drowning of myself.

In a convenience store I buy the vitamin C tablets, anti-cold and a six-pack of water bottles. The entire afternoon in a hostel, a half-sleep state that feels like drugged. In the evening my throat is razorous with every swallow.

I text, *No I'm not. I don't know where I'll go after. I can visit Toronto.*
Leaving Toronto soon.
Where?
Windsor lol.

Then, last chance, I text, *Been to London before? I might go there next.*

The next morning I wake with a pain like a leech had denned in my skull. My nose and throat are pumped with mucus. Eat breakfast, drink the crappy coffee. I go in the bunk and attempt sleep.

• • • •

I YELL, "TURN OFF THE alarm!" The phone alarm shuts at 6:03 AM.

"How can you leave an alarm running in a hostel, you asshole." My heart is like a drummer caged in my chest.

I step down and see him staring at me from his top bunk.

"You're in a hostel," I tell him. He looks away.

The person in the bottom bunk says, "Leave him alone."

"Go back to sleep," I say.

"Stop yelling."

"I said go back to sleep."

He gets out and postures.

"You're in a hostel letting your alarm go off," I say. I stick the key into my locker.

"Now you are so shut the fuck up."

The standing one stares at me. "Get back in your fucking bunk," I tell him.

A woman-hag from another bunk yells, "Chill out, it's over. We're trying to sleep."

I walk past the standing one. He is in basketball shorts and a t-shirt and his hair has morphed flatly skewed to how he slept. My direction curves to him and he steps close. "What are you going to do?"

He says, "Touch me, touch me." I stare into him and get out-of-body, no self nor ego, a raw spirituality. He tells his friend in top bunk, "I want him to touch me."

His friend pulls him back. He tells his friend, "No, I want him to touch me, why won't he touch me?" The woman yells, "Chill guys." The friend whispers in his ear. I eye my bunk and then my locker and try to think. I turn to the door. Outside the door I realize what I had forgotten was my pack.

I buy a new pack and smoke along the St. Lawrence and fantasize about seeing both of them in the streets or me going back to the hostel.

Later Melody texts, *We can go Tuesday*. Tuesday comes in five days.

• • • •

SAT AT THE FRONT DESK is the scrawny worker who welcomed me in. I tell him, "Cancel my booking."

"Is everything okay?"

"I want to cancel my booking."

"How was the room?"

"Just cancel the room."

"Okay. There is a charge for cancellations. It's in the policy. Did you read it?"

"How much is it?"

He tells me the charge and it seems more worth it to let the booking run.

"All right. Cancel the thing."

"Did you prepare the towels and the bed as needed?"

"Of course."

He goes through the procedure.

"All done?" I ask.

"You're free to go."

"Thank you. This hostel is trash."

"Anything I can do?" I hear him say. I walk back.

"I'm sorry," I tell him. "I didn't like it."

"What's the issue?"

I feel warm and relaxed and emotional. "The bunkbeds need curtains."

"Is that all?"

"I don't know. You don't care about privacy?"

"I do. But I guess we never thought of it. Thanks for telling me. Was there a problem at all with the amenities?"

"Which?"

"Showers, rec room or dining hall."

"There's a rec room?"

"Down the hall here."

"Oh," I say. "Showers are fine. The dining hall. I don't know. Be more hygienic if you used disposables."

"Thank you for the suggestions...are you okay?"

"I don't feel well."

I walk on. Bright engine oil pools toward a curb, slow moving, shining brilliantly in crispy sun-warmed streaks of blue and yellow. Past the depanneurs and boutiques and magasins. "Bonjour, bonjour. Bon matin. Au revoir."

While waiting for the train I take out the book I had brought with me, the one I had forgotten about. It is an introduction on Mahayana Buddhism. My bookmark is more than a third of the way through. I try to remember the peculiar stages of enlightenment in this tradition.

Remembering these stages is like digging up an artifact and I've only my fingers to pierce and mash the top layer of soil.

I recall the first which is the pursuit of enlightenment. I search the pages to find the detailed progression which I remember is slippery for comprehension to hold. The second stage is emptiness, that is the emptiness inherent in the pursuit. A word the author uses to describe this stage is *disillusionment*.

My tongue skips on the syllables. *Disillusionment.*

One may consider the word to be synonymous with *delusion* but it is best paired with *disappointment*. The base *illusion* with the negative prefix *dis* denotes the dispelling of an illusion. If the semantics inheres a psychology then the word signifies the necessary precondition, an illusion, needed to allow a state best described by the word's antonym, *contentment*.

Appear, appear, whatso thy shape or name,

O Mountain Bull, Snake of the Hundred
Heads,

Lion of The Burning Flame!

O God, Beast, Mystery, come!

. . . .

Euripides, "The Bacchae of Euripides III"

Part 2

1.

THE CASHIER WATCHES me from behind his spotted glass. I shove a two-liter of milk in the basket, a dozen eggs, peanut butter and a honey bottle, pancake powder. I hand him the items through a square opening in the glass. He is a big man, big chest and shoulders and forearms, with skin like crushed tamarind. He mouths a deal for chocolate bars and I tell him it's okay. He continues on the deal. "It's okay."

"Can you give me the change in loonies?" I ask him.

"Loonies or toonies?"

"Loonies."

He pulls the register. His new-shaven face is lit with sweat. His scalp twinkles in fading hair like a bush of electrical wire.

"No loonies today," he says.

"You have zero loonies?"

"I'm joking."

"What?"

"A joke." He grins.

"A good joke."

Then, "Thank you," I say looping two fingers in the first bag. Then, "Thanks," as he slides the second. With the last bag I loop two more and say, "Thank you."

"Can I get a pack of Philip Morris? King size. Or you don't have?"

He turns his head. "I have." Big and full teeth like white piano keys.

I hand him my ID.

"Windsor," he says.

"Yeah."

"My family in Windsor. Rajumuar."

"I don't know them."

"I thought maybe you know." His head shakes and a gold ring in his left ear remains inert.

"Thank you," I say.

Then, "I also need a lighter."

"Friend, please don't hurry. We figure out everything you need. What lighter, which colour?"

"The small one," I say. "The green."

He plucks it out the tray and stamps it standing up on the counter. "Okay. Next."

"That's it."

"Okay. Are you happy?" He hovers his big fingers at the counter, stretching them above the lottos, wiggling them.

"Yeah," I tell him.

"If you're happy, I'm happy."

"I'm happy."

"Two for three." Two fat fingers like chocolate bars in the glass.

"No, thank you."

Some giant cord in his forehead lifts his eyebrow. "You're happy?"

"Yes."

"Two for five drinks. Monster. Red Bull. Look."

There's a small fridge with drinks by my feet. I take two blue Monster. He reaches a gorilla hand to clutch and pull and scan. He pokes his pink tongue out his tightened lips and licks two loonie-sized fingertips and rubs a plastic bag apart. He tosses all in the bag.

"You're happy?" he asks. Another cord tugging those hairy meat blocks together.

"I'm happy."

"Now I'm happy." He pushes the bag to me.

"Please, don't lie to me."

"I'm not and I won't."

"Thank you. I am happy now."

"Thank you."

I walk to a liquor store. By the sliding doors is a man playing the guitar. The long tuner strings wag with the strumming. I drop two damn loonies in his case and walk in.

Modest shelves of whiskey and vodka and rum, the wine cached in a separate room worked in tawny wood. Mildly cold fridges of bitter craft and domestic and international.

I grab a six-pack of cheap malt and stroll into the liquors where my eye catches a discounted cinnamon whiskey.

The cashier asks for my ID. I tell her it's my first time in London.

"Welcome," she says. "Nice to receive you."

"Like I'm a gift."

"It's my special way of treating people."

I pay and walk out.

The guitarist tunes the guitar, humming a song. He strums a few chords to get the pattern and once set begins again a rhythmic trance. His head screwing in the torso, the eyes lidded tensely. Fragile singing strengthens in the chorus. The metal twang of his overworked steel strings, spit and sweat, boozed memory and improvisation and random discords of emotive untensing. The untamed redemption wrenching by sound out his fleshy husk, the feeling and knowing biology of demise, the empty-full paradox of it, by the sliding doors of the liquor store.

A black Kia SUV drives towards me. I open the rear door and place my bags in the seat and the driver says, "Trunk."

I drop the bags in the trunk. I sit in passenger side. A clustered mass of fresheners hangs deceptively on the rear-view mirror.

"Hello," I say.

"Hello."

"I've never been to London before."

"Welcome."

"Do you like it?"

"Hmm."

"Do you like living here?"

"Why not? Quiet and cheaper than Toronto."

He accelerates out the lot. We enter a neighbourhood where the sidewalk has dark traces from dried leaves. A children's park with swings and slides and the ground is the smallest pebbles. Trails of rubber pavement disappear in small woodland.

The house is old, light-green panel siding sprayed recently to shine, and two-storied with pots of plants on the porch, a hanging bench. Almost like the dorm house I rented during college. My roommates were four Indian men and they cooked me curry. I wrote one's writing assignments in exchange for twenty dollars. He questioned why I stayed in my room all day, what I was doing, and I told him I was reading novels, one fiction and one non-fiction, or watching YouTube videos. I told him I read the entire textbook for every class. I had read textbooks for subjects I wasn't taking, like physics and molecular biology. I was killing myself with outdated textbooks found in thrift stores. This was after I abandoned reading philosophy for something more grounded. He recommended me to go outside because outside things were happening for real. I assumed he figured I was masturbating compulsively and he never mentioned it again. He owned many four-wheelers in India and he said he leased them out to foreigners who wanted to do excursions.

We park in the wide driveway, next to a blacked out van. I open the trunk and grab my bags. I pass the driver side and say, "Thank you."

He says, "No worries," and backs up.

The lawn is cut and smells green. The cracked porch fibres shift against my feet. I look at my phone at the instructions. I look at spider-flower, white lilac and vibrant heliotropes. A digital intercom. I press it and hear the ringing inside. A female voice in the intercom.

"I'm the guest for today," I say.

"Read the instructions," it says.

"I did," I say. "I don't understand them."

"Go to the path on the left and lift the lock then enter the code in the door to the right."

"Thank you."

The path on the left is square concrete plates dropped in the grass. I lift the lock and push the gate and there is a white door with a cross-framed window on the right. Empty clay pots or pots holding soil where tiny weeds have sprouted. I enter the code in a button pad and the mechanism clicks.

Downstairs there's a large and low-lit living room with a couch and television. There is a wood counter with a coffeemaker and microwave and portable stovetop and sink. Two bedrooms.

I turn on the stovetop and take a pan out of the sink and a bowl. I pour in milk and one egg. I find a stick of butter in the small fridge. I cook two pancakes and plop them on a styrofoam plate. The pancake is soggy, some parts uncooked. I lather peanut butter and squirt honey. The styrofoam has melted on the pancake. I eat on the couch while staring at my warped reflection in the television screen. I peruse through the two bedrooms. The first one by the stairs is smaller than the other. The sheets smell good and clean. I masturbate and go to sleep.

Later the coffee machine gurgles and spews coffee in a porcelain cup. I chuck it in the sink. I sit on the couch with the jar of peanut butter.

I text Melody, *I'm here.*

I tongue a few spoons of peanut butter and squirt honey onto the spoon. I sit back on the couch and open the television. It is crucial to have lazy days since they allow you to perform consistently well through a longer amount of time.

We'll go out big when I come.

I also bought beer and whiskey.

When are you meeting your friend?

She'll get back to me.

Sounds good.

I haven't seen Tracey in over a year but we talk online, here and there. Her persistence in meeting me again has sustained warmly my memories of her. Even though I haven't been persistent or engaging about it. And I'm nervous. Though nervousness is an interpretation. What I am feeling is a stimulus that can be registered simply to mind as excitement.

I throw my jeans and underwear and shirt in a hamper and put on new clothes. I walk up the stairs and slip my feet in my moist shoes and open the door and lift the fence lock.

The large branches of trees swoop and make a sky-bed of golden leaves through the street. There is a woman walking a dog and the dog is craning its neck at me. The ladle-like tongue pulses. She yanks on the leash because the dog wants to sniff the grass. She allows the dog. I ask her if I'm allowed to pet. "For sure."

I graze my hand along the torso and a twitch crawls through its flesh. Its fur is short and grey and spotted wine-red. I scratch its wrinkled scalp. "Nice doggo."

"He's super friendly," she says.

"He loves to sniff," I say.

"He can be stubborn with the sniffing," she says.

The dog stares with rich burgundy eyes. Eyes like the scalding imprints of flamed iron. Like whole worlds left extinguished by celestial fire yet wheeling still in cold space.

"Do you think he'll care it's my first time in London?"

"Uh yeah, he's welcoming."

I scratch under the saggy chin. Warm spit in my fingers.

"Thank you for letting me pet."

"Glad you enjoyed it, stranger. I'm sure he did. He loves scalp rubbing."

"Have a good day," I say.

"Safe travels," she says.

I continue walking into an outdoor shopping plaza. There is a small café designed in the European mode. Behind it is like a grove and a company has been hired to trim the trees, their trucks are parked in front.

I walk inside and sit near the windows. Large and generic paintings of flowers or landscapes. The tile floor resembles somewhat the stony slope of a mountain captured in print.

The waiter's head is bald at the top with tufts of hair on the sides. He wears a white apron, his chipped hands on his waist and he asks what I want. Later he comes back with an espresso.

"Thank you," I say.

It tastes like burnt pretzels.

I remember another similar café. It had boarded windows so the patrons could smoke. We would drink alcohol in the café even though I was underaged. The last time we met he asked me how I was in Albanian. I answered that I was good in English.

"Good," he said in English. He withdrew a pack from his leather jacket. He pulled out one long cigarette. Then he asked, "Really good?"

"Really good," I said.

He chuckled and took a drag. The smoke was like water out of a firehouse. His teeth were stained but robust. He picked up packets of real sugar and shook them and ripped the tops and laced the espresso and stirred with a tiny spoon. "When are you getting married?"

I wanted to say something in Albanian but did not know how to parse it. The smoke was stinging my eyes. "I am taking my time."

"Take as much as you can," he said. "How is your mother?"

"Mother is good." I did a thumbs up.

"She is working?"

"Yes, full-time."

"How is your sister?"

"Good."

"Good, good." He sipped the espresso. A metal-sharp slurping. "You have a girlfriend?"

"If I did I'd marry her." I expected him to laugh but he looked upset.

The waiter filled our waters. He cocked his thumb and winked. Then the waiter came with the liquor. He held the shot glass and frowned and nodded. We toasted. The shot burned.

"I married your grandmother at eighteen."

"It's too young," I said combatively.

"She was young. No worry. No drive and no care."

"That's a shame. Her not driving."

"Do not worry for her."

"I'm not."

"She sick. You do not worry?"

"Of course, I worry for that."

"You love her or me?"

I said nothing but smiled.

"You suppose love her," he said. "I die first. You love and care for her. Men die first."

"You are not old enough to worry about that." He was sixty-seven.

"I feel." He grabbed his forearms to indicate the presence of death in them.

Then he asked, "Do you worry a lot?"

"No."

"You are quiet. Worried."

"I'm a quiet guy."

"You worry for your father?"

"No, I don't."

He said an Albanian idiom to show how little he cared about his son. His Albanian speech moved quick and imperturbable like the cascading of artfully placed dominoes. "Mos mondo shumë. Të lutem."

Two out of the three men at the table were leaving. One patted him on the shoulder. He had a moustache and a golf cap on. He was very skinny and his large leather coat looked ridiculous on him. He stared at me while talking to my grandfather. Then he said he did not want to curse me by staring so long and left. "My good friend," said my grandfather. "You make friends at school?"

"Yes, I do."

"Good to make friends. In school I make friends."

"Yes, I know."

"But you cannot make friends worried."

"No," I said. "I'm fine."

I finished my espresso and stood and walked to a corridor facing the counter. The bathroom was small and yellow and tremendously clean. I washed my hands quickly. There was no mirror. When I got out I saw my grandfather left cash on the table. "Are we leaving?" I asked.

"You want espresso?"

"I can't."

"Shot?"

"No way."

"You want food, tell me. Good food. Trust me."

"No, I can't."

"You are hungry after the shot. You eyes betray you. Please see the food."

"No, no."

"Sandwich? Juice?"

"No."

"We buy pizza."

"I really am no hungry."

"We go restaurant and buy steak."

"No, I can't. I can't."

"Okay, okay. So what?"

"Let's go."

"Okay."

He was at the counter with another man. The man was shorter than my grandfather who was a short man. I walked to the small fridge and took out a strawberry flavoured soda water. I saw my grandfather waving his hand at me idiomatically. "You face look like yellow wax," he told me. The man brought out a take-out box. In the parking lot my grandfather handed me the box. It had a pastrami sandwich which I ate in the car.

We drove to his house where my grandmother was sallow and crooked on the couch watching TV. She kissed me severally on each cheek and she cried. She pointed to the bruises along her arm where the IV was inserted. "My skin like paper," she said. She pinched up the skin on her backhand and it stayed up until she flattened it. My grandfather yelled from the kitchen for her to stop crying. He said her crying was a disgrace.

I remember my grandfather used to throw full meals on the floor or out the window. When I was a child he threw a tray of pork chops with a bowl of salad over his head while lying flat on the couch. I did not see the throw because I was watching the television. I heard the dishes clattering. I saw his face in lethal apathy. My grandmother scrubbed the carpet with a towel and bucket of soapy water. The olive oil in the salad had soaked in. It was not told to me why he had thrown the dish. After these events they would not speak. My grandmother stayed busy in the kitchen or went in the bedroom. Sometimes the silence lasted an entire day but never two.

When I got older I read Tolstoy's *War and Peace*. In the novel Tolstoy mentions a *peculiar Russian feeling:* when one revokes what is pleasurable or helpful to make themselves disadvantaged. By doing so one attains a higher power as if they are above what people consider good and necessary. And so they become above other people entirely. I told myself that this was what my grandfather was doing.

He had said that he wondered what time of the day he would die. Morning, afternoon, evening or night. Whether it would be during his favourite seasons or not. He said he never thought about death when younger because he was busy working but in retirement all his thinking was death. No one told me the time but it happened in the winter. I imagine telling him this and him being ambivalent about it.

I remember telling him about my trip to Vietnam. He had not known I was going. When I came back he said plainly that it was good for me to open myself to different people and places. He said he was proud of me. He said he'd never travel so far and to a place so foreign. I felt good for him to regard me as a reckless explorer. But he never asked what I did or what I saw. He spoke admirably for the Vietnamese because he thought they were still communist, which was a system under the renowned obsessor Enver Hoxha who took him from a labourer picking grapes to interviewing potential employees in a civic office. He told me how in his youth the most important goal of living was being fed, feeding family, and then when he came to Canada it became hoarding money, giving money to family.

I thank the barista and walk out and smoke in the plaza. The gas-powered tools of the landscapers irritate me and I continue walking. It's a long walk to stop hearing them.

2.

IN THE MORNING I PLAYED pool with two girls from Germany.

I told the tall one, "Sehr beeindruckend" when she pocketed a ball and she looked at me with her restrained European surprise. The other German was short and depressive. The sole hostel receptionist joined us for a short time, handling the pool cue like a sword.

I offered the Germans slender cigarettes given to me by a man from Spain. He had been in the army and he enjoyed riding the train. He had told me train travel was the ultimate experience and he loved the Trans-Siberian, the sitting and watching of the varied country wheeling before him.

The tall one said she only smoked when drinking and the shorter shook her frizzy head no. I sat smoking by myself and eating scrambled eggs. I liked the tall one. She was dirty-blond and tanned and curious and happy. These two friends had been motorbiking through the hilly plains of Sapa, northern Vietnam. I noticed Europeans did things that those in North America would consider remarkable. But the Europeans never thought them as such. They had grown up riding bikes and traveling countries, sometimes solo and sometimes in groups, and they spoke of their travels through Europe and Asia with a restrained European sentimentality.

"We met a Canadian friend here too," the tall one said. "He took the wrong passport yesterday. Another Canadian's passport."

"I'm Canadian," I told her.

"Check if it's yours."

We laughed about it even though I was nervous. Then I was nervous and euphoric. I imagined the bureaucracy of the Canadian embassy.

I asked the receptionist for my passport. The receptionist spread the passport. It was a picture of a long haired and smiling Canadian.

"What do I do?" I asked her.

Her face was tightening. She said quietly, "Come back soon."

"Where is it?"

"Safe," she said annoyed. "Come back here soon. Today. A driver pick up."

"I'll text my friend," the tall one said.

The short German ate cantaloup slices with melancholy and the tall one was on her phone waiting for the friend to text back.

"No reply?" I asked.

"None."

I smoked and imagined myself with no passport in Vietnam. No formal identity and no chance to get home. I will have to pay ten-thousand dollars for a new passport, I told myself. It will take them six months to a year to first legitimate me and then issue a new one.

I asked the tall German if she had plans for the night. "We'll rent scooters today," she said. The short one nodded yes like an infirm. "Riding a new road in the hills. The ride is all day."

"Where do you rent scooters?"

"The hotel upstairs."

"There's a hotel upstairs?"

"The hostel and hotel are one company. Take the elevator and find out."

The elevator was behind the receptionist desk where the receptionist sat like a dead body. She was an eighteen-year-old from one of the local tribes. Yesterday she had hiked with me through villages, rice paddies, grassy mountainsides, explaining the culture and snapping pictures and sharing platters of local food prepared by her relatives.

"Hey," I said. "Don't worry about it."

Her eyes lifted to me.

"Don't worry about it."

The elevator opened to a hotel lobby. There was one man working the hotel desk. His business suit was too tight and he was spectacled and pale, his teeth like rotten corn kernels. He said a worker went out to go grab my passport from the Canadian in the upper north. "Today," he guaranteed.

An elderly woman followed me as I walked in the dusty road. She wore an intricate dress of rainbow colours, cross-stitched, pleated, and flowery embroidery. She presented a colourful collection of flimsy cloth bracelets. I mindlessly asked how much they were. She continued following me. Then others like her began following me too. The three of them presented their bracelets and I told them I can only buy from one and so I bought from the original follower and walked on. But she followed and begged for me to buy embroidered cloth purses too.

"I give you five-thousand dong," I told her.

She explained the worth of some small purses.

"No. I give you dong for free."

"No," she said.

"Leave me alone now."

I walked into an outdoor restaurant and ordered salad rolls. She was in the road, standing and smiling. I ate the salad rolls quickly. Outside I told her with determination that I'll give her dong for nothing.

"No," she said.

"I don't wear purse," I begged.

She grabbed a handful of bracelets. I bought one and then she left. Then I sat on the restaurant's porch smoking in the hot noon. The lazy dogs yawned reposing in the dusty and sloping road and there were no cars or motorbikes, some bloated tourists hiking down into a village where more of the rainbowed women waited for them. They were called *mamas* to the tourists. They spoke great English and they sold handmade ornaments carried in baskets roped to their shoulders. They looked different than the other Vietnamese. Broad faced, darker skinned, and flat headed mountain folk. Some of them would give invitations to a village house where they'd serve you traditional Hmong cuisine. Their grandchildren would dress similar and sell the same uninventive wares.

The young man that served me the salad rolls said, "Hey, bro." He pulled out a cigarette. My type of guy.

"Hey," I said. "Your brother?" A small shirtless child was by him.

He looked down to the wandering child and grabbed his wrists and danced with him. The child was laughing and he lifted him by the wrists and swung him fiercely.

"You good, bro?" he asked me.

"Oh, yeah."

His eyes poked half an inch out his skull and he was horribly veiny.

"You have girlfriend?" he asked.

"Yeah."

"Good, good. You white. Big dick."

Then he asked, "Vietnam girl?"

"Yeah."

"Good. You fuck condom?"

I wrinkled my nose. "No condom."

"Fuck you."

"Condom no good."

"No. Fuck you."

We sat smoking well in the silence and the heat. Then the child came again and he grabbed him by the wrist to pull closer and scratched his belly and armpits and the child squealed.

"Good day, bro."

"Good day."

Later at the hotel I asked the receptionist if my passport had come and he said it will soon. I lit a cigarette and tipped the ash in a tray shaped like a conch shell. Then I asked him about the motorbikes. He didn't ask if I had a license or any experience but I told him I had neither. "Ah," he said. "Be careful." He slithered his hand to show the terrain I'd be driving in. Then with a random document and pencil he sketched a route of attractions and explained a sequence of left and right turns.

A custodian showed me how to turn the motorbike on, to throttle and stop. The seat was hard and ungiving. He gave me a red helmet that was like a plastic ball-cap. I moved cautiously down the road. It felt like a bike except for not needing to find a natural balance. Then I throttled and the steering became lighter and I glided down smoothly. At the end before the swaying bridge to the village I tilted left and continued on a path into a forest that soon ended to a toll gate. I turned back and up the road and into the flat streets of Sapa. At every stop the afternoon heat grew burning and then faded totally with the throttled rush of wind.

Behind the timbered lodges and food shops were tall pines inclining to the highlands. A range of modest mountains and ribbed valleys of green rice crop. The streets were massively wide and cracked. Cliffs overlooked a plain of fenced hamlets cratered between furrowed hills and rivulets, the open shacks and animal pens and bricked wells, long-horned and yoked caribous standing like iron statues. Dark human shapes stomped across the hills, their rain boots sucking into the water of the paddies.

Along the highway were paths that cut into piney wilderness or twisted around mountain ranges. I swerved into a long ridge where below on either side were stony banks, a few watering holes. There was a cabin. I eyeballed where the ridge would lead me. In the distance it curved behind a wide muddy hill. I stepped in the cabin and a woman greeted me and I paid the fee to enter and then I started the bike and sped on until stopping before the hill. The ground was lumpy and grooved deep with tire marks pocketing brown water. Small grainy puddles and pudgy piles like clotted shit. The front wheel caught and spun in place, flinging hot wet earth, and my left foot shot into the ground and sunk and my right leg swung out from the bike which nearly crushed my left leg. I sat on the bike and trudged through the mud. Then the ground became dry, my calves and shoes hardened thick with grey mud.

Then it was up and down, up and down, through an empty dirt field. Then while downhill the motorbike stopped running, the fuel gauge needle below zero. I lumbered on pushing the steering handles.

I found a house that was like a military outpost enclosed by a metal palisade. There was a man watching me, laughing. I pointed to the fuel tank of the motorcycle and he told me to wait and he got on a motorbike and zoomed off. I cleaned the mud off me using a spigot. Some woman showed me it. She smiled as I was cleaning myself. "Sorry," I told her. She said it was okay.

The man came back carrying two canteens of gas. He opened the gas cap and looked inside. He looked at me. "Full," he said. I didn't feel stupid because I was a tourist who by default knew nothing. He capped the tank and turned the engine. It started. I wanted to pay him for the gas but he refused and said he'll keep it for himself. I drove off and later nearly toppled over on a hill.

I entered the highway and continued on. Located among the side vegetation was a noodle shop. I sat in the cool and ate beef and noodles and smoked the last of my pack, Marlboro Green, refreshingly cool.

Behind the shop was a man spraying with a hose the windows of a service store. My bike was crusted with mud that looked like hard clay. I stood watching him and I didn't need to do anything for him to shout, "No!"

I yelled back, "I pay!" and he yelled, "No!"

Then I drove back. I was exhausted from the riding and the noodles and my ass ached on the bike. The custodian saw in disappointment the caked mud. I shrugged my shoulders like a tourist.

In the lobby the receptionist said, "Gift for you, sir." I had forgotten about the passport affair, stimulated enough to not be rational, and so I was delighted. He opened a drawer and handed my passport. Some of the pages were watermarked. Then he asked how the bike was and I said it was easy. He asked about visiting the hill tribes or idyllic waterfalls and I told him plainly that I only rode in the streets.

3

THE THICK AND DIMPLED glass is streaked by helical swirls of red syrup. There's heavy cream up top cut by paper-thin strawberries. It all moves thickly and pink through a clear straw. I push the glass to her. The beer washes the strawberry sweetness.

Four men sit in the table next to us. All in tucked button shirts, dress pants and large analog watches, leather or steel bracelets. They talk in a way easy to listen in.

First I tell Melody about Eric and Lyndon and Gabriel. From a short description she says she doesn't like them. She says she can't imagine me around them. She says in traveling you'll meet people you'd never be compatible with and only traveling makes it so. I tell her traveling removes the social filter. I tell her that it is true the people you share experiences with act like filters for what you are. She agrees and tells me the filter of the night-world she lives in is filtering out her saner qualities. I tell her that that's the main problem of her world. She tells me the money is too good and the consequences of getting it is what she'll bear. Then for the second encounter I tell her, "I feel inappropriate." I don't but her reaction would interest me.

"Think I care?"

"No," I say. "I don't know. I'm stupid. I met her on an app."

"I love dating apps."

"Well, I met her on one since it's hard to do in real life."

"What's that mean?" She pauses. "Real life."

"In the wild."

"Same shit."

"It's harder, honestly."

"How'd it go?"

"We fucked."

"Was she good?"

"She's a good athlete. Ask me what her sport is."

"What?"

"Fucking."

A plate stacked with sweet potato waffle fries. The burger meat is oozing on the porcelain. Heavy flaps of bacon. The bun is smooth and shiny. I bite and the bun cracks and shatters and caves to the soft centre. Melody drinks her beer like water.

"You're shy about it," she says.

"I don't know."

"You know I'm a stripper, right?" She laughs her squeeze-toy laugh.

"I don't know."

"I guess I'm way too open about sex and stuff than other folks are."

The waitress asks how the meal is and we both say it's great and I order another beer. Indeed, Melody knows that I drink to affirm my satisfaction.

"I'm not uncomfortable though," I tell her.

"No? I can't tell with you."

"I'm not uncomfortable."

"Okay. Just the way you talk. There's no intonation," she laughs, "I can't figure out anything. You're interesting though."

"There's bad and good interesting."

"The good."

"Good."

She drinks the milkshake until only foam is left.

"You're a student, right?" she asks.

"Yeah," I say. "Maybe there's a course I can take on intonation."

"Ahaha. I was going to say I want to go back to school."

"Go back?"

"I finished one semester."

"For what?"

"Psychology. Mental health is a big issue for me."

"How long has it been since you left?"

"Two years."

"Going to be hard to get back with all the stripping you've done now."

"Stripping's my back up plan."

"What's the main plan?"

"Therapist."

"Unexpected."

"If you knew me you'd expect it. What are you studying?"

"Social cues," I say. "I'm failing."

Does her wondering head have me all categorized? That tinkering stripper-head that auto-gauges sexual and social profiles. The laughter compresses out her lungs, her accentuated voice-box. "Seriously," she says.

"So, at first I was in neuroscience. I took some psychology classes too. Then I switched out to a general major just to explore more subjects. Then what I was basically doing was cognitive science. Which is an umbrella term for any subject of the mind and brain. Then in the second year I declared a major in linguistics. Minor in neuroscience. I wanted to be working in academia, actually. Now I'm not interested in it. Or at least for now."

"What do you want to do now?"

"Travel."

She agrees that aimlessness can eventually help find an aim.

"Can you give me career advice?" I ask.

Is she high enough to look down to see the comedy? Or is her position looking up from the bottom, from tragedy?

"It seemed you were smart with all the sciency shit you study but now..."

"I know, I know."

"I'm the last person."

"True."

"Come on. I'm good for some things." She sweeps her hands across her chest. "Look." She picks up a braided dread. "Did it ma-self."

"Artful," I tell her.

"You sound like a robot when you say that."

"Artful," I say louder.

"Yeah," she's squeaking, "you're awkward."

The men beside us are talking about their business. They are loud and depressing.

"You use dating apps a lot?" I ask.

"I do. The apps are great but the girls are a gamble."

"You use it only for girls?"

"Yeah. Men are nasty."

"They are, huh?"

"They get nastier on the apps."

"Like what's nasty?"

"The shit they'll send or text or whatever."

"I might be nasty too and you don't even know it."

"Let me see what you're doing."

She looks at my phone. "It's so innocent I don't know how you get a date ahaha." She continues, "I don't think I'd be all that interested to reply to you."

"Why?"

"It's so innocent!"

"Boring?"

"You're not doing anything to show an intimate connection."

"How am I supposed to show that when they're a stranger to me?"

"Oh, come on. You can. Why are you even using the app in the first place?"

"I'm not up to being instructed."

"Are you upset?"

"No. I'm saying shit."

"Oh, okay. I can't tell. Like at all."

"Don't worry."

"What's your dates been so far, anyway? They go how you expect?"

"Yeah. They do."

"What's your type, anyway?"

"What's your zodiac?"

"Mmm. Gemini. You believe astrology?"

"Not really. I'm a Virgo. I do very well with the empty-headedness of a Taurus."

"I know a lot of tauruses. They're not empty-headed. What makes you say that?"

"I'm just saying kind of what my type is. I'm using the zodiac signs to say so. I think it'll be more interesting to describe my type using them."

"What makes a taurus empty-headed? You just dissed an entire zodiac sign."

"That's not what I'm doing. I'm saying things for the conversation."

"Okay."

I take chance looks at the men. I wonder if one of them considers himself like an appendix which can be cut without altering function.

"You ever do things with girls at the club?" I ask.

"Kind of part of it."

"But like in the back?"

"Yeah, I'll fuck a dancer at least once a week."

"Seriously?"

"Yeah, in the backroom."

"Just to like relieve tension, right?"

"Just to fuck."

"You fuck just to fuck?"

"Need a reason?"

"Maybe for like a goal. Like to cure a headache."

"Is that what Montreal girl was? A human Advil?"

"Boredom, I guess."

"Ahhh, right."

Soon I tell her, "If I had a daughter and she had her female friends over and they were in the basement and I am in bed with my wife and she asks me, 'Please check on our daughter and her friends,' then I'd go down and have a peek and then go back up and tell my wife, 'They're doing lesbonic activities and it is the plainest thing in the world.'"

"Dude," she says. "What?"

"I did have this suspicion since I was young that girls during sleepovers kiss and hump and it's like nothing for them. They'd be good friends after."

"Is this serious or sarcasm? For real."

"I'm being provocative. For conversation."

Then after the meal we walk into an empty lot where Melody lights a pipe. I smoke a cigarette and watch her. She sits cross-legged on a concrete blockade. She tells me she's pansexual and polyamorous. I tell her I don't know what I consider myself as. "Typical white cis-male," she says. She tells me to sit and we kiss.

"Wait," she says. "Not so aggressive. You're literally spitting in my mouth."

"Stop laughing."

"I can't."

We kiss again. Her dreads jerk back. "Oh my God, you're so awkward."

"Yeah."

"No. I mean it in the most endearing way possible. I didn't even know you were into me."

"Obviously, I am."

"Okay," she says. "That's good."

Then we walk on past a farmer's market and a parking lot with a van for TV news and soon Melody sees a bong store and we go inside. The cashier tells us he's from Bangladesh. He has a childish voice and a carpet of sideburns along his fat head. He tells us he longs to sell weed in the store.

I look at the tall bongs in the glass case. Memories of dreams as a child walking through stores of giant unmanageable objects. Usually massive Halloween costumes and masks, the flayed skins of sea and space monsters. These dreams were at times scary enough to be nightmares. I realize I've had no nightmares in adulthood. I've had bad dreams but not nightmares. Not the living fear of childhood nightmares. The rooted fear as if a tincture of fear-concentrate dropped in the heart where it soaked and spread to begin the process for a higher baseline of fear.

Melody has been talking to the cashier for a long time. They both laugh, here and there. Then she buys a glass pipe that looks like it has trapped within its glass a colourful dust storm.

. . . .

MELODY IN A RED KIMONO dress, a thin cloth belt wrapped around her waist. Clothes sprawled on the floor, the suitcase gutted. From a backpack pouch she pulls out a rolled zip lock baggy. White flakes that look like paint chips. She taps the flakes out on her laptop cover and crushes them with the hard corner of the baggy. She uses her pinky to craft slim lines and she hands me the laptop.

Then a shot of the cinnamon whiskey. It is like melted candy blended with alcohol. The cinnamon-reek spitting out my nose.

I imagine myself facing a giant grinder like those for trees and thrusting my head into it in a rage so primal. I imagine my insides squishing inward until becoming a sludge. The bones crackling and breaking like firewood. My forearms are sweating as if they're blocks of ice.

I crush a chip on my fingertips and rub it in my teeth. Numbing gasoline mixing with the sweet cinnamon. The sensation of falling hard into the ground but I'm standing still.

Then she is in booty shorts, an oversized varsity jacket. Black stomper boots. "You're going to freeze," I say. Her legs are spider-like. "My legs don't get cold," she says.

"You look so hot."

But you cannot be nice for if you are you present no goal and every goal is a challenge and people love challenges.

A black Honda parks. "Hello!" He has rounded features like he is made from buns. In the rear-view he watches us both. He shifts into drive and the backside tugs. "Fun night tonight, guys?" The vowels round and fat and liquid.

"Hoping," says Melody.

"Why hope?" he says like a clown. "What are you doing tonight?"

"Clubbing," says Melody. "We never been."

"You new?"

"Yeah. Toronto."

"Oh. Same, same. But Toronto goes crazy clubbing and expensive. I love it for me here because it is not so crazy. You know?"

His eyes search the rear-view. They talk about the Toronto Raptors. There is a red light. "Is your friend sleepy?" he asks.

"I'm not sleepy."

"Okay, relax," he says.

"I'm okay."

The light turns green and his foot skims the throttle and he continues staring. "Hey, don't be so serious," he says. "Serious guy." He smiles.

"I'm tired," I say.

He pats the air. "Don't be serious."

"You get sleepy at this time?" asks Melody.

"No. I'm a little bit tired."

We step out the car.

"Have fun guys," he says. He drives off.

"You liked him, huh?"

"Kind of my type," she says.

"What's your type?"

"Dad bods. Greasy accents."

"You're disgusting."

"What?"

We walk past the crowd. The crowd can see her and they can see me. They'll make sense of us in their own way. Make sense of those booty shorts. Who else has an ass that gets paid just to show itself? The peekers, they wonder how I have won it.

There's a loud and manly *Beewop* in the crowd. Sneers in those surrounding, mockery. "Beewop!"

"Shut the fuck up," one says lowly.

"Beewop!"

Friends laugh and taunt, drunk in friendship. "Beewop!" Those that are not friends speak their criticisms with no intent to be heard by those that are doing the noise. The friends continue it until reaching the doors where they're told to stop by security.

Our wrists get stamped with the club logo, a circle and initial.

The dance-floor is packed with hot bodies. Platforms with mirrored stripper poles. We drink shots of tequila. Then we sidle through the crowd and step up on one of the platforms. I hold Melody's large purse. She clutches the pole as her booty shorts whip like tassels. The white girls in tight skirts are hysterical. She introduces me to some white girls as Max and her as Clair. Her purse strap is nestled in the pocket of my arm while she dances with them, her movements inhering a burning wilderness of fuck.

Then we follow a hall to an outside bar where the music from inside clatters senselessly. We get another tequila. Her pelvis bone scratches whirligig shapes in my thighs.

I cock my head to the bar. She follows holding my hand. She walks to the counter. I see high-schoolers talking to her. She comes holding two plastic cups and gives me one. "They want to buy me drinks," she says. "But I told them I was with you."

"Right."

She holds onto the round standing table as if she's falling and she pumps her rear hydraulically. Her slender shape with the sensually tuned proportions wobbling in the shadows below pink strobe lights, her body slick with sweat. A high-schooler latches onto her waist. He nods a puny sophomore head to his friends who look on exhausted. Remember me, the one who allowed you. His weasel hands glide. As soon as they rim the breasts he grinds on air. It looks like he apologizes. He walks away.

I lick her neck, salt slime, the inner cheek. "I wanted it," I whisper. Security breaks us apart. "Can't allow that," he says.

"Okay, okay," I tell him. I search his broad face for signs of recognition. Do you know the cravings of our communion, our need to connect intimately in this place and your own past of connections in similar places? His face is stone-blind to any signs, a face of apathy in the flesh.

There's a hall that leads to a backroom with a small stage with no people. The stage has a turntable and there's couches and chairs in front of it. A bar in the back. We close the door and sit on a couch and make out. Then I walk to the bar. I step behind the counter and uncork a bottle and drink. I hand her it. She drinks.

"You got any nina?" I ask her for I am a member of her. She'll act accordingly. She is not strange to me and neither am I to her. The sense of strangeness is a sign of ignorance. If I reveal something strange to her it's only strange because she didn't know it but when she knows it it no longer will impress her as strange. She is a tolerant and iconoclastic person. She integrates strangeness in herself with a cosmopolitan ease.

She runs a hand in her purse. She sprinkles a bit on the counter. We inhale what little there is. I search the counter for the register. It's locked. She asks if I'm really trying to rob the club and I tell her yes. I am flattened, stretched and squeezed, under a world-shouldering anger.

We sit on the couch where her smooth wet tongue couples and uncouples with mine.

"Um. Excuse me. What are you doing here? Are you the set?"

"Yeah," I say.

"What are you doing?"

"Preparing the set."

"What the fuck, guys. Get out."

We walk out the room and out the club. She orders a ride on her phone. The car comes and the ride is restfully quiet.

• • • •

I STAND OVER HER, AFRICAN and atavistic female, the fuck-eyes like flashlights, fear or excitement, coil the dreads in my hand and drive her face in. "I kept you after class," I say. "You're failing."

I give her breath.

"I said you're failing my class."

Her mouth engulfs.

I step off to the floor, long drip out her mouth splattered over the tight breasts. She reminds me of seeing deer in a trail. The fabled quality of the deer, its accompanying kick from out the common. But she may also be like a coyote which steps on the trail and as it walks ahead you do not know what it is and then you realize dogs do not have foxtails.

"I've come here with my crew and our ships are docked on the shore. We've been on voyage eight months. Finally discovered this here new world. I venture out into the jungle and find you picking berries. You in your lonesome. You're giving me the look of fuck and I've never seen a thing like you before. Never could dream or imagine a thing like you."

"Oh, God."

"You never heard of the Christian God. I'll show that to you later."

"Bye."

Resound the pin drop of adrenaline. "I don't want to force you out of your own will to pick those berries."

"Bye." Intuit beauty of death-signature.

Then we both lay under the bright ceiling light, the wet heat of our bodies. "I don't know how to feel about what you did there," she tells me. Her voice is the texture of matte if sound synthesized to touch. I stare in her eyes, the two pupils obscure in her amber black. The spinal erectors like two hollow tubes my fingers press and release. I pull her in, her leg over my hip like a sodden log.

4.

I REMEMBER THE DAY I left Saigon. She kissed and hugged me and I didn't care that it was in public. I told her that when she'd fly into Ontario she could call me to give her a ride from the airport. She never called me because she considered it rude. I loved her considerations for things I did not consider to be serious. I loved her light attitude which could harden like mortar. And like mortar if you were handling her it would shock you how quick she'd harden. It was a hardness that did not harm you but acted as her defence. I loved her instinct for self-defence. She answered in lies to my personal questions like if she had sex with other foreigners before me or if she kept talking to them after I left. I knew they were lies because she'd tell me later.

The restaurant was designed in a Japanese style with block-seats connected in a square to allow a table in the middle. In the old and yellow walls were narrow glazed windows displaying a tangle of sprigs, a rain-boiling summer.

Tracy covered her face when the first dish came. A domed rice cake on a metal plate. She had only come to the restaurant because it was my last day. She was red-faced and constantly squinting as if the restaurant was too bright.

I lifted the rice cake where underneath was a pasty coat of bee larvae on steamed rice. There were winged insects and large ants among the premature globs. They were all the same fleshy colour. In my right ear, during the massive forking of insects, was an earphone blasting death metal. The next dish was lemon pepper grasshoppers. They were crunchy and tasted only of lemon pepper. Tracy sat squinting at her phone, pinching her nose or covering her mouth, drinking rice tea.

I asked the waiter for scorpion but he said it was not in season. Soon I realized my request of quail was ignored. The three servers in the corridor looked and talked in a way that indicated it was about us. We were also the only ones there.

Now she texts me that she is in Lululemon. I stand in the entrance. She looks up from her phone, the head askew, smiling, face half-hid under the curved, dark bangs. She is wax-toned. The hair wiry like a broom head. She hands me a renewed plastic bag holding a can of Vietnamese coffee. She smells like sweet perfume and feels skeletal in my arms.

"How are you?" I ask.

"Good." She makes glances at my face. "Good to see you." Her accent is real.

I direct the walk to the Starbucks.

"It's been so long, huh Tracy?"

"One year."

"Why're you making that face?"

She says I need to shave my stubble.

"You look good, Tracy."

"No. Not true."

"How do you like Canada?"

"Good."

"Good?"

"Great."

"Not as great as home."

"Different."

"More drinking for Tracy?" It is like lifting a boulder to yell underneath.

"Oh, no. I need to study."

"What do you want?" I ask her.

"Strawberry frap," she says.

"Take a seat and wait for me."

I order her a large strawberry frappuccino and myself a medium black coffee. I wait for the drinks and watch her. She is texting.

I sit down with the drinks and she is on her phone. I sip my café and the frap is facing her while she texts. "Drink." She sets the phone down. She sips delicately.

"Hungry?" I ask.

She pouts. As if for a kiss.

"I know you are. Fatty."

Her jaw hangs loosely below her skull.

"Fatty. Fat, fat. We will try the food court. Get your fat belly exotic food. Big shopping today too?"

She nods, a smile covers her teeth. I see the coated hairs in her upper lip.

"Okay, we'll shop first to build appetite."

"Fine."

In a jean store she pulls a faded pair from off the rack. She goes in a changing room. She is in there a long time. She comes out and the jeans show her legs as two blue-fade poles.

"Stylish. I see many of the Asians wear them. Are they too big though?"

"Need to be big."

She goes back in. She comes out with the jeans tucked in her armpit. "Cost a lot," she says. "Ugh."

"But do you like them?"

"Yes."

I lead her to the cashier and pull the jeans out her armpit. She is embarrassed. I tap my card on the machine. We leave the store and she tells me that I am very kind.

"I want those other Asian internationals to be jealous of you."

She laughs, covering her delicate mouth with her delicate hand.

"What else do you want? Shoes. Purse. They will know who you are, those damn internationals."

"No, no. I must stop you."

"Why?"

"Sonny, it is too kind of you."

"When Tracy comes to school she will be like a celebrity among the internationals. The Canadians will think she is a princess from Asia."

She grunts like a man and shoos me away. We walk to the food court. It is busy.

"Want to try Indian?" I ask.

"No."

"Non-spicy. Sure?"

"No," she says. "Get for yourself."

"How about Korean?"

"It's okay," she says. "No."

"Thai is pretty good," I tell her.

We both get Pad Thai, mine beef and her chicken.

"Have you made any friends?" I ask.

"I met another girl from Vietnam and she is my best friend."

"Very good."

"We hang out a lot."

"How is the family treating you?"

"They have a big dog and he is so cute and fluffy. I take him for walks. The sister stays in her room all day and sometimes she takes me out. She is nice."

"Everything sounds great for you."

"Sometimes I'm lonely. At school no one talks to me. Only other foreigners talk to me because of a program. They are boring."

"Make the best out of it. Schedule hangouts with them. You're all shy at first and it gets better the more you open up and then it can be fun."

"No," she says. "They are boring."

"You should be the one out of all of them that goes out drinking. Everyone will want to hang out with you then."

"They'll call me irresponsible if I do drinking."

"Do you remember when we went out to the bars and drank all night?"

"Yes. You made me drink a lot. I never drank like that with guys."

"But you had fun, right?"

"Fun. Yeah. But lots of drinking."

"Oh, you loved it."

Her eyes roll.

I imagine asking her if she wants to go to the Starbucks but we already went.

"Not a lot of time," I tell her. "My friend's waiting for me."

"Leaving?"

"We're only passing through to meet up with some more friends."

"But are you leaving?"

"I have to go."

"I took the bus *here*."

"I know I should have told you before it could only be a little hangout."

"What are your friends doing?"

"Getting together. Traveling. Drinking."

"Is it a girl or a boy?"

"Girls and boys."

"You are going to leave me here?"

Then I say, "I should have told you. My minds so gone with the traveling, the drinking."

"What am I going to do here alone?"

"You are joking."

"What?"

"Shop or go to the Starbucks. You're in a pretty large mall. After all."

"I drank a frap already."

"Call your best friend. Ask if she can hang out."

"I'm not calling her."

I slide our garbage off the tray and into a bin. She is texting forcefully with her face hidden by her trembling bangs.

"You want a boba?" I ask.

"No boba."

"Ice cream?"

"No ice cream," she says. "What I do here alone?"

"Are you scared?"

"No. I'll be alone."

Then she asks, "You leaving?"

"Yes. Fatty."

"Okay, leave."

"Will you take the bus?"

"My friend'll come."

"That's great."

"Leave."

We hug tightly. I move away and she extends her hand and I clasp it. Our fingers interlock and she stares in my eyes. I walk out the entrance of the food court, to the open air, and light a cigarette behind the supporting columns.

• • • •

IN THE MORNING THE musculature of my skull tightens to produce a cephalic vice, my lungs struggling against the electric quickness of my blood. I stand dizzy and walk to the sink to pour a glass of water.

I beg Melody to get out of bed.

We go out walking to the shopping plaza and then go in the coffee-smelling breakfast diner.

She shakes salt until it creates a white crust over the eggs. I cut my omelette in the middle and flay it open. I spurt in hot sauce. Melody chews on the cold bacon.

She tells me that in the club she was giving a man a lap dance and he requested more for the compensation of one hundred dollars. Melody told him no. The man then talked to her friend. He wanted to pay both of them three hundred dollars if necessary.

"I refused. But it was tempting. Really tempting. But he sent me vibes."

"Vibes?"

"Weird vibes."

"Interesting."

"Interesting," she says. "Guys love that word. Interesting."

"How is the club itself?"

"Low-key. Simple. Chill. Yeah. Check it out for yourself."

"Me?"

"Good club for a first timer."

"Maybe. Will knowing you give me cred?"

"None at all but you'll be a level ahead anyone in there. We did sleep together."

"That's right. I know that."

The waitress pours us more coffee. I eat the last of my everything omelette. On her plate is only bacon and cut cubes of ham. The ham splashed with ketchup.

"This is good coffee," I tell her.

"I know, right?"

"It's free refills, right?"

"I think so."

"I'd hate it if it's not."

She raises her hand. "Excuse me. The coffee is free refills, right?" The wrinkly waitress eyes both of us. "Of course it is," she smiles villainously, "need a top up?"

"I do." I lift up the cup and she pours it in. It flows out steaming and smelling like good coffee.

"What was your first impression of me?" Melody asks.

"You were easy to talk to. Attractive. The artful dreads. What about me?"

"Cute and aloof."

"Okay. I got it."

"In a wholesome way," she says.

"Anyway."

"I like messing with you."

"Do you think I like you doing it?"

"Yes. I think you like it."

"Maybe. Maybe not."

"I'll never know. You're impossible to tell. Even if you say it. You're impossible."

We drink the satisfying coffee.

"So. Polyamory?"

"Yep," she says.

"Isn't that what people do when they're still searching for the right person?"

"Not at all. Do I need to give you a lesson right now this early?"

"I'd like one. I'd like to understand this so complex relationship status."

"I'm not in love with labeling. Labels just help getting things clear."

"They confuse things."

"Depends. But I think they're more useful."

"Monogamy is a legitimate status because it's a sacrifice. You're not having fun all the time. You're forced to problem solve instead of giving up and going to the next person."

"There's a lot more dynamic to polyamorous relationships than you realize."

"Let's not argue in the morning. Let's have a good morning, please."

"You're the one ruining it."

"Good morning," I say smiling.

"I didn't peg you as a such a wholesome good morning guy."

"I wasn't before but I've taken a lot of mornings for granted, so now I'm a good morning guy."

"Oh my God. Pathetically wholesome."

"I know. It makes me sad. How do I unwhole myself?"

"Spend more time with me."

"Uh oh."

"Top up?" the waitress asks wickedly.

"Yes, please." She pours.

"How are you going to unwhole me?"

"It's kind of early to say."

"Early in what we are or early in the day."

"What are we by the way?"

"Do we need to have your other partners here to make it official? For me to be included?"

"What do you want us to be?"

"It's better it happens organically than us saying it."

"I agree with that most of the time."

"What's the best time for you to agree with something like that? Is it the morning?"

"Time I be moving on." She stands. "I got to pee."

I drink coffee and wait for her.

"How many coffees have you had?" she asks.

"I think this is third."

"We have to get out before you collapse."

"I don't care."

"You should."

"I was absent for that lesson in school."

"What?"

"I missed the class where the kids learned to care about their health."

"Huh?"

"Not funny?"

"I don't know."

"I'm saying everything I know I learned in classes."

"Why be so harsh on yourself?"

"Sometimes I need it."

We pay and then walk out. I light a cigarette and offer her one and light it for her. She is hotter with a cigarette and I tell her this, though she gets lightheaded and reserved. The neighbourhood is quiet and still impersonal. This suburban staleness inspires us both to never be suburban in our tastes and lifestyle.

We relax in the house. I cannot imagine going out again. She looks up things we can do before her shift in the evening. I tell her to come closer on the couch and we kiss. I push her head down. "What?" she asks.

I push her head down.

"That's a joke," she says and wiggles away.

"What is it?"

I kiss her again and pull my pants down and grab her hand and smack it on. She squeezes. Use your instinct and turn your head off. I push her head down. She locks on it. She pulls back. "Listen, what are you doing?"

I pull my pants up.

"Sorry," I say.

She says nothing and looks astray, her head oscillating on the neck like a malfunction.

Silence has varying qualities. It does not exist as one singular thing. This specific quality is piquantly violent.

• • • •

THE DRIVER POINTS TO the building and looks at me. It is a squat building. No windows. A big board sign out the roof displays a blond woman in a pink bikini, her viperous crotch.

"Okay buddy," he says. He stops at the entrance, a dark purple wall with double doors that look painted on.

"Are you around this area?" I ask him.

"I drive."

"Will you be around later?"

"How late?"

"Past midnight?"

"Take my number."

I enter it. "Thank you."

"Have fun."

I look at the doors and the parking lot.

"Ever been here?" I ask him.

"How old are you?"

"Twenty-two."

"You knock and a bouncer opens," he says. "Sorry. I got to go unless you want a ride somewhere else."

"No. I'm fine. Thanks."

I knock on the door and a man in a dress jacket opens it. "How's it going?" he asks.

"Good. How are you?"

He looks at me confused.

"I want to come in."

"ID."

I hand him it.

"Got another card with your name on it?"

I hand him my credit card.

"Got cash on you?"

"Cash?"

"ATM inside. Twenty dollars cover charge. Cash only. ATM inside."

I enter a dark room where he sits on a stool. Across from him is an ATM. It belches one hundred dollars in twenties. I hand him the twenty and he opens a door. The sound of the club shoots into the room. It is submerged in dark. There are woman dancing topless and one is nude. She looks like a noodle with two lumps. Woman walking around topless. Few disparate men sitting along the lip of the stage.

A woman asks if I want a drink and I tell her whiskey sour. I sit in the far corner in the dark. The woman comes with the drink and asks me if I'm alone tonight.

"Yeah," I say. "I'm waiting for my friend to perform."

"Your friend?"

"Yeah. She's a stripper."

"Cheers."

She walks off. Her singlet folds into her muscular ass.

I imagine walking into the back and watching Melody prepare for her performance. The other strippers would be there facing the big mirror and inspecting themselves. Melody would introduce me. They would walk around naked and I would even be able to smell them as they passed me sitting with Melody who is layering eyeliner. In the corner, two of them would be kissing. One would spread her legs on the chair and the other would pump her fingers inside her. I'd peek out the curtains watching Melody dance on stage. The desperate men watching her.

Soon Melody in a red bikini rides a pole on stage. She dances a carnal splendour with herself and another stripper. I finish my drink and the waitress comes.

"No thanks," I tell her.

"You want company?"

"No."

"Do you want the bill?"

"Sure."

I inward scream.

She comes with the bill.

"Machine?"

"Cash."

I hand her a twenty and say it's all for her.

I walk to the front door and a waitress tells me to use the back door. I walk back and pass a tall bouncer who nods pleasantly at me. The door shuts and snuffs the sound.

I light a cigarette and walk the solitary street and imagine myself in a bed, my limbs releasing and the warmth under the sheets.

I walk into Melody's room and shuttle into sleep beautifully.

• • • •

OUTSIDE THERE IS A stocky security guard with an orange beard. I light a cigarette by him and he watches me. I imagine asking him what he's watching. If there's something so interesting as to continue watching. Short and big boned and lumpy ginger freak.

"How's tonight?" I ask.

"Slow night."

"It's bad for you?"

"Want some action. Not all the time. Sometimes. Good action."

"I guess it's boring, eh?"

"Sure is. Sometimes"

I imagine asking him if he saw her. I imagine him saying it's good for me.

"All right," I flick the cigarette, "Hope you get some good action soon. See you."

My beer is resting flat-headed on a coaster.

"Melody," I say.

"Yes?"

"Nothing."

Then she says, "I've seen shit...I think you don't get what I'm saying. I suffered depression most of my life. Abused, sexual and mental, so many times. By different men. You don't need to know about it. Not your problem. But I'm telling you because we've gotten close now."

"Okay. I understand. I would never want you to feel uncomfortable. Are you okay?"

"I'm okay. I'm a mess on stage if I'm drunk. I get too angry too. I haven't been really drunk in a long time. Once I tried to kill myself when I got drunk. Admitted to a hospital for six months after. All this is just coming out."

"I'm not judging you for it."

"It was at the worst period when I was working as a waitress. I hadn't even started stripping. Sometimes the thought comes back. Weak but it gets strong. And like you I felt misplaced too growing up. I was a troubled kid. With everything that happened. Fuck this has gotten serious. Fuck. Didn't mean for this to happen. I'm not going to be able to dance tonight if we continue this." Then she says, "I want to be a therapist to help others get out of the shit I'm in. With depression and trauma. Now you know that about me. I'm sorry. I have to say this. I have to let it out. It's fucked up for me to be stripping. I want to leave it soon. The whole sex entertainment shit. It's hard. But I'm making my way."

She adds, "Want to know the reason why I liked you enough to give you my number? I never, ever, do that with guys... You gave me a safe feeling. Didn't try hitting on me, sexualizing me... It was safe and fun. A little childish too. I liked it. It's soothing...Why did you keep talking to me?"

"Because I liked it too, silly."

Then later she goes outside to smoke her pipe. Why did you not go out with her? She comes back.

"We still have time?"

"Yes," she says.

"I found a plan. Let us be fun-loving idiots and go bowling."

The bowling alley is decorated with flashing lights and on the walls above the pins are giant screens playing 90's music videos. I order a pitcher of beer. I type into the bowling console, entering her name as *Melixara* and mine as *Mandingo*. She laughs as she has laughed in previous times and it feels right for her to do so, her smile travels beyond herself.

The alcohol has padded my movements and I feel great. She is challenged at bowling. I make fun of her and she is laughing at herself too. It is enjoyable and renewing to bowl with her and watch the old music videos and share the pitcher of cold beer. Then two games have ended and the beer is gone.

The car comes. "I'll see you," she says and steps in the back. I watch the car recede in the road. I walk in the urine-stained sidewalk and the empty intersections and see in blurry astigmatism the green-lights like wayward signals and a taut banner stretched long across the poles.

• • • •

"CAN YOU PLEASE SMOKE a cigarette?"

"Why?"

"I want to see you smoking."

"Fetish?"

"Yeah. I think so."

We smoke tobacco together.

"Are you hard?"

"Hardening."

She laughs and inhales, exhales through beautifully round nostrils.

"I want another."

"Okay," she says.

"Have another with me?"

"I think I'll get too lightheaded."

There is a mass of pigeons chipping the ground.

"Come on," I say. "Just one."

She smokes.

"You look good smoking."

"I'm scared you're enjoying me too much."

The sky has swirled clouds, gaps of blue. I tell her they are like the swirls of her pipe. She says she wants to buy a bong.

"Do it later," I tell her. "Me and my big mouth."

"Okay. I'll do it on my own time."

"Sorry. If you want to get a bong we can go."

"No, we won't."

Not every instance is a challenge. An instance can be that and nothing more. A ground does not have to be laid with every instance. Time can pass without that time being the duration needed to form a ground. You can lose a challenge and it will not be a loss to you because it does not enter into awareness as such. If you widen the scope then the losses will make you will feel alive in the worst way. What you need for the good way is a narrowing, a limit, a rest.

We walk to a Starbucks.

"This is a nice Starbucks," she says.

"They're not usually like this."

A man with a neck tattoo looks at the top menu. Melody says he's cute.

"Do you have any tattoos?" I ask.

"You looked at all of it. Did you find any?"

"No. Thinking of getting one?"

"I can't decide."

"Me neither but I don't think I'll ever get one. I hate the idea of a tattoo. It's like a profile description on these stupid apps."

"I was debating of getting a panther on my arm."

"I'd like to get the head of a pigeon on my bicep. Have you seen the head of a pigeon seriously? They are funny and ugly."

"But what'll you tell people when they ask why you got a pigeon head tattoo?"

"Different response for everyone. That's a pigeon head tattoo."

"I see."

We consider options of what to do before the evening but we do not decide on anything. I order a ride and we get driven to the house. We go into the bedroom and she strips nude and cradles me like a massive leech.

Later on in the night she spills the residual powder of a baggy on a plate. Another baggy drops a half-cut tablet. With a butterknife she splits and minces it into dust. She trowels the residue together and pats it down with the knife butt and fashions two strips on opposite sides of the plate. She sniffs half and sucks in hard and sniffs the other. She looks like an animal gulping meat. I sniff the other strip and it lodges shut in my nose. I pick it with my finger and breath in.

She plays music on her laptop. She asks me if I like the music and I tell her yes but I do not. We share the bottle of cinnamon whiskey.

Then Melody wants me to dance. I am able to dance. It is true that I am dancing. Dancing is in me. Dancing is natural and simple and nourishing. She grinds in me. I sense the music not as sound but as an emotion. It buzzes in my nerves.

* * * *

IF I WANT, I CAN RECALL some of the memories with her. They will grow heavier and brighter. Whatever god or process has designed it beautiful like that. But also very sad.

"Do you know when it comes?" asks a young androgynous person.

"I'm not sure."

"I think it's late."

Soon we are both looking at it driving through the lane. We step inside and they sit in the far back. In the next stop a woman sits next to me. Her big body is touching mine so as to cause a friction-heat. I look at the digital panel displaying the upcoming street names. I know I will have to press into the women by me in order to lift my hand to pull the wire. Or I will have to wriggle my other arm against her. My phone pulses.

Should I wait to touch the wire or do it immediately as the street name appears? Does my preparedness indicate to anyone here my preparedness? Some touch the wire when the street name has not flashed. They know their routes and their streets.

From the centre of my life came
a great fountain, deep blue
shadows on azure seawater.

. . . .

Louise Glück, "The Wild Iris"

Part 3

1.

THE ROOM IS NONSENSICAL, my position is too. It is not that I do not know it as a room or me as laying in it but it fails to lock a past reference, a schema of intention.

There is a feeling like a lead ball in my pelvis and my equilibrium spins harder the further my malfunctioned head lifts from the floor. I lay and breath and stare in the ceiling. The room is cold.

I pull on the blanket above me and my left shoulder feels shorn as if it whirled like a grass-cutter string. With eyes closed the equilibrium feels as if corkscrewing out of my skull. Lay and breath and remember and stare and move your extremities and focus on loss of touch or strength.

I remember the airport. There are several to remember and they blend with each other. The best one was in Seoul, South Korea. I was there for a two-hour layover. Washroom stalls like fortresses, wandering wheeled robots that you can press for directions, designer coffee in cafés playing Brian Eno. I could live as an expatriate in the airport of Seoul. But Seoul is not the airport. For me it is the exemplary model of an airport.

The observer of my mind is floating in a living bog which is my mind. It lives and moves, murky, hot and populated with bog things, alive with noise and feeling and synchronic reaction.

The airport in Toronto. Think of the bus routes. Where did they lead and what did the ticket say. Patterson or Pearson. The airport is complex, city-sized and subterranean.

Complex and complicated are different.

What I mean is complicated. *Complex* is a feature, *complicated* is an error. However, it is both complex and complicated. The best word for that is *chaotic*. I try to think of a less sensational word but I can't. A good airport though chaotic. It's not bad for it to be chaotic. It makes you feel like you're traveling. There's adventure coming.

But the Toronto airport is not the one. It's the most frequented but it's not the one. I can't think of the name but I can think of the features of the one. Small and parochial. The perfect one for the observer to discover in the breathing bog of my mind.

The Greyhound bus drove me to departures. I waited a long time in the terminal. But which departures. International or domestic. I'm sure it's domestic.

I arrived in either Vancouver or Abbotsford.

Abbotsford, the rural west, almost like Harrow, Ontario, where some of my friends in high school were from. Country friends that took Facebook pictures with slain ducks and camo hats and varmint rifles. Did those country friends ever go traveling? They don't seem interested in being outside their communities.

My phone is on the table or the bed. On the table is also a paper bag. I had ordered Skip the Dishes. "Hi," I said to the delivery man. "How are you?"

"Good. Did you order food?"

"Yeah."

Remember him. He told you he was from Burma. He used *Burma* specifically, not the current name, Myanmar. He said that because you're white you might know better the older name. He was hurrying to leave, it seemed. I told him I was traveling and he gave me his Snapchat. I don't use Snapchat but I redownloaded it to add him. I pretended to be looking for it on my phone while it downloaded. He said to hit him up for anything. *Anything.*

Vermicelli and chicken and spicy prawns and pork chop. After eating I felt a burning headache.

But the brain does not feel pain. It is the thin encasing membrane which has nerves to feel.

The macabre images of the brain, the wrinkled and throbbing jelly, and knowing its personal fault, in a bucket of kerosene.

My uncle and his popped brain. An aneurysm from diabetes when he was eight. They had to saw his skull to find the bulging nub to stop the hemorrhaging. My fate authored by the malady of his putrid genes.

Fate and *destiny*. Similar meaning but strangers in connotation. It is my destiny to arrive here, it is my fate to die here. As it was his destiny to have a brain, his fate for it to bulge a diameter of four millimetres.

I won't think of the brain and its working and unworking. I imagine complete evacuation of physical matter. I am thought stuff, cool and non-aching and non-bloody, non-smelly, non-sweating, cosmically derived and divined thought.

It was raining all day. Dark turbulence on the plane. "Welcome to BC," said the taxi driver, a Punjabi man from Pakistan. I listened to the rain in the room. It beat on the windows and balconies and like gunfire through the puddles in the lot. Dark clouds and beyond the street was darker, rain-glazed to look plastic, a road exploding to the rain drops.

The cable television bored me and I turned it off. Non-stop advertisements. I took two ibuprofen and slept.

I roll away from the bed and push up and ease on my knees. I grope in the paper bag. Only empty containers, dried napkins.

There exists a thirst in me so craving as if to be like an organism fit with its own consciousness, hopes and anxieties.

In the bathroom I punch fingers in my throat, scratching the tongue. My hands shake, my stomach, and my breathing bubbles in vomit.

The unutterable and unalterable completion of my life. Not unpleasant or sad yet my eyes water. The last of my brain as yellow and pink strands in the toilet. A hemorrhage, a cancer, an unknown epileptic, the curse of Caesar, wandering until a seizure ends wandering.

Then cleaning myself, a perceptible emptiness, then dressing, slowly, walking the bright hall, slowly.

If the man at the desk heard the thud or scream, the convulsions. He stares at his computer and I walk outside in the dark, the cold, the wet.

The gas station is behind the hotel.

Keep watching me. I walk to the drinks and grab electrolytes. I walk to you with the two drinks. You see the pallid face, the crumb of vomit, bloodshot and dishevelled youth. Maybe he is sixteen or twenty. What is he, a junky, a homeless, a thug? If he's traveling, you want to see his smiling photos in nature's perfect landscapes and hear of his learning about different customs and meeting strangers and becoming less strange to them. You'd like to know if he opened his mind to new ways of life and his life to new potential.

"Can you help? I passed out. Has passing out happened to you?"

"You passed out," he tells me.

"Yes."

"Need a doctor." He makes a heroin gesture.

"No. I took two ibuprofens for a headache."

"I can call you a doctor."

"No. I never needed a doctor."

"If you inject drugs a doctor can help you."

"No. I don't. And I don't need a doctor. I'm fine now."

"You're not healthy looking."

"I think I'm dehydrated."

"You will go crazy if you do not talk to doctor. I'm not doctor. Drinking this is good for you but a doctor will do check-up."

"Thank you."

Then, "Is it possible I can get another breakfast package?" I ask the hotel receptionist.

"Didn't get one when you checked in?"

"No."

He goes through a door and comes out with a brown paper bag.

"Thank you."

The elevator is out of service, a hall is blocked by plastic sheeting. I go up the stairwell, pulling myself, both hands remarkably sensitive. Dropping too hard in the bed. The buoyant brain bouncing in heated blood. I sip on the drinks and chew a granola bar. Time passes in the bed. I watch my phone repeatedly for the time. I want to stop relying on my phone so I need to buy a watch. A luxury watch which is a talisman providing protection against the awareness of death.

If a watch can be a talisman against death then people can too. Tracy is a talisman. It would be kind to text her. She has never talked about death but that is not what makes her a talisman.

But there are others who invite death without knowing. There are others who do it with knowing. They are talismans in their own way and it is not clear they are good or bad.

So much of what living is is living after the fact. Upgrade or degrade.

But the fact has not happened. You know it will be happen. What you mean is living *before the fact*. But before that there are many other smaller facts you must deal with. But why do these smaller facts have to be bad? How does one live after the fact of a good? Maybe it is best to degrade after. Maybe upgrading is like raising your defective head to touch a chainsaw.

I attempt to believe that a healthy precondition to existence is the acceptance of total loss. It is easy to believe and comforting that there are numerous prior loses I must accept too.

The blanket consumes me and I breath and the air grows hotly dense. I unravel, sweaty and cold. The blanket consumes me again.

The matter of my brain may kill me. The knowing of having this brain problem changes my identity.

I can use standard language to express myself idiosyncratically. It is a malleable template but only if I work to make it so.

I remember disappointment to words that equated to my feelings. The words were trivialized. Books and songs and movies could be made out of them. As if they originated in these things and these things gave them content and the means to interact with them.

It is not identity that has changed for me. It is the signature of myself that has changed. I like the word *signature* rather than *image* because it denotes a personal marking. I like it more than *identity* because it is more personal to me and the associations of it feel realer.

A signature is the psychological mark of a person. I have an innate and intimate signature of myself which I cannot communicate to others nor can others communicate theirs to me. The reality of it is purely subjective, untranslatable to language or even visual expression. It is disorienting for me to think about what the signature of myself is for other people.

I shower, slowly as if watering my diseased body with liquid medication, and then lay in the bed and watch the dim morning slit through the blinds and then cover the walls.

I call the taxi driver who drove me to the hotel. He gave me his personal number and a card. He was not a licensed taxi driver. He waited in departures with a van asking people if they needed his service. In the windshield he had glued the Uber logo and a tiny picture of himself and a card with his name. He was not working for Uber, not full-time, and he only accepted cash. Why he worked like this was not clear. I tell him it's me and he asks, "Who are you?"

"Sonny."

"Oh. My friend Sonny."

He told me if I were to call I needed to make it friendly.

"I need help today."

"Oh, yes. I help. The Ramada?"

"Yes, my friend."

"Okay."

The receptionist is now the woman from yesterday morning. She asks, "How was your stay?"

"It was disappointing the free breakfast was a bag of apples and bars."

"Sorry to hear. The hotel is currently renovating. Services to offer more breakfast is not available."

"You should state online."

She walks to me, holding a brown bag.

"Sir. I can offer another free breakfast for the troubles."

"Okay," I say. "Thank you. Sorry for seeming rude."

"No," she says kindly. "Our fault."

Outside is the driver in his rusted van. He gets out and waits by the door. He can see me and he waits either for me or for my signal to come in.

I open the door and, "Hello, my friend," he says. His name is Placit. I told him it's like *placid* and he said I was the first white person to tell him that.

"My good friend," I say. "How are you?"

"Wonderful today." He has a large Punjabi bracelet on his wrist, a small and blurry tattoo on the back of the hand, near the thumb. I shake his hand. It's big and hot and strong.

"You look beautiful today." He has a massive wrestler neck, balding, big bearded, a dimpled scar above his left cheek paler than his brown skin. He eyes the lobby, the receptionist.

"Good hotel?" Placit asks.

"Nope. Let's go."

He turns the ignition and the mass of keys in the keyring jangle and the engine coughs and starts and he smiles and drives to the exit and watches for a turn.

"You well?" he asks.

"Last night I passed out in my room. Maybe dehydration."

"I know something happened because you quiet. How feel now?"

He enters an opening and I wait for the engine to dull.

"My friend, I am only tired."

"Ah, happens me too," he says. "In bathroom. I was your age. Sick by fever."

He speeds in a hill where ahead is only the clouded sky. Then on level ground the horizon appears, barred by the trunks of trees so tall. So much grassland. The passing semi-trucks shake the wheel.

"A bad headache too," I tell him.

"Exhausted."

"I think so too."

"Drink water and rest for today." He does the Punjabi head motion. "You'll be good."

"Thank you."

Yesterday he told me how he prided himself on his ability to go anywhere no matter the danger. He said he loved the mountains of Nepal which British Columbia reminds him of. Bangladesh was particularly important for the people and the geography and cuisine was suited to him. In a market he met European foreigners and for a few days he banded with them through Jaipur and to New Delhi where he tried alcohol for the first time. He hated the taste and never tried it again until moving to Canada where he admitted coyly to have gotten drunk several times.

"One day I was so sick in clinic. Disease not exist in developed nations. Called dysentery and if you read lives of soldiers in the world wars you know they suffered dysentery and doctors give me medicine soldiers took. Called sulfa. I suffered dysentery two more times. Then I always carry with myself sulfa."

"I carry ibuprofen and a bottle of vitamin C."

"Good," he says. "It's boring and everyone knows. Exercise and eat healthy. No smoking. Maybe little drinking. You need a strong immunity to travel."

"What about coffee?" I ask him. "I love coffee."

"But not too much coffee. One cup is good. Two is good. Three and more is bad. Heart tires."

"My friend, I drink a lot of coffee."

"For this you are not good."

"You drink tea or coffee?"

"Tea and coffee. Coffee in morning. Tim Hortons. But I buy food. Expensive and not too tasty. But I will buy."

"It's convenient. The food."

"Yes."

Yesterday he talked about Pakistan, its detachment from the rest of India in the 20th century. He said as a Punjabi born there he was harassed by the Muslims. Pakistan for locals can be dangerous but as he said and as other travellers have told me, it is the nicest country to travel. He tells me that people will invite me to their homes and they will cancel work and other obligations to host me. I told him that that sounded great but I'd prefer hostels.

We drive on a bridge where below are long harbours. Far in the distance is an inclined stretch of mountain land with neighbourhoods one can see the layout of as if flying overhead or as if the land had upturned to fold itself into what burdens it.

"Hello mountains," says Placit. "It's me Placit."

"And me. Sonny." I wave at the mountains as my friend Placit had done.

We reach a hill where he speeds hard, the pistons jiggling the seat. He taps the brake as we go down. We continue on a narrow and flat street with traffic. The adjacent roads are flaring upwards into suburbs. I can see behind glassy complexes the raised platform a sky train shuttles through.

"Better than hotel?" he asks.

"I think so."

"Higher price?"

"A bit cheaper, surprisingly."

He gets out and opens the trunk and grabs the backpack and spreads the straps. I shake my head. "I hurt my shoulder too."

"What other hurts?"

"Head."

He palms my forehead. "No fever. No problem."

On either side of the building are homes with a low glass fence. I lift up a gate latch and walk to a glass door and enter a code in a keypad. The numbers do not light nor make sound. Then I knock on the door. A man opens. "I booked for today," I tell him. He is short and built like a box and smells of cologne. He looks behind me.

"Only for one."

Placit laughs.

"He's my friend." I almost say *driver*.

The man gives me a key and flips a switch which gives power to the keypad and then he leaves.

"Modern," the Punjabi says.

"Is it?"

The walls and furniture are white and faultless, the floor is of dark grey laminate. There is a futon, a flatscreen TV fixed on the wall in the small living room, a kitchen-island with a deep sink. A chandelier that looks like the snapshot explosion of a star. The bedroom is small and citrus smelling and its corridor opens to the bathroom. On the bed is a folded turquoise paper with **Welcome**.

The Punjabi shakes my hand. "Take care, friend," he says.

"My friend, take care."

I pull on the beaded cord to draw the curtain in the living room. The view is sheeted grid-panels covering what I think is the pit for a new parking storage. Beyond is the sky train on its high rails, reeling in soundless speed.

On the granite kitchen-island there are two cylindrical packages of wheat biscuits. One package is wholewheat, the other sprinkled with sesame. They are crunchy like over-stale bread. The crunch is like boots walking on gravel. The lactic acid like minuscule metal threads coiling in my jaw. I pour a glass of water from the tap. The water is refreshing yet hurts as it pushes down biscuit.

It is right for me to concern myself about hydration. I wish I had the concern Placit has for my hydration. Most likely he has forgotten about his concern but he has stored it without knowing inside a surface pocket of his heart. The deeper pockets of that heart are reserved for concerns of family and his wellbeing.

I focus into the pockets of my heart where the different concerns are organized. What is the deepest pocket and does it contain myself or some fragment of it.

The deepest bottom pocket contains people, not concepts or euphoric states of nicotine and caffeine. You know it does. Coward.

• • • •

IN THE SKY TRAIN I stand to view the city's backdrop of blue mountains, a smoky mist skirting their snow-capped or bald peaks, the shadows of cloud colouring them blue. The many clouds are breaking to pass the sunlight which in the sky, among banks of furrowing grey, glows a dusty white. The sunlight presses on the forested country of mountain a golden green pockmarked by the underside shade of giant trees. Dipped portions of the mountainside, a darker blue, with the neighbourhoods that are so like clusters of painted rock.

In comparison to these mountains the commercial high-rises and multi-storied condos look like a school project of erect crystals growing in a crater. They are reflective, a metallic gloss, pale blue and ribbed to each floor, the windows looking knocked out as if they are pieces in a shooting gallery. They are new constructs, spaced far from each other, few in number, a modest and clean-seeming city. There is a crane with its huge, protruding arm taller than any of them. It rises across the neighbourhoods of perished low-rises and skeletal structures.

The doors slide and I wait for these new passengers taking their warm side-seats. Then the train beeps and the doors slide closed. It rolls on with a sound like a choir of maybe fifty people singing one drawn-out and unholy note.

I pass the tollgate and then wait at an intersection, watching these micro-movements of the city, the random bird or dog, easy traffic, tactically dressed and bag-burdened vagabonds who with their walking, their pin-point presence, fashion enigma trails through the streets.

In the distance is a large dome anchored on top a low building. It looms over an urban creek loaded with sailboats, like an engineered moon. Now crossing the intersection, walking closer, I see the dome is formed so by crisscrossed triangular panels which make it angular and glinting. A frame of fasted bars in hexagon pattern wraps it whole like a cobweb and nodes throughout the connected joints stud it with dynamic light.

A walking trail loops around the dome and along the creek. On the right side, far behind the dome, a stadium, its spires massive and sharp and wide, rises like a god's crown.

I walk on a straight and pavered path between trees, the sides bedded with grey rocks, wood benches set for views of the creek, the sailboats so still and many in the water, their tall and tied masts like bright roman pillars flashing among dark trunks.

The trail branches into a hump of thicketed land rimmed with gritty sand and rock beds. Hacked tree trunks pitted in the soil, the bark flaking away like a rust, placed strategically in the outskirts.

Soon the trail's right-side expands in a base of cracked stone sloping down to the water. The bottom edge, kissed by the waves, is bloomed with algae and shiny. Crows and pigeons peck and totter in the crevices and soar down pointlessly and fly back. Crows perch on the stones, a primitive jury, beak-scratching their wings in the fierce way birds do.

A restaurant is supported on a pier with a dock alongside it. Carpets of hairy green scum grown around the underside pillars rock to the delicate waves.

The restaurant reminds me of scenes I imagined in books or scenes I've seen in movies. Multi-levelled, all wood, classic diner arrangement with a nautical theme. Nights in Mediterranean ecstasies, citrusy fish and Turkish coffee and strong non-filtered cigarettes. Hushed conspiracies and lover dramas. The esoteric happenings of seaside living.

I buy a black coffee and walk out to a boardwalk. Far away over the water is a bridge where underneath in the shadows and rusty abutments seagulls are spiralling like toys hung by wires. The bridge is an arched mouth opening to the vast and clear inlet. Farther is an island of mountains wrapping the horizon in velvet blue.

I walk down a matted ramp to a dock of ferryboats and then into a cabin. Paddles and nets and pictures of fish and boats and happy people on the walls. "Hi," she says. Her hair is a sun-kissed brown, soft and splitting. She has freckles and sunken hazel eyes that look on insanely.

"Hi. I want to rent a boat."

"Is it your first time renting?"

"Yeah."

"Super cool. I'm going to give you some information before we get you on your trip. First you need to book an appointment."

"Okay. I'll do it online."

"I can set you up right now. I do have to ask first though. It may sound scary. But there is a one thousand dollar safety deposit just for any damages to the boat. You get it back right after."

"Right."

"I will give you the form."

"I can do it online."

"Awesome. Please take a brochure. Included is a map of the trips you go on and the prices and boats... Have a great day."

"Thank you."

If I lived in a boat it would not be a yacht or a big boat. A sailboat with a quaint cabin is enough or a basic engine boat with the same cabin. I'd live on the shores of an island resembling some Polynesian island. I'd fish for food and drink the juices of tropical fruits and boil water and hunt jungle rats and, during monsoons, shelter in caves, maybe build a hut, and live brutally true to my biology.

I imagine the island having a bar I'd frequent. The bar would have a friendly bartender and he'd give me drinks on credit since I'd not have access to my first-world bank funds. There'd be the usual characters in the bar and there'd be domesticated cats and birds I'd feed and have drunken discussions with, here and there, when human beings are not worth it.

I'd have a few lovers in the bar, traveling in from wherever, for a few nights. They'd ask me what I was, what I was doing, and I'd say I'm a plain fisherman living on the island. They'd think it romantic, my lifestyle. But they wouldn't want to live it themselves, at least not more than one week. To them I'd be not only romantic but rugged. Soon they'd find me distasteful and reckless.

My consistent lovers would be the local Polynesians. They'd love me in the spiritual way, the way that binds individuals together to transcend them as the same entity. They'd always maintain their desire to be with me even though they'd know of my encounters with those passing through. And to them my lifestyle would seem an element of me and not a phase of me. They'd consider my faults with humour and a quiet fondness, a mark of my intrinsic and inscrutable foreignness to them, which could never be reconciled but only forgiven.

Incidentally, I have read on the voyages of an Englishman named James Cook. I was very interested in the voyages of old-time explorers. Cook had circumnavigated the globe, discovering parts of Australia, New Zealand, Micronesia and Melanesia. He was funded by England to find Antarctica, what in the eighteenth century was called *Terra Incognita,* which he didn't realize he discovered when he did because it was all ice and snow.

Cook's crew members joined his journeys to experience what they regarded as paradise. Beaches and exotic foods, simple living, and islander women who were bronzed and wild, partly or fully nude, untainted by Christian ideology, and willing to fuck, sometimes for nothing and other times for metal nails. Their civilization never knew metallurgy and so metal in any form was valuable.

Cook never slept with islanders in all his voyages. He wrote about his marital fidelity in his journal, his temptation. He was also a great and free hypothesizer. He burdened his ships with jars of pickled cabbage. He was ridiculed by other captains but his crew were the only ones never to have suffered scurvy, the disease of Vitamin C deficiency.

While walking on a bridge I see the city of Vancouver rising and falling to the contours of its tectonic bed. In the multibillion dollar bonding of metal and glass, the business and international recognition, the meeting of cultures, there is me taking part and not being without. Even if I have not contributed to it by mechanics of tax or proprietorship. There is a common mind helixing like a DNA in this brick and mortar landscape.

To the right are tracts of grassy parkland between inclined residentials, square office buildings. The round and tall treetops are like a massively expanded green foam that blocks most of the buildings and streets. To the left is glass and metal, pale blue city buildings, penthouses, few terraces flashing bushy tops, the long stretch of medium-height condos showing a latticework of beams so redundant and orderly as to be a landscape of overlapping graph paper.

Below me is a concrete plant with large silos painted as caricatures, yellow faces fixed in drowsy states. There are rubble filled industrial dumpsters and house-sized containers of gravel. The rows of warehouses with arched roofs like steely hillocks.

The bridge peaks over the water, a few cruisers cutting in fast its grey sludge-like surface, causing tremors which rock the anchored boats. Soon I see the floor plan of nearby condos, the empty kitchens and living rooms. A glassed school is spearheaded between the highway ramps, the classrooms all visible and bright. The bridge pavement narrows and goes into an offramp.

I pass a shelter house, a construction zone, restaurants and fitness centres. Donair and Asian cuisines. Speciality stores selling band merchandise and gas masks, army fatigues, sex shops. A long passageway of plywood and a wire meshed fence shielding demolition, the rubble like a coral reef dried and blanched.

The long pole-arms on trolleys clip onto a network of wires laced above the street. The trolleys drive through a special lane and the wires jostle and twang electrically.

There are people squatting in front of cannabis dispensaries, closed night clubs, bong stores and a disused theatre. One is bent down at the waist as if her lumbar spine was removed, her legs firmly straight. A man is slanted sidewise like his hipbone was removed. Perhaps in the street is a robber of bones, a nocturnal stalker waiting for the overdose, a hobbyist plucking vertebrae like gems out of numbed backs, developing somewhere a subprime market of bones.

Among the department stores, in front the space of a drugstore like a town square of hot dog trucks and standing pedestrians, is a greasy long-haired man sitting on a crate, a cardboard sign of indiscriminate mark folded by his sandaled feet. A shirt of wolf's eyes, bead necklace with wispy feathers. A fat girl sits facing him on the hard city floor, lumpy and bruised in unsuitable dress, looking up to him with autistic passion. She listens to his slurred talking as if he's telling her fables she will remember opportunely.

One patroller of the streets is wearing a flat brimmed hat, a hoodie and sweatpants. His assistant has a black hoodie with the hood up and a vape pen between his lips. They talk to a hunchback resting his elbows on an empty shopping cart. The one with the hat likes to walk back and forth in the sidewalk. He likes to look at people as he walks. He passes me and asks, "You party?"

"Huh?"

"You party?" He asks with care.

"No cash."

"Get cash," he says. "Hook you up."

He walks to the hunchback.

I imagine going up to them. You all get on this rusty cart and I will push you the fuck out of here.

Who the fuck are you? asks the up-craning hunchback.

I am someone looking for trouble. I'd turn to the hatted one. Took the words out your filthy mouth? He would be looking at me woolly eyed. He would say, Is that a threat directed at me?

You bet your life it is.

The hooded one would reveal his vape pen as a disguised stiletto. He'd run pointing it at me. I'd grab his hand and direct his force to the hatted one. Then I would elbow the head of the hunchback and he'd fall like a tower of blocks.

"Classic dog," I tell the hot dog griller. "And water."

He grills the brats quickly, singeing it with crusty grill marks, then snuggles into a baguette-like bun. The crate-sitting man looks ahead with machined tranquility. "Hungry?" I ask him. He startles and nods and smiles, reaching for the bunned sausage. He hugs it to his belly.

Standing by an entrance to the train station is someone in a dark and stained hoody and coat. Inside the hoody I see his webbed eyes wheeling back and forth at the floor. He repeatedly says, "Starving." I pass him and he says it louder.

At a kiosk I buy a ticket to enter the tollgate. In the tunnel before the train arrives there are many others waiting. They never look at each other and they stay quiet except for talking on their phones.

Within the scream of the coming train as it bounces in acoustic turbulence I hear the word, *starving*.

2

"HOW ARE YOU TODAY?" she asks.

"I'm good," I say. "How are you?"

"Good, good, good."

"That's good," I say. "You really got a great voice."

"I was born with my voice."

"Nothing to compliment then."

"Oh, you can compliment me. No one notices my voice."

"They notice those nice earrings. Very nice." Her earrings are metal lime wedges, neon green.

"Finally," she says. "Thanks."

"Okay." I squint. "Huh." She waits for me.

"Can I get a simple espresso?"

"Sure."

She bangs the espresso handle on a woodblock taped on top a trashcan. The grinds fall like a sack.

"This café is cool. Looks half-done."

"Freshly set up."

"You should keep it like this. It looks cool."

"Tell my boss," she says. "Save me some work."

Along the window two women sit with their laptops. The back of their heads look beautiful and washed.

She hands me the espresso in a baby paper cup.

"I'm traveling here," I tell her. "Coming from Ontario."

"Welcome to the westside, Mr. Ontario."

"Are you busy tonight?"

"Actually, I am."

"Nice. I'm just looking for cool people to hang out with. I don't know anyone."

"I'm not interested. Sorry."

"For like a walk or just a coffee?"

"Thank you but I'll pass."

I tear a package of brown sugar and lace the espresso and stir it. I sit on a stool by the two women. A textbook lays face down. I see the name on the spine. "Hey," I say. She does not look. "What do you study?" She looks.

"I'm a student too. What do you study?"

"Biology." She is embarrassed.

"I guess you're in nursing, eh?"

"Yeah," she says.

"How is that? I heard it's hard."

"A lot of deadlines."

"I wish you could give your deadlines to me. I love deadlines."

She laughs the nervous laugh. "You'd save my life."

The espresso is warm and soured from the sugar. I check my phone. She has called two times. "Hello, boy," she answers.

"Hey."

"I missed you so much. Where are you?"

"BC," I say. "British Columbia."

She says nothing. Then, "That's amazing. I'm so happy for you. If you need money tell me. Don't be ashamed."

"I'm okay right now."

"Are you staying in a good place? Eating good?"

"I'm going to go eat right now."

"What are you eating?"

"Good food."

"I'm so happy to hear from you and that you're good and it's okay you're taking time off. It's not a big deal."

"All right."

"How was Montreal?"

I tell her about beautiful and distinct Montreal, how it had a creative and young energy.

"Did you speak French at all? Everything is French down there."

"The context was too different."

"Okay. Did Mae call you?"

"No. Why?"

"Nothing. For the best, you know. But, you know, these things still hit the heart. For me, I prepared myself long before. Chained my heart up and protected my heart."

"Let's not talk about your heart."

"It's funny though. But now it's final it's quite sad. That's what it feels like for me."

"You said you felt good about it."

"Did I?"

"You said it's for the best."

"Yes. Keep throwing my words back at me. I need that."

"You're an emotional fool."

"Thank you. You are a necessary pill to swallow. My therapist but better than a therapist because you don't care if you offend your patient."

"Whenever you need to get necessarily offended you call me up."

"Okay."

Later she tells me about her virtual workshops every weekday morning. She tells me she's opening a personal website. I want to cry because she has worked hard in ways I never imagined her to work. She suggests that I move back in with her and then we can go on a trip through Ontario like she planned a long time ago. I tell her it would be nice but living with her would be hard since I've been on my own during the last two semesters. She said it would be hard only at first, she would like the company and she won't bother me.

"Now," she says. "We can say goodbye."

"All right. Goodbye."

"Have fun. I trust you. I love you. Goodbye."

Throughout my teen years my parents took me on Caribbean trips. In the Dominican Republic we stayed at hotel resorts that cost nearly two-thousand dollars for two weeks. My mother and father woke early and ate breakfast at the buffets and then they sunbathed until the afternoon when they went back to the buffet for lunch. After that they had a nap in the air-conditioned room. Then near evening they went out, ate a light meal, sunbathed, a dip in the water to refresh, drank and then ate a big buffet dinner.

My older sister, Mae, was mostly absent at the spot we settled in at beach. I watched people sunbathing in the sand, forming sand sculptures, playing volleyball, swimming, and sometimes I saw her walking along the tide, listening to music on her iPhone.

In the evenings we frequented the mini bar where I drank virgin Piña Coladas and Shirley Temples and listened to my parents and the pop-music. I remember feeling like I had no justification to be on a vacation with smiling people drinking and enjoying their vacations. The music didn't feel made for me, the friendly service and beachside leisure. I never communicated this feeling because it felt shameful to express shame about vacation fun.

My sister was again absent in the evenings. This bothered my father but not my mother. I imagined my sister was walking around the resort, listening to music or eavesdropping, imagining herself with a group of friends or a boyfriend.

The only activity my sister and I did was collecting molluscs in mason jars. We plucked them off rocks. They stunk our hotel room.

My parents were insistent on taking us with them every summer to these Caribbean trips. They mentioned traveling with them as if it would inspire us. It was enjoyable but not fun. The possibility of going out the resort to explore the actual streets maintained some excitement in me for the duration of our vacations.

There was one vacation where we visited Cancun. My uncle lived somewhere around there. He was a short man of fifty-six years old, a large nose and large hands and feet, his lower goatee always moist with spit. The aneurysm surgery at eight years old left a slash by his right ear where no hair grew. He learned Spanish from his Mexican wife and he lived a kind of half-dreamy Spanish way, attending house parties hosted by Mexican friends. Sometimes he made road trips with his wife and only daughter, other times he made road trips alone. We were unsure what he did for a living but typically he was a truck driver.

My father didn't like to stand from his sunbathing when my uncle was with us. His belly button was bulging badly from a herniation and my uncle would shout, "Belly button!", no matter the people around. My uncle swam and shouted, "Belly button!" and got out dripping, shouting, "Hey, belly button!" and walked to him and said, "Belly button, come for a swim. Why are you not swimming, belly button?" They were both obese men in their fifties.

My uncle stayed in the resort for two days. When drunk he was ready to fight the hotel guests at any sign of threat or offence. He'd look blank-eyed at the guests to see their reaction, their compliance for a fight in the lobby or mini bar. He told me he was in over two-hundred fights. He'd fight anywhere with anyone and he didn't care about winning or losing. He said one time he was an *enforcer*. He used the word specifically because he didn't know what else it was called. For some reason he ripped the skin on a man's arm with a handsaw. I told him, "You're an intense guy."

"I'm a nice guy most of the time," he said.

I felt powerful around him. As if he was a weapon I could use on the cocky hotel guests.

He routinely reminded me that he was my uncle. "I'm your uncle." He'd give me a beer and say, "You're my nephew." It seemed he was obsessed or confused.

"If somebody fucks with you, you tell me, okay?"

"Okay."

"Look at me." He watched my eyes. "You tell me."

I didn't know how to behave right with him, which made me nervous.

"Okay," I said.

"You tell me?"

"Yes. I tell you."

"You're my nephew and I fuck them up."

He made me feel both good and bad emotions, which is what made him so fun.

On his last day he drove us out of the resort and into the streets of Cancun with the thousands of palm trees and crystalline beaches and neon nightclubs.

We entered a party area and drank beers at an outside bar. I saw women dancing and women with tight clothes walking in the street. Thinking of the resort depressed me intensely.

We ate giant steaks at a westernized bar. Being there with my parents and sister depressed me. I imagined myself only with my uncle who I imagined would invite women to our table. He and my father knew each other since childhood. They had a lot of stories they didn't share. I imagined myself growing up back in the 80's with them. It was good to imagine with them drinking and talking in front of me. They seemed changed and admirable, these stewards of manhood and private stories.

After two high-end tequilas my uncle started speaking Spanish to Mexicans at the bar. He stared at me with a delirium of interest and said, "I love my nephew," and kissed me wetly on the cheek. "Remember since you a little kid I protected you. I gave you everything. I didn't have a lot but I gave. Ask your mother." He pointed zealously at her. "Toys and video games. Who bought you all those toys? This asshole never bought you anything," he pointed in drunk ecstasy at my father, "and he's made more money than me. But look, he's boring. He can't have fun. Only work work work. Who cares about all that money? Your uncle is a fun community guy and he doesn't have as much money as a boring money-maker."

Later my uncle drove us back to the hotel. He was drunk and he drove fast but not reckless. He wanted to leave but my mother insisted he sleep in the room. In the early morning he woke us all and told us he was leaving. My mother insisted he at least have breakfast but he said he didn't like the menu and there were preferred menus in some local places he knew. I haven't talked to my uncle in over six years.

Outside the café, a block further, on the sidewalk there are wood crates packed with nuts and vegetables, mini-shrimp, chicken feet and leathery fish. Elderly women sit by the crates, discriminating. There are meat markets where the floor is slippery and red carcasses are pierced on hooks, gutted fish staining red their beds of ice. A butcher, heavy duty apron and rubber boots and gloves, walks in the sidewalk, smoking, his apron pink with blood. Across him, someone hugs a blanket by a church. He seems wanting to move. One man lights aluminum foil on a bus bench and inhales.

I walk behind a woman, old and thin and short. Her walking is grace. Her feet straight and close, her hipbones paddling the air shyly. Her arms swing like pendulums so light.

Then there is a hard stench of piss, the sour tang of unwashed. Rotting food and sweet drinks sticky and dry in the ground. Chunky orange brown puddles and masses of cardboard soaked so thoroughly as to be like oatmeal and stomped cigarette butts and wrinkled sheets of foil that look glued to pavement. Syringe packages. Hordes of people sit or stand in the street. They are filthy and wasted in a waste that exists on a spectrum. Their display of apocalyptic post-earth modes in fashion and behaviour. Laid blankets where on rest the hot refuse of clothes and snacks, a pork leg and packages of steak, books and movie discs.

"How are you today, sir?"

"I'm good," I say. "How are you?"

"Good to hear."

A slipshod flea market, chemical-grown culture flourishing in this open subconsciousness of the city, and the sellers sit cross-legged, relaxed against brick walls, some smoking or lighting bongs, fiddling with glass objects.

Walking to me is an Indigenous youth. It looks like he's been punched forever in the face. Squashed lips, a toothless smirk. "Hey, you slutty whore." We both wait for the light. "Where you going to go? Back home to whack off?" Then the light turns and we walk.

In the next street is a man curled in the aspect of death. Others stand around him, gawking and whispering. One of them, a leader perhaps, shirtless, tattooed, his skin oversized, hovers a hand over the fallen one, detailing his circumstance or insulting him or incantating necromancy from lack of naloxone, a medicant for overdoses. The three others look on with bovine stupefaction. The conversation is too oily, too city-birthed, for me to understand.

I pass a man vibrating in the corner of a closed pharmacy, a filthy woman bow-backed, wearing only a bra and jeans, no shoes, sitting in the curb, her spinal bumps like copper rivets, and a skinny man lurched with his legs outspread and his head twisting as if a morbid conductor is yanking his back muscles.

A craggy female walks ahead, chancing glances at me.

"Stop," she says. "That's enough. Stop following me. Go back right now and stop following me."

A wiry and sunburnt freak boxes a tree, a man wearing a foul sweater and snow pants has his chin hunched to his collar, the cervical bone like a nubby spear. He drools and slurps and stares up sightless.

Among the many people are some bars that have accepted in their planned or not design the fate of the street. Barred stores and shelters, ruined churches, thrift stores that look burglarized, charity kitchens and nomadic tents.

The people walking are seldom of the type huddled in the street. Some are tourists passing through. I know they are tourists because of their dress and their watching which maintains neutrality, forces neutrality, perfected in a neutral and judgeless gaze. Do not comment on the smell, look but with objectivity and no-contacting eyes, their faces seem to say. Other walkers are the more mobile, less dispossessed inhabitants who look either to be new immigrants or the forgotten old and poor.

There are some that walk with possession. It is not of money or knowledge or status but high-revving and narco-lacquered delight. It is an obvious and non-envious positivity that glows in their walking and manic head-darting, the surge of non-compulsive happy action, springy cloud-steps, which energizes you alert and anticipative.

A thing zigzags through the sidewalk, asking questions to mind-wasted standers. They look like a child enlarged two times, a giant skull harnessing a nebula of rusted slinky toys. The dwarf features which are abnormal for a dwarf, a face so plump as to be undefined, and skin which looks smeared by the bile-coloured analgesic cream used by surgeons. Thrifted and motley clothes, 8-inch boots and elbow-patched blazer and holes in the pale green corduroy pants. I can't control it. I step off the sidewalk and walk in the road.

These desperate questions of East Hastings Street. Maybe they are questions in a chain of questions without length or boundary. For to define length and boundary requires an endpoint, a set measurement that stops and makes clear the final answer, the last chain-link. Maybe at their bottom, the anchor, exists a semantic nightmare or they are entirely beyond the threshold where reason breaks.

• • • •

AN OLD ASIAN MAN WITH a violin. He places it in the case and walks back and forth with his hands held behind his back. He grips the bow and whips it as if it is wet. With the pad cupped to his jaw he raises the bow quick and then slow at the moment of touch. His flat cap hides his face, the summery button-up pinned to his midsection by sweat. The first note whines and his wrist swivels to sharpen it. His finger grinding into the board a tremulous chord.

In a fountain is a short pool of algae-green water. Pennies vault the bottom, winking like rusted stars. Crows dawdle or poke their beaks in the metal trashcans. Their wings are a gothic-plate of feathers. They leap on the border of the fountain and look to the water. Black reflections, absence of edibles, skirr across, peek, still nothing, and jump off.

A skinny young man rolls a hard-shell suitcase out of the train station gates. He stops in front of the violin player who plays for him. His body is like a hanger for his brown trench coat, padded shoulders set long and straight and phantasmic. Equally unreal is his standing and staring as if the violin was a rifle, the player his executioner.

Wait for him, your death-maker, the terminal soul to see whatever life lives in you leaves you. And shuttles maybe into the womb of one of the expectant crows who win souls like yours. Souls with chambers either filled or empty, no half-stuffed. Weighty souls that rest with a clamour, buzz and roil and wail, but move silently like moon-sized hunters through the ether of lighter souls that spread and separate to the movement.

He descends a hand in the inside of the trench coat, searching, spreading the coat out massively. It looks like a wing of human skin. He pulls out a pamphlet and drops it in the violin case. He plods on. His slated ribs shuttering out the coat, his stomach smooth and hollow. The suitcase looks like it weighs one-hundred pounds.

"You liked the playing?"

"Hmm?" He revolves his shaven head to the player. He nods at him.

"Traveling through?" I ask.

His eyes slit. "Yeah."

"So am I."

"Cool."

"Where are you going?"

"Waterfront."

He stares at the ground like something was lost.

"Got a smoke?"

"Ha. I recently quit."

"Lucky guy."

Then I say, "I've been trying to find stuff to do all day."

He laughs like a nob was turned in him. His shaved face is muscle-stringy, high-boned cheeks and testosterone sculpted jaw. In another time, with more meals, he would have been a male model. It is possible he is one of the many who come to Vancouver, the Hollywood of Canada, to pursue acting. An extra in shows and Indie films. Lover of theatre, Shakespeare, and even Marlowe and Ben Jonson. He must also be a lover and analyzer of Doctor Faustus and Goethe's Faust. He couldn't pay tuition or accept campus culture and so experience will be his institution and what comprises it, his cohort.

"Fine," he says. "You want to do something?"

"What?"

"Tell me a joke."

"I don't know any jokes."

"I know jokes."

"Do you want to tell me one?"

"All right."

"Well."

I shrug.

"Listen. Listen."

"All right."

"It's like a puzzle. Not a joke but a puzzle-joke."

"Do you know any pure jokes?"

"I like this one."

"All right."

"A guy walks into a bar," he says. "The bartender flips out a shotgun. Points it at his head," he makes the movement with his arms. "The guy says, 'Thanks.' Walks away. Why he say thanks? Not really a joke is it?"

"I can't think of a reason why."

"I'll tell you then."

"Not yet."

Soon, "The guy's hiccups."

"It's good," I say. "Clever."

"I told you a joke, can you afford a few dollars or whatever you got?"

"You're an entrepreneur too?"

"There's no surviving this city without a business."

"You can sell your own course and teach the others." I laugh and he laughs. He talks to me about stand-up comedy.

I search my wallet. "Take a five."

"Right on," he says. "Thanks."

"No worries."

He walks down the concrete stairs with the suitcase wheels banging in the steps. The violinist smokes a cigarette, sitting in a flat seat carved in a jagged boulder.

· · · ·

"FIRST TIME OR COMING back?"

"First time."

She smiles effervescently. The warmth and fizz of her smile, its star-shined texture.

"So glad I found this place." I laugh. "I love the décor."

"Special treat from back home."

"Where is home for you?"

"Mexico." She pronounces it the Spanish way. The breeze of her pronunciation, its sensual refreshment. "If you love Mexican food you'll love Mexico."

"If they have that there then I'll never leave."

"You're funny," she explains. "In time for happy hour too."

"What do they drink in Mexico?"

"For what?"

"For beer."

"Sol."

"Naturally, I will have the cerveza Sol."

"Coming up with cerveza and agua."

It's easy to love her privately. But you used the word and she might be intimidated. She has gotten many lovers coming in here loving this and loving that.

"What's Spanish for *thank you*?" I ask.

"Gracias," she says. She sets the bottle and glass.

"Gracias," I say. "I'm so stupid to forget it."

"You say it perfectly."

"I know poquito Spanish." I show the size with my fingers. "I traveled in Montreal weeks ago so I know French better."

"I went to Montreal," she says proudly. "Gorgeous. But I know poquito French." We stare at each other and laugh.

"Did you decide?"

"Yes, I'm going to Mexico." I pronounce it the English way.

"The menu."

"Tienes beef enchiladas," I say proudly.

"It comes large or small."

"Grande."

"Perfecto."

"Do you recommend the enchiladas?"

"Yes. The beef enchiladas is delicious."

"Like in Mexico?"

"I apologize. In Mexico is another world of ingredients and preparation." The meaty syllables of *preparation,* the razored hiss at the penultimate.

"I love your honesty."

"You have to for these things. Nothing compares."

"Even for the beaches?"

"My soul is in the beaches."

"Gracias," I say like when hiking a mountain and as you go higher you view the supine lethality above and you do not have the skill nor equipment and so you go down.

I drink the beer quickly. Then she comes out the flapping kitchen doors with the plate.

"What else do you recommend for the Mexico experience?"

"For beer?"

"Non beer."

"You drink margarita?"

"Never drank one."

"Do you want to try? Make it special. Not like normal margarita. Your first should not be basic. I recommend you a smoky margarita made with mescal."

"Mescal sounds delicious."

"Mescal is a serious drink more than tequila."

"Good."

Then she comes with the smoky margarita.

"Gracias," I say. It is pink with a murky white on top, a peppery crust rimming the glass. She stands watching me. The margarita hits electric in my tongue, burns my throat.

"So happy I found smoky margaritas," I tell her.

"You like it?"

"I love it."

"I'm happy for you too."

The enchilada is warm and small like a hairless animal in my palm. I bite and sop it on the cilantro mayo and bite again.

I tell her the meal was great and she's been a great waitress with equally great recommendations. We're neither in past nor present but future, neither loss nor gain but potential. Both beautiful and terrible because the imagination is infinite.

"Receipt?"

"No, just gracias."

"Mucho gracias," she says.

"Mucho gracias."

3.

HER CHIN IS TUCKED and cutely doubled and her forehead hangs over a cold face. Her long-lashed eyes blinking like glitched flytraps. Oily lashes, thick like boar bristles on a paint brush. "Sonny?" she asks. They are big and black and ill-defined eyes.

"Yeah. Chrissy?"

"Yeah."

"This is it," she points in the window to women in hairnets. Her manner, tone, is best described as *glacial*.

Inside a woman scoops saucy and metal-black pork chunks, shredded pork fat, in a plastic bowl. "Dinuguan," she says, pointing at the black sauce. Then she speaks to Chrissy.

"What's she saying?"

"She asks me if I mentioned it's blood sauce."

"It's made out of blood?"

"Yeah."

"I want to try."

Chrissy tells her. The woman's face stretches vertically and she speaks rapidly.

"She likes you," says Chrissy.

We walk out and pass a bar patio seated by men. They are drinking beers and talking. I am shy walking past them.

We go inside her car. It fills with the smell of musty pork.

"How do I say *thank you*?" I ask her.

"Salamat," she says.

"Saalaamat."

"Salamat."

"Salamat," I say and she nods. "I wanted to say it before."

She starts the car and pulls the gear. Her hands are big and meaty, the nails falsely gemmed green for middle and ring.

"Why you here?" she asks.

"I need a reason?"

"Just asking."

"Traveling."

"That's nice."

"How long you been here?" I ask.

"Five years."

"And where you from specifically?"

"Cebu."

Her driving is fearless on the highway. In the nervous quiet I see the black thickness of her medium hair. It curves like snapped wings down her cheeks. Her short blade of nose, sharp skull ridge and flat brow, the islander size of her swelled lips. We drive a long time in a dark and slim road winding through forested mountainside. Pay attention to the calm aspect of her face, her fatal symmetry. Meritorious selections of archipelago life. When I compliment her she smiles a ruinously beautiful smile. She must fight her skin to smile.

"I'm kidnapping you to the mountains," she says.

"Please do. I want to stay in the mountains forever."

"I like going hiking and camping in the mountains."

"Your profile said you love the sun?"

"I love sunsets."

"What about sunrises?"

She says nothing.

"Still asleep for those?"

She laughs. It is quiet and deceptive and breathy.

Then she says, "My English isn't good."

"I didn't notice."

"You're lying."

"I've been with more severe ESLs than you."

"Bet you have," she says with flirty indication.

"Oh, yeah," I say.

"Oh, yeah."

"Say that again."

"Oh, yeah."

There is a jeep here, a canoe strapped on its roof. She parks away from it and then we walk up a rocky hill to a bench overlooking the expanse of a bay. The green mountains are like a moss growing on it.

We stare at the bay and eat the bloody pork and rice. There are furrowing clouds that expand at the borderline between the sky and the blue bay which is as faultless as glass. The sun is a blood orange soon to be pocketed in the mountains.

I kiss her mouth. She flings one leg over me and mounts. I run my nails on her hard ass.

Then we walk down.

In the backseat she undoes my pants. It is black outside and the windows are fogging. I undo the button on her pants and the zipper. In the dark I can see it as a fleshy mass. It feels very natural.

Later she says, "Stop. I'm not ready. I want to see you again too." There is heat inside of her now. Steam in her breath.

We sit wet and silent and tired, the foggy windows lowered and the heat flowing out, coolness in. It is very black outside even though the sky has revealed its stars.

Then she drives back, the headlights beaming in the blackened road, and I say, "I only see girls." Then, "You know what I mean."

"Thought so," she says. "It's okay."

"You meet guys like me all the time?"

"Uh, yeah," she says. "Mmm. Whatever."

"You're really hot," I say. "I enjoyed it."

"Did you?"

"Don't think I didn't enjoy it."

Then I ask, "Did you?"

"Hmmhmm."

Out of the winding roads she speeds violently into the highway. We enter the city so bare and changed to its true perspective or given a new one or shifted to one within its collection. The other-side suburbs look like once plucked stars lodged throughout the black mountain.

Then all I see are spangles of multicolour light. Light from building windows, poles, headlights, shop lights, electric banners and signs. The road is golden and sharp with detail, its grit and cracks and marks of tire and paint, like an endless scroll reeling into your eyes.

She stops.

"Thanks for the ride and the food and the view and the other stuff," I say.

"Thank you too."

"Damn, I should say *salamat*."

"Haha. Good night."

"Good night."

I walk in the street for a long time, passing busy restaurants and speakeasy style bars, casual live music bars and youngster clubs, bushy and dark walkways between overpriced poor-looking apartments, a Circle K sprayed with the lacey words, *food* and *sober*.

• • • •

HER NAME IS PO, SHE is a twenty-four-year-old from Northern China, a place once called Manchuria. She settled in Burnaby eight months ago by herself. Her clothes indicate that she does not have social media, the best word for her fashion sense is *pedestrian*. You know exactly what the word implies, what image it evokes. Her almond-toned hands are tiny and delicate like the limbs of an insect.

She tells me she does not like busy public places. One time she was touched on the breast by a man somewhere in the lower market. Her English is good but she spends too long between words. I tell her that she needs to talk more English and she says it is hard because all her friends talk Mandarin. I tell her that the most important aspect of language learning is being interested because interest is what allows you to engage attentively for a long time. I say that she can abandon learning material and courses which for her have made English a thing stripped and dried. Primarily, I tell her to not worry about progress because it invites frustration which ruins the fun. She nods as an ESL will sometimes do when they have not understood. Naturally, she changes the topic.

She mentions her family of four and asks about mine. I tell her I have one sibling, my older sister Mae who lives in Michigan and takes disability cheques due to a car accident. She was the one who got me a summer job in landscaping. She worked as a lead hand for a company started by the father of a high school friend. Before that she assembled cars at a Chrysler factory. I don't tell Po that my older sister has a wife. Po may consider that a misfit piece in the evolving puzzle that is my personal signature for her.

During the rehab period of my sister's car accident she wrote a memoir. She said she wanted to honour her life and writing about it was the truest way she felt of doing that. It was a coincidence because I had then recently read a memoir by François-René de Chateaubriand, an 18th century politician and novelist who considered himself the greatest romantic of his era. He talked a lot about dying, his coming death, the death of an old world stocked with old memories, and the degeneration of the aristocracy, having once tried suicide with a pistol but failing, and the illusions of life, ambition, love, rank and honour, that sustain one in gripless moments from the ultimate conclusion of death. I didn't mention him because I knew that wasn't the type of memoir she wanted to write.

For parts of her memoir she interviewed me, asking me questions like what were my best experiences with her and how I felt about her coming out.

While growing up we shared a room together, sleeping in separate beds across each other. There was a television with an Xbox in the room. We played Halo and Halo 2. Then she bought an Xbox 360 and we played Halo 3, both so amazed by the graphics. I said these times playing video games were my favourite. A specific favourite memory was when I was ten years old. She made me laugh on the bed, bouncing and flailing, and I sat on my middle finger and chipped the bone. I had a cast on my finger for two months.

After high school Mae cropped her hair, abandoned sideburn trimmings, and wore jeans and hoodies and makeup only to cover acne. She made weekend trips to Toronto to visit the largest gay district in Canada, where she befriended gays. She told my mom and then me. It was a secret from our dad. I told her it didn't hit me as anything at first but as I started to understand more of what it was, what other people thought, the surrounding culture, then it hit. The reality needed time. Or it was given a reality by the social reality it was in. Whether this was a corruption or the fundamental of its reality, I am not sure.

At twenty-eight years old she saw a woman sixteen years older than her. She made sure to say that they were *seeing* each other. "Seeing is believing," I told her. She continued on the merits of *seeing*. It was non-exclusive. But it was different than a casual relationship. "It's preparatory to the other four senses," I said.

"You need to see someone for a while before you can say you're dating," a meditative sister told me. "Dating is serious. It's healthy for both people to look around before they decide."

"There's one person you have for touching. One for smelling. Hearing and tasting. Then you at some later point decide to combine all five into one person."

She dismissed this.

"I don't want to spend all of my time with her. Not every week. I go on a lot of first dates. But this is the thing. I don't do anything with them. Because I'm seeing her. Though I want to test other people. No, wait. That doesn't sound right. I want to explore other people. Does that even sound right?"

"You want to see other people."

"No. That makes it like I'm not seeing her."

"Figure out what you're doing here because it's a lot of people's senses you're playing with."

"I'm looking around."

"How's looking going?"

"Lame," she said. "I'm looking for her in them."

"Then why waste your time with dates?"

"To make the best decision."

"But does it matter?"

"I don't know."

"People aren't products you bid on."

"Is that how I'm treating her?"

"I'll say one thing. The last and only thing I'll unsarcastically say...Don't deny her the potential to be the best decision you make."

Later they married and Mae moved to Michigan. In Ann Arbor, past midnight, she got hit head-on by a drunk driver going sixty mph on a rural road. After that, shattered pelvis and snapped femur, hairline cracks across her skull, she was bonded to her wife in a bond I'd not try to define. The best word to describe that trying would be *sacrilegious.*

Po has been through Michigan, Ohio, Virginia, following Florida. I tell her I've been to Del Ray and I liked it. She attempts to say *small world* but *small* is trapped like a lozenge in her throat. She has traveled to four provinces in Canada and she wishes to live in Newfoundland. I tell her I've been to three and she is overly shocked as someone who substitutes conversation for emotive expression might be.

She talks about how her family felt about her moving to Canada alone. She has the courage and resilience people living in circumstances that demand action often have. She has somewhat the immigrant understanding that options subvert the best one can do.

She mentions her love for nature, the beaches and mountains. Cities are horror for her. There was a time in Old Toronto when she was lost trying to find an Indigo bookstore. She had gotten off the train at Union Station. Her phone redirected her, confused the layout, lagged, shut the GPS application. Frustrated, phone depleting, she managed to find an exit, and continued walking in a half-imagined route, each traveled street presenting itself anew.

A middle-aged couple discovered her attacked by anxiety, overwhelmed, wandering. They led her back to the station. She charged her phone in a Chipotle and then face-timed her father in China. Her father did not know how to help. She said she still regrets calling because she frightened the family, she legitimatized her father's claim that the world outside of China had real problems with fake solutions. But with her phone charged and after asking a worker, she found the hotel where she passed the next day planning an itinerary, then leaving finally on the third to explore a freshly dawning Toronto.

She walks back with a bowl of soup. I tell her, "Smells scrumptious."

She says *scrumptious* and laughs.

"If you see someone who is handsome you say they are looking psychedelic."

She says it. I laugh with her.

"If someone is wearing good clothes, you say they are looking scientific."

She says *scientific* about me and the food court and the soup bowl. I teach her the words *ameliorate* and *apoplectic.* She says that they are crazy words.

Then after our meal I buy coffee jelly bubble tea and she buys oolong with one hundred percent sugar. She teaches me one to ten in Mandarin and we spend twenty minutes practicing it. Then she teaches me *fuck.* She warns that someone will punch me if I say it.

"Let's pretend we are strangers and I talk to you."

"Okay," she says.

"Ni hao."

"Ni hao."

I say one to five in Mandarin.

She bounces with laughter. I say five to ten but slower.

"This is not conversation," she says.

"But to people that don't know Mandarin it seems like one."

"Is if ask me how I am doing in English and I reply one, two, three, four."

"Yes, exactly."

"Five, six, seven, eight," she says.

"Two, three, four."

When we go out I walk slow with my hands behind my back and scrutinize the ground. She shrieks. I worry she will hit something.

"This is how I always walk."

"No, you are a big liar. You walk like my dad," she says. "I am apop. Apop?"

"Apoplectic," I say.

"I am apoplaytic."

We continue walking. I guess that our hangout will extend the entire day, the next day, the one after that and so on if nothing is said. Then she sees clothing stores but I tell her, "Not for today. Come by yourself next time." We depart on the sky train.

I text her about when she wants to meet again. She texts back that she doesn't want my friendship, that I'm rude to her.

• • • •

A MAN IN XXL ARMY SURPLUS jacket, cargo pants and boots. Dark green, shaggy and bloated and alcoholic. Erotic glancing to the cars. He waves them in at the intersection. At the red light he talks to the cars intensely. As if they were whores. His fermented speech of catharsis, sallow and heady, soured alley brew in the flesh. He gestures equal nonsense with his dark hands. Then before the green he stands in line. He drops a raised arm, shouts, and the cars begin. A race or start of journey. Some cars honk. He reacts with nothing, this trafficker of what is within, walks back to his corner and watches with perceptible heaviness, planet-heavy conviction of his purpose, waiting for the red.

"I can't anymore."

"You're just driving."

"It's gross," she says. "Weird too."

"Weird, huh?"

Against a wall people are sitting up or hunched forward, snuggled in blankets or in sleeping bags, some standing morbidly bent, some eating out of food boxes or smoking, some with their heads sunk profoundly between their knees.

A man's cheek is planted to the sidewalk, his shirt drawn down to his shoulders to expose a starved torso where the once-big belly hangs like a droplet. He is as still as a fire hydrant and coloured like one too.

Chrissy clicks to third, accelerating.

4.

"WE NEED TO GET YA A vest." He has a fake Australian accent. His blond beard blends to the whiteness of his lean skin. He escorts me to a wall of safety vests. "Here ya are." I strap it on.

"Perfect," he says. "I have an eye for safety. And I hope ya do too."

I follow him to a dock. He steps in a boat and the boat bounces.

"Is this ya first time in a boat?"

It's a cuddy boat. Basic cockpit, two passenger seats, a low horsepower engine.

"Yeah."

"Great." He pauses. "Is it the other's first time too?"

"Other?"

"Are you alone?"

"Yeah."

"Oh. My bad."

"You recommend being with someone?"

"Doesn't matter. I never had a lone," he draws out the *lone,* "rider."

There are two canisters of fuel hidden in the back. He says that I might not use both but it's guaranteed I will use one. He unlocks the fuel hose and locks it again.

"Questions?"

"Nope."

I sit in the driver's bench and turn the ignition. He yells for me to strap the safety cord to my wrist. I push the hand throttle up and it vibrates hard. The propeller is silent for a few seconds and then suddenly bursts in noise. The wheel is like a plastic toy. I turn it three inches to the right and the boat moves in a long arc past the docked cuddies and ferries. A band of scratched glass lines the cockpit and I stretch my neck to look over it.

Ferries are passing. I swerve right when they come towards me. I spin sharply in place. I throttle and turn the wheel and continue on.

The throttle is lowered on the resting RPM and the boat floats along and I watch the walking trail, the runners and bikers. The water is smooth like a marble and there are kayakers slicing into it their fibreglass blades. They flow on mutely.

I turn the engine off and the boat spins slowly. The security cruisers pass quick and launch waves tilting the boat. I start the engine and lift the throttle and cut through the waves.

At the end the creek is the domed museum. Science World. It is there to inspire children to do science.

Then I go back, all the way to the first dock, tapping the throttle up, here and there. I turn under the bridge that opens to the inlet bleeding so thoroughly into the blue of the sky. Jetskis skip in the water and a ripple hits my boat and lifts it up enormously.

Beyond the huge freighter ships are the mountains, a field of cloud sweeping upward along them, a living network of buildings and roads in their woodland. There is a beach with buoys that mark its swimmable perimeter. There are people with towels spread on the chalky sand, sunbathing. Outwards from the shore the water grows shades lighter. Open and light blue expanse, a trembling calm. I use the distance of a buoy to gauge how much the boat has moved. The buoy has minimized with every look.

Waves hit the hull in a chain of pounding slaps.

I spark the engine and throttle in short bursts and shut the engine.

I feel alive in a good and bad way. I start the engine and drive on to the distant and still freighters. Around me is monstrous with blue water and sky. I feel as one atom of this monster and not trivial in my scale. The boat beeps for me to turn back.

In a single move I raise the throttle to its upmost. The engine screams and rumbles the hull and depresses the backend where water pulses and foams. My organs pull astern and compress, the skin tightens. A massive air breaths in like menthol. The frontend lifts to block my view.

Two workers wave me into the dock. One instructs me with his hands on how to turn. The boat slides in without touching the edge.

"How was it?" he asks.

"Awesome. I turned into the creek and at the very end I realized I took the wrong way."

"I totally saw it," he says. "Didn't know what you were doing."

He offers a hand and I push my foot down the sideboard and the boat lowers and I squat up with the one leg. I peel off the safety vest and he tosses it in a barrel. I walk into the cabin and to the desk.

"Impressive," the woman says. "Nine pounds of fuel in four hours."

Another behind her says, "Took a pleasure cruise, eh?"

"Yeah."

"Is it weird?" I ask impulsively.

"What?"

"I mean the nine pounds."

"No. Of course, no."

"Did you enjoy yourself at least?" asks the other.

"I did."

"There you go."

I pay the cost of nine pounds and ask about riding a sailboat.

"We don't rent out sailboats. They're pretty advanced so you need skill to drive them. We do courses though I can set you up with if you're interested."

"It's fine for now. Thank you."

Then I walk out and up the ramp where my feet nearly trip.

In the indoor market I judge the rainbow macrons. The sugar-crusted donuts.

A father with his young son hugged to his arms looks in the glass and tells his son how good the pastries are. The son does not look in the glass. He looks at me and the father nudges his chin to the good pastries. He asks him what he wants and the son says nothing but looks on in the wonder-gaze children have. The wonder of total novelty, first-time experience and emotion and figuring. Though it is not fearful or worrisome, not for most times. It is fun and curious and motivating, both for the children and the adults who at times look to the children for secret guidance.

"Let this gentlemen order first, Davey," says the father to the son. "We're still deciding," he says to me. The child burrows in his neck. With the baby arm he hugs the neck and peeks out the father's bristled throat. The father presses a cheek to the child's head and then his lips. To hear some suggestive whisper perhaps. The father hugs and rocks the baby child. "You're not so hungry, Davey?"

"Half-dozen macrons," I tell the pimpled cashier.

I eat the macrons standing. They are like as if gulping air that has been crystallized in sugar. Then from the same patisserie I buy a café avec crème.

Outside I sit in the log bench and view the inlet through the mouth of the bridge. I am happy about the water and weather and the speed of the boat and my conservation which cost me twenty-two dollars extra. There are not many people outside but there are seagulls plopping with their large webbed feet. They tap those feet smartly on the brick.

Then there's a circling gang of pigeons. Some have purple discs about their necks and fading skirts of grey and green and purple along their black-dotted backs. Pigeons like machines dawdling past the runtime of their software. I imagine asking someone what their favourite bird is.

Pigeons, they would say.

I would ask, Really? Have you heard of the arctic tern?

No, they would say.

Let me tell you. The arctic tern travels from the north pole to the south yearly. A journey of over thirty-thousand kilometres.

Among big and dark trees, fanciful cherry blossoms, paths padded in pink shrivelled leaves, there are crows gripped to branches or the grass and they caw to each other and they spin in the air and fly into treetops and walk on the trail like mammals. They are weary of me and wing away unlike the pigeons which tramp and poke their bulb heads mindlessly. The pigeons unlike the crows are brilliantly crested and amusing in a lighthearted way.

• • • •

HE IS IN A FLANNEL shirt and stomper boots, long and wet hair, rogue and dirty, sitting in a campstool in the sidewalk. He stomps on the ground strumming a dark and stickered acoustic and he does not sing but shouts. He stops to drink a tall can.

He is the best street performer you have ever heard and he plays neither generic songs nor covers. When he plays he stomps on the ground not in anger nor frustration nor for attention but to discharge the excess within him, to truncate the abundance. He does not care for your money or money in general, at least not in the more than practical sense, but I care to give it to him. It is the fact of care, the primary morality of it. And I hope he does not care. So I can know that he has traced himself a horizon where he wakes and sleeps in his own morning and night. He should by now know his own seasons and be habituated to their successions. He sings like he knows them.

I drop a ten in his guitar case.

"Damn," he says. "Thank you, bro. Thank you."

"You sound great."

"Appreciate it," he says. "Means more than you know."

"I've been wanting to learn the guitar for so long. I don't play any instruments. Except for the recorder and the clarinet they forced me to play in grade school."

"Hard to get into it when you're playing twinkle twinkle little star," he adds on.

I agree. "Was that a cover or an original?"

"Original."

"I can tell. It was good and raw."

Then he plays stomping a song.

WALKING IS AN ACTIVITY I have not always enjoyed. It is true that easy satisfactions are worthless. To struggle is the mark of true ownership. What I own is my satisfaction of walking.

I started walking three years ago. That seems like I had been living without using my legs. When I say *walking* I mean the routinized activity. The making of a habit and time-specific and expectant nature of routine. Though the reward of routine was not expected. The start of satisfaction was the departure of expecting a reward. That was when I could say I am a *walker* and *walking* is my activity and *walking* is important to my lifestyle.

Before walking I was a homebody who considered walking to be another exercise or a method of arrival. I did not understand what walking could be for someone who owned it in themselves. It took eight or ten months to own my satisfaction.

I first started in the morning, before school, but quit on the third day. It was bothersome and boring and I didn't yet feel its therapy and refreshment but I understood of these things for I was told about them through podcasts and articles. My understanding was not useless, though. It made goals for me. I assumed that If I didn't understand then I would be more limited in the experience. The range of experience would be narrow, plain and painless. I say *painless* because I have a presumption that pain must be included in the range or else the entirety of it is trivial. It feels true that experiences without this serrated edge are worthless. If the capacity to understand is large then the scale of both pleasure and pain are doubly so.

My toes, carpals, shins, heels did ache. Chaffing between my thighs. The exposure to sun and rain and snow. There was a time even when I didn't like the heat of the sun. Now that heat is a craving, a cuddle from something greater than me.

I walked in the evenings after school but I was usually too tired to do it consistently and the evening lost an essential quality which the morning always had. The mornings were metal-sharp, refined, colder, at times crueler, and allowing for longer walks. Then I restarted in the morning but instead of walking in my neighbourhood before driving to school, I walked around campus at least two hours before my 10pm class started. After the walking, half an hour or more, I went to the campus café and drank a large coffee.

Walking in the early hours helped me discover areas I would've never either because it was pointless or there were too many people around. But with walking as an activity there was neither a point nor lack of point. The concept didn't work. It was just discovering and thinking or not thinking and movement, blood-flow, sunlight, and coffee after. With the coffee came sitting, more thinking, watching the campus café fill with the students and teachers, hearing the clicking keyboards in the backdrop of Taylor Swift or Post Malone, conversations of daily hassle, and small breakfasts.

Within three months of this four- or five-day routine I noticed the top outer soles of my shoes had become smoothed. I was wearing outdated running shoes and I had to buy another pair. But after two months of scouring the campus paths the outer soles smoothed out again. I looked online for what cause or symptom. An article said that I had under-pronation, a defect in my gait that put pressure on the outside of the foot.

I videotaped myself walking in the basement. We had a large basement where my mother would have parties. I looked at the videos and could not see a problem.

I asked my sister about my walking and she said she always knew. She said, "You have a very unattractive walk."

"Walking like a duck," she continued, "Or an obese penguin."

She videotaped me walking in the driveway. My feet were skewed out and there was a lift at the ball of my feet in each step, as if I was doing calf raises. How many people knew of my defect and why did they never tell me? I had been walking the campus like a freak for three months in the mornings.

"Begin each step with the heel hitting the ground and the ball coming down," an enlightening sister told me. "Point the toes forward. Start that by turning in the hips."

She showed me her normal walk. I tried her suggestions and she said it looked better.

"But not good?"

She searched on her phone. "Book an appointment with a podiatrist."

First I walked in the neighbourhood trails with my new technique. I was self-conscious about my morning walks on campus. I made new discoveries by focusing on how I walk. My head was usually downward, my shoulders tightened upwards, my hands moving too quickly, stiff hips. Consciously forcing my feet inches more inward made my glutes sore.

I continued my usual campus walks and started new ones. The soles still smoothed without any difference to before. I must replace shoes in around four months, the mark of my defect apparent in all my pairs.

I don't like buying new shoes. If I do they're always a pair of casual hikers since they're more durable. I'm not medically bothered by the soles smoothing but they eventually rip a hole which lets in water, the rubbing ground irritates me, and I'm aware that when sat and resting my calve on my knee, as I like doing, the smoothed upper sole looks bizarre.

6.

THE BAR IS LIKE A KITCHEN in a studio apartment. I can stand and reach to grab the bartender and pull him over the zinc-topped counter. Far to my right is a lounge, some occupied tables, a middle strip of fake grass to play mini golf on. Not many people enough to create that buzzy noise of conversation.

"Figured something out?" he asks.

"I can't find the drink I want."

Then he says, "It's only served at the cocktail bar next door. I don't have the ingredients here or else I'd make you one. I can get you over there if you wish."

"It's not a big deal."

"Know what you want instead?"

"I need more time."

I look over the menu. I watch the television. I am more so standing on the stool and my jeans are cutting into my scrotum. I feel like a puppet for a ventriloquist.

"Sour daquiri?"

"Sour daquiri."

"Yeah, sour. Not sweet. It's not popular in North America, I don't think."

"Where you from?"

"Ontario. But I'm saying it's more popular overseas."

He crafts my drink quickly. The daquiri is in a martini glass and it looks like bathwater.

"How is it?" he asks.

"Very good, thank you."

"Let me know if you need a fill up."

If the bartender was more extraverted with me I would tell him that I've been an introvert for most of my life but now I am discovering my potential as an extravert. A potential that is activated when one becomes more familiar. Familiarity is probably how all potentials first activate. What is too unfamiliar is too difficult to see a direction into. The world is as pointless as you are ignorant.

I would say, Listen here, barkeep, *integration* is an interesting word that appears frequently in my thoughts. There is likely a hidden feature of myself that is obsessed with integration, those foreign shapes that are unwieldy for me. There are likely hidden, ancient, desires that compel me to wield them. If I wasn't of the type to guess them as desires then I'd guess them as a god. If not a god then as fate.

Hey barkeep, let me tell you, the metaphor of taking something unsuitable and making it suitable through the manipulation of dynamic shapes is significant for me. Much of my adult existence has been integrating misfit shapes, compressing and stabilizing them to fit, to be easier held and carried. They are like trophies in a bag. I was not born with many. I had to go out and collect them, oh my introverted bartender. It's a fearsome activity to do. Some people were born with these trophies. But those same people do not know what it takes to win them.

Soon there is a light release in my legs.

"Another daquiri?"

"I'm curious about getting the other cocktail."

"Absolutely."

Then I follow a server to the cocktail bar. It is dark and narrow and the counter is long, pewter-style, and there are adults sipping cocktails. Dark glassy shelves of bottles, warm lights, and fake leaves. She takes me to an even narrower section deeper in.

Across from me is a mirror in where I can see myself on the stool. I sip and stare at myself in the mirror. I feel happy yet I want to intensify it. Obviously, I am not as happy as I think I am. It is greed and ungratefulness to always want to intensify it.

Then I look at the bill and she looks at me.

Finally, I say, "At the other bar I got a drink that would be transferred over to my bill here."

She comes back with the new bill. "Thanks for letting me know," she says.

"What could I do?"

I walk in the street where a prowler picks up tarps and wrings out the rainwater and folds them into a shopping cart he pushes on and on like an immortal in exile. His hands are ridiculously giant. Engorged knuckles, red like cherries. Loose steel bracelet and buried rings.

• • • •

THEN, "WHAT'S YOUR name?" he asks me.

"Sonny. You?"

"Teal." He extends that slippery and swollen hand to me.

"I don't mind at all you eating a slice," he says.

The slice is heavy and hot and wet.

"Damn good pizza," he says. "Taste good. Good for me too."

"What are you doing around here?"

"Nothing. Asking for quarters all day."

"Screw quarters now."

"Folks more willing to give me their shoes."

"Where you from?"

"Calgary."

"Nice. I'm from Ontario."

"Been there."

"How was it?"

"There's a lot to Ontario but when I went not much different. It was the nineties last I went. Maybe you weren't born then, I bet."

"I was born in the nineties."

"Know when I was born?"

"When?"

"Sixty-six. You know what the people call me?"

"A boomer."

"Yeah. You know. I'm a boomer. Okay boomer, they call it."

"Do you think it's funny?"

"It insults me."

His hose-like fingers are glistening.

"I'm kidding," he says. "I don't care what they call me."

"You've done a lot of traveling?"

His chest rises. "Yep. When I was a kid my dad took me all over on his boat. I'm grateful for my dad. I saw the world on his boat. From the ports of this Pacific here and back again."

"That sounds awesome."

"I'd like to go out on a trip like that again."

"How old were you when you went?"

"Sixteen, I think. After that," he shakes his tousled head, "I was one bad kid growing up. Got into selling pot. Making three hundred bucks a day easy. Smoking and getting girls. Got caught and put in jail a few times. Then fucked my life up with more drugs. You seem very young. Don't do what I did. My advice. You can fuck up a lot but don't ever lose your license. At least with your driver's license you can still get a decent job."

"But I'll admit you something," he adds, "I've been clean eight years now. Nothing but some beers, some weed. I'm okay."

"That's great."

"Yeah. I don't wish addiction even on my worst enemy."

"You were on Hastings?"

"Yes, I was." He raises his sleeve to show a tattoo on his forearm. *East Van.* "I cannot say I'm ungrateful. Regrets, sure. I've probably done millions of dollars worth of drugs. Can you believe me? Millions shot up in me. One time I carried eighty-thou of pot across the Windsor-Detroit border...Just got it in a suitcase with me. Went up to Detroit and bought a gun. Every time we'd go to Detroit we'd buy a gun and then dump it when we'd go back to Windsor. I sold all the pot and the same border cop asked me where my suitcase was. He knew it. But what he didn't know was I'd get scared shitless just for a whiff of getting caught for trafficking the dope and I'd never do it again."

"You didn't get caught?"

"No. His mistake was letting me know he knew... Let me explain. The cops won't take you down the first time. They'll let you keep running until they bust you for a big one. Because that's what they expect. For you to get cocky with the runs. There's lots of dumbos that'll keep going even if it's obvious they've been tagged. I was a dumbo but I was a scared dumbo."

"You got eighty grand for that?"

"A portion of it. Blew it up my nose, in my veins, sucked into my lungs. All of it inside me. It's disgusting."

"How'd you get clean?"

"A girlfriend of mine OD'ed in front of me. We were both street sleepers, drug-heads, thieves. I had a kit. Always carried one. Too high to react. She died and I stared at her. I sobered and she was a corpse. Tried ending my life. Failed. Got clean instead."

"Damn."

"I live with it every day. Still sleep in the streets. But I don't touch any junk. Because of her, I don't...Not many people'll do this for me. Not any, actually. You're the first that did this for me."

"Yeah. Why not? What are you going to eat with a quarter?"

"You need a tour guide or something out here."

"Maybe."

"I'm saying it has a lot of history, this area. Tours come through all the time. I see em taking pictures and talking facts. You like history?"

"Here and there."

"Yeah. I like it. I know a lot. Like this area is named after Jack Deighton, a sailor. They called him Gassy because he could talk and talk. Back then if you did that they said you had a lot of gas. Like me. I got a lot of gas. In both varieties. Don't worry."

He takes a pack out. "I'm stuffed." He lights a cigarette. "Know what I'm tryin ta do? Buy a camera I can go around videotaping. I saw online so many guys making money doing that. And you don't need a lot of money to start off with. You don't need to busy yourself much. There's a guy that just walks. Doesn't talk. And he has thousands of subscribers and people pay him to just walk a city. I've been walking a city my whole life and I could be rich now with a camera. All that I see and everything. Crazy stuff. I should be rich. Look at me. I'm like a Seinfeld episode."

He looks at me strangely. "Seinfeld episode," he repeats. "You know? I should be this because I look like it. But I'm not. I'm like Kramer or somebody."

"Do you have a phone?"

"No phone."

"There's a camera on a phone. If you had one."

"What phone you got?"

I show him the camera on it.

"I see," he says. "Incredible. That an expensive phone?"

"Yeah, it is."

"Damn. Everything is. Going to need lots of quarters."

"It's a good idea. But do you have a laptop?"

"No."

"Well, you need a laptop or a phone like this to post the videos online."

"Explain again."

"A camera can't post the videos on the internet. Unless you hook it up to a computer."

"I use the library computer. It can it do on that?"

"Yeah. It can."

"Okay then. I don't need to buy a computer then." He sucks his cigarette. "You're standing a long time. You want to sit?"

"No. It's okay."

"Okay."

Then I ask, "How long you been living in the streets?"

"Man, I've been on and off the streets my entire life. I was a squeegee kid. A hitchhiker and squatter. I was a fisherman too. I escorted people around a resort, fishing. It was a good job. They gave me a boat. Before that I was living in Alberta but didn't like Alberta. Cold Alberta. Can't be homeless there. When I came here I knew I never wanted to leave. That was the eighties that I came here. Fell in love with fishing here. Just worked at the resorts. Back then I told them I had experience driving a boat and fishing. No experience in it, actually. At all. Been on a boat and that's it. Maybe some fishing when I was a young kid. But they gave me a job anyway and I learned on the job. That doesn't happen anymore. Now you need certificates and proof. Back then you didn't need proof. It was okay for some things. Bad for others. Know what I mean?"

"Why aren't you fishing?"

"Who says I'm not? The fish changed to quarters, Sonny."

I laugh.

"See. I got a personality. I can be popular on videos. Get more views than those jackasses...But what did you ask me?"

"You not fishing anymore."

"I'll fish if I get to it."

"In the resorts?"

"No. I haven't done that in a long while. I fish as a free agent now. If I get to it. I think what you want to ask is what the hell did I do after to land me here asking for quarters?"

He lowers his voice to say, "Prison."

"I didn't kill or anything. I sold stolen cars with me and a friend. Some friend. And after getting out it's pretty much you're either be homeless or back in prison. If you're smart you'll just find some other work but if you're smart you wouldn't of ended in prison, you know. Fishing never provided the money to live in a city like here. But my expenses were paid by the resort and...they got me my own boat. It was a very good job."

He has a few-toothed smile of skewed dark malachite teeth. He says, "Don't do what I did. Don't sell stolen cars."

"Well, now I'm not considering it anymore."

"I'm done with the pizza if you want it."

"No. It's all yours."

"And don't ever, ever go down to Hastings. I'd hate to see a young kid like you there. One of those dumbos'll try to hook you. They don't give a shit how old you are. They're fucking low-lifes."

He shuts the box.

"Take the drinks."

"I won't forget you," he says. "Elephant memory." He taps his skull.

I watch the tourists taking pictures of themselves or the street. At the entrance is a large bodyguard. A very blond woman waits by the guard. "If you're alone you can sit with us," a biker in line says to her. The bodyguard tells him that she is all right. One of the bikers passes the blond. "Seriously," he says. They get led to a table, without her.

"Bar side," I tell the muscled guard. He bends down. "Bar side."

In the walls of the entrance are tacked license plates. The rosebud Alberta, Ontario, mine to discover, Nova Scotia, the big waterpark, Québec, je me souviens.

"Sir," says the guard.

"Yeah?"

"How are you, tonight?" a waitress asks.

"Busy night, huh?"

"Yeah, a popular act tonight."

I am led to an empty side of the bar. I sit and imagine people sitting next to me. The bartender asks me what I want. I tell him to sit somewhere else. He says he'll check. Then he waves across the glass clutter of the bar.

I sit facing the pull arms of draft beers. Behind me is the singer. Beside me is a man drinking a beer. He looks like a classic burglar. I get a beer.

"You're alone too?" he yells at me.

"Yeah!"

"Nice."

"How's it going?" I shout.

"Great. Been here two days. Not from here. From Toronto."

"Me too!"

"Yeah? Great. My name's Jim."

"Sonny."

"Tony?"

"Sonny."

We chink glasses.

"Where you staying?"

"Hostel upstairs."

"How's that?"

"Not great. Shady."

"How much is it?"

"Fifty a night."

"Fuck that."

He agrees.

"I was in Alberta. Banff. Beautiful. Been to Alberta? Going again. Sunday. Got to go. Live there for sure one day. Banff, Alberta."

He shows me hiking pictures.

"I'm on a big ass road trip. Canada." He shoots his hand forward like a plane.

A few stools away is the yellow-blond woman. She asks the waitress if she can move. She sits next to me. "Want to talk to a stranger or no?" she shouts.

"Want to talk a stranger!"

She tells me her name is Kelly and she is from Tiny, Ontario. She graduated in biomedical technology and before starting a career in pharmacy she is traveling through Canada. Tonight is her first in BC. She smiles unendingly at what is around her. She is positive and engaging and friendly and all this can reverse fully and efficiently.

The burglar-looking man winks at me. I nod at him and he keeps winking and I talk back and forth to the two of them.

"Tofino!" yells Jim to Kelly. "You'll love Tofino. Trust."

"I hear good things," she tells him. "I'll go."

"Nanaimo island. The islands are all good vibes. Victoria is a hangover rest stop."

"Victoria?"

"Very, very chill. Go to Whistler for partying. Trust."

The singer thanks the crowd but the crowd begs and he continues singing. I order another beer and soon the burglar disappears. Then Kelly and I leave.

"You don't know anything," she says.

"No, I can figure this out."

"You're drunk and you don't know anything."

"I'm not drunk."

The street is dark and irregular and the restaurant seems in a location different than before. The music is festive and booming though few people are here.

In the dark by the fake candlelight the enchiladas look like two snuggled rabbits on the plate. Within a few blinks the meal is over.

• • • •

KELLY'S IDENTITY IS described as *small-town girl*. However, her identity is like a marker in a forest only signalling the way and not the way itself.

Her encouragement of my desires to travel make me feel right about myself and her. I knew she would be like this. It feels good to know something and have that something be true. She responds to my few accomplishments with, "I'm proud of you." She thinks she is being wholesome and fun.

She says, "I was obsessed with aliens growing up. I'd go to space if I could. I'm in love with anything space. I'm hoping we communicate with extra-terrestrials in our lifetime. By the way, do you think there's intelligent life beyond our planet?"

"Sure."

"You don't sound confident. I mean, it's a statistical certainty."

"Most likely there is."

"They'd have a lot to teach us. They could have no technology like ours and that's why we haven't found them. Their intelligence might be in their interpersonal communication. Might be great conflict resolutionists that don't start wars. Most of our technological advancement has been from military innovations. If a species has the intelligence that allows them to not get into war then it makes sense they won't develop communication technologies like ours, so we'd never hear about them. Their societies would be perfectly like organic systems, very little contradiction and conflict, just well-functioning."

"Interesting," I say. "So, our computers are actually the result of how bad we are at dealing with each other."

"Yeah. We really like to think a species goes through the same stages of civilization development as we do. It's our inherent anthropomorphism but so much of our development is actually random."

She continues, "I hope we'll be able to figure out within the next few decades how to best live on this planet. I don't think we've reached civilization yet. I think it's all been experiments. Civilization is coming. We have the technology and the know-how for it now."

"You can feel it coming?"

"Don't say it like that."

"But what does the ideal civilization look like, Kelly? Like Tiny but scaled up?"

"First and foremost, it's decentralized. There's nothing to distinguish people from each other."

"What about bread? Where will people get bread?"

"At the bread line," she says.

"Where will people buy shoes?"

"The perfect civilization will be filled with people who can make their own things. Grow their own crops. Live sufficiently on the land and use technology in the best and less harmful means."

"What about those who don't want to make their own shoes? What do you do with them, Kelly? Is there a camp you put them in?"

"You're asking me if I'd be a leader for the new civilization. I'm telling you it's decentralized. No one's in charge."

"That only matters for the crowds and media to pinpoint their blame or praise. Decisions need to be made still. Who's the governing body to make decisions?"

"It's pure democracy since there's no difference between people according to their class."

"Where'd you read this stuff? Are they spreading it around Tiny Town?"

"There's a place under an old, abandoned church."

"I'm worried, Kelly."

"I'll be fine. They're my friends."

"The books are your friends?"

"No, I mean the people that hang out under the church."

"The literary types?"

"Some of them. A lot are just working-class types."

"You get those people into reading and they'll never go back."

"You're a classist scum."

"Look what's happened to you. Am I right or wrong?"

"I'm not going to say."

"I'm saying books give people ideas."

"Books changed my life," she declares.

"I bet you've read Walden. I bet fifty bucks you read it."

"Waldo?"

"Walden. Henry David Thoreau."

"Nope. I read Kropotkin though. The Conquest of Bread in all translations. Changed my life in Spanish and English."

"Is that why you knew so well where to get bread from?"

"Yeah. And I know how to make my own too."

"Self-sufficient Kelly."

"Don't bandy my name around town like you own it."

Then we drive through a road between a wilderness of pines.

The car careens to the side and dust shoots out the tires. I try to fix the phone syncing problem as cars and trucks speed past. I then sync her playlist.

I get in the driver's side and we continue on the road listening to alternative rock. She is drinking her coffee and talking about her electric guitar which she has been practicing for four months. I tell her I love *buskers*, the people that perform in the streets, with their spontaneous and bootstrapped charisma. She says she loves Van Halen and Led Zeppelin. What other music did you expect her to love? The mind-waste played at the clubs?

She talks about living in her small town. It is the absolute standard experience of such. Though she is not standard and if you were to ask the right questions you will see the standard exists to only manage and sort and instrumentalize. Its existence is owed to a natural mechanism tinkering each individual to function in a condensed whole, both socially and psychologically. I do not tell her this. I am driving. It is morning and we are enjoying each other.

I notice her looking romantically at the trees.

"Look at this, I love nature," she says.

"What do you get out of it?"

"Peace. Happiness."

"Loneliness?"

"I wouldn't call it that," she says. "Solitude is a better word."

She knows synonyms convey valences either negative or positive and sometimes a synonym grows so negative it dies to become antonym. Then from the new flesh of that antonym spawns a new set of synonyms. She knows all this. These are the stupidest things to know.

"I'm trying to escape my student loans," she says.

"Are you serious?"

"I want to run away," she says coolly.

"That's okay. That's how you find perspective to fix your problems. What problems do you have?"

"Think I'll tell you?"

"Sure."

"There's a commune starting in the Interior. Looks interesting."

"A cult?"

"Commune."

"What's the difference?"

"A cult has a leader and an ideology and beliefs. A commune is people living somewhere isolated, working for themselves, tending the land, as a community."

"Communes grow into cults."

"No, they don't."

"Didn't you already live in a commune back home?"

"No. I lived in an Amish settlement. I escaped."

"Kelly, I won't support you joining another manmade trap."

"Fuck you, dad."

"You'll get murdered up there."

"So?"

"Shut up, Kelly."

"I really think it's how society should be split up. In self-sufficient decentralized communes."

"It's your Amish prejudices saying that."

She watches thoughtfully the trees. Then she says, "There's so many old-growth forests here that need protection. Protests are happening. There's one coming up."

"You and your commune friends go."

"You're the only friend I know here."

"You're mine too."

"Seriously?"

"I've been here but a week."

There is a parking lot with many cars. There are people tramping with their barrel-like backpacks. In the open grass people play badminton or lay to the sun, drying their aching feet.

I park and we get out with our gear and we walk into an opening in the forest, sided with muddy soil. Among the giant hemlocks are tents and the further we go the darker the path and the cooler and wetter the air.

Two people in matching polos. "Welcome," one says. "Do you have your code?"

We ask what code and they tell us that we need to pre-book our hike for the day. Then we try to book on our phones. We show them the code.

"Do you have proper supplies? Hiking shoes, water, food, mace, whistle, sunscreen?"

We both say yes. I point down to my casual hikers and she observes their tactical nature.

"Are you both hydrated and physically prepared?"

We say we are. On my back is a drawstring pack and Kelly has her hiking backpack, frayed holes and dirt stains. I have two water bottles, boiled eggs, a bag of trail mix, moon cakes. Kelly has foil wrapped peanut butter and jelly sandwiches, a purifying water bottle, and a tiny canister of bear mace dangles off a carbine on her shoulder strap.

"Does someone know you're here today?" she asks us individually.

"Yes," I tell her. It's a lie.

Then we continue on.

There are different trails going to camps and hiking areas. For each forking there is a large board sign with a map. Kelly's finger follows one out of the three peaks up the mountain.

"Then we can go," her finger winds, "to here and then down here."

"Okay."

We continue to the left, following a ravine where the water is flowing rapid and loud. In the end, before the official hike's start, is the waterfall that powers the ravine. Behind the endless fall is a dark cave, the water glides smoothly off and on stone, surging into bubbly mixtures and flowing on.

Ahead of us is a series of strategically made stairs fixed with handrails. They are scattered about the steepest gradient of the trail, a richly forested groove through a mountainside of rock. We lunge in huge steps, stretching the entire backside of our legs. The speed of my heart is shocking. I feel wetly entombed in my heartbeat.

Throughout the less graded sections the soil has been fashioned in wood-framed steps. Massive ferns sprawl chaotically between trees, their lobes spilling out the overhangs, like green flame. Moss beds are glued on trunks and the boulders by the steps. The moss is so soft like petting an animal.

As we go higher the crags on each side widen, we sink in the hot glow of the now sinister sun, and the steps give to the untouched land. We step on rolling mounds of hard soil, boulders, glossy and giant roots. There are serenely fallen trunks, monolithic and decayed, some settling on perennial plants, others caught mid-fall on other trees or stony cliffs. They are thick with mushrooms which a sloppy foot, a resting hand, or misplaced seat can crumble fragile as ash.

We rest under a cliff with underground gaps streaming out what is like fridge-air. I chew a moon cake. We are both breathing hard. Kelly takes a long drink of water. "We stay a few minutes longer and it'll be more difficult to move," she says.

"Okay," I say.

We continue on to a slither of a path running up the crag. Below us is a downgrade falling sharp to an unscalable and high wall of rock. Soon we reach a brown chain pierced throughout the crag. Along it is a floor of boulders wedged tight together. She grabs the banging chain and steps widely in the crevices. Then I grab it and nestle my feet in the sharp corner. There is a fearsome stretch throughout my ribcage. She has hiked to a peak and is taking pictures.

The small town of Squamish is like a pit among the mountains and touching it is the bay. It's like a perfectly collapsed sheet of blue sky. The houses and stores and the layout of the roads are in fine resolution, the mountain trees so visible as to be counted, the granulations in the stone. A rim of planetary mountain along the sky's boundary. The bay spills in from between a hazy and cloud-blocked opening of mountain, an endpoint where the world falls off.

Here the world no longer requires us to redeem it. Redemption is law in this vista of its authentic heart. To look at these mountains is a calming, restorative, graceful stimulation. The religion of beauty, a signature of sacred mystery. Mystery which eludes corruption, which is what makes mystery so vital.

We sit in a dip that has collected reeds from the few tiny pines that poke out the rock-smooth top. Surrounding us are other hikers laying sprawled like ritualists, taking pictures of themselves or other mountains.

Chipmunks scuttle up to us like spiders. A chipmunk dashes sideways like a pinball until nearing my hand. It snatches an almond. It spins the almond as its incisors chip off the skin. The cheeks swell enormously. Kelly takes a picture and says the chipmunk is cute. I tell her the chipmunk is a rat bastard.

Ravens circle and disperse, circle and disperse. They are tremendous dark-purple and dog-sized and unreal creatures, black beaks and claws and eyes, and auguries of death or fortune. One lands and views its rest spot with biblical magnitude. It flaps its wings to lift its massive frame and becomes aerial in a way, slow and heavy, as if the air around it is of firm substance.

Kelly stands and pulls out her loose shorts scrunched in her crotch. Her legs are not tan and not pale, a hue like wheat. Thick but not from fat and bone. She walks, ponytailed head down and hands in pocket. Blond helical hair-threads tied back, which makes her look like a barbarian, her round trapezius muscles, this sun-golden and lionized young woman. She takes pictures, a landscape portrait and selfie. She points the camera at me. I'm sitting with my head turned to her, over my bad shoulder, not smiling, no expression but breathing and staring. She walks back.

"Ready?"

"I don't want to."

"Come on. Remember what I said."

"I forgot everything."

"The longer you wait, the harder it'll be."

"Kelly. How did you get so strong?"

"I live for this."

She lifts up her backpack and straddles it. "Yuck," she says, squirming her shoulders against the pads. She drops it and unzips a pocket and wrestles out a towel. She covers her back and straddles it again.

I stand. She laughs and points. "What?"

"What?"

I look down to it.

"What's that?"

I run my hand along its sizeable circumference.

"People are going to think you're the moon if you stand like that."

"It's from the moon cakes."

She takes pictures as I pose against the town and mountains, like a pregnant woman, hugging the stomach bloat.

"We're definitely not going to the second peak," she says and then continues on.

She gambols down a slope of bulgy rock, pebbles, boulders, random dried trees. The best word to describe it is *gambol*. A playful, dextrous movement. Also more suitable because it sounds like *gamble*. Daring steps, lunges, jumps, inviting injury and maybe death if misplaced. Yet she executes all gracefully, skillfully, esteeming herself with the beautiful danger of the mountain.

Along a lip of overhang there is another chain. Her feet pinch on the overhang, she goes down pulling on the chain, her torso bent. It is hot in my palms. I pull it tight and stay close to the wall. Then we step down a metal ladder where at the bottom is a tall cleft. There is only blackness inside, too slim to go through.

Then we zig-zag down a dusty slope that cuts into the forested side. My knees and ankles pound against the soil and stone, my sweat-soaked shirt clapping on me. I settle my back on a tree to release some of the weight on my legs. All around has become frozen. I do not know many of the names of what is around me, the trees and plants and even the mountains. I have meagre knowledge of the fauna or funga. It would satisfy me to know and in time I will grow my knowing. It will never be complete but processual.

Then I continue down and see the clear water of a stream rolling on the rocks and splitting to draw out two wavy tails around a boulder. It spills out a shelf of jagged ground. There are dark logs lodged in the stream. Bright pebbles in its floor.

Kelly is sitting on a log. Her backpack rests against the log. Her Merrell high-tops are off. I sit by her and pull my shoes off and peel off the socks and she pinches her nose. I tuck the socks under the log. I soak my feet, her's are pure white in the water, my toes are crinkled and they sense the water with psychedelic intensity.

I take my feet out and wriggle my toes back in my shoes. I stuff the damp socks in my pocket. She rolls her tall socks back on, laces her boots. We continue down to wood-framed steps. Now I notice how massively spaced the steps are. I twist my ankle and we rest a short time and people pass us and some ask if I am okay and Kelly tells them I am. Then we go on but she accommodates her speed to me. Soon my ankle heals spectacularly. The stairs appear. After the last step we are finally walking. It is cool under the crowded pines. The mental images of the hike are exact and fierce. I feel the sting of sunburn on the back of my neck, the forehead, the forearms.

Later from the car we take out fresh clothes and go into the washrooms to change. As we are walking back to the car in our dry clothes, new socks, our old ones heavy in an Ikea bag, she tells me she wants to drive. She syncs her phone and she drives into the town.

We buy coffee and two large oatmeal cookies. I regret not getting my coffee iced. A regret like a gravitational torsion-point cranking a futile counter-clockwise.

7

I HAD A SIMPLE, PRIMITIVE, equilibrium before traveling. The equilibrium is a balance between desires, desiring, and expectations.

My desires before were like a small and trickless cuboid of which I could feel fully each dimension. The same desires are now more of a cuboid cut and coloured to be like the six-by-six Rubik's, a much specialized construction than the three-by-three so easily solved by beginner algorithms.

My desiring has grown thicker, more heart-pounding, and flooded with varied streams. Like a river. The main body is water but the branching rivulets contain enough compounds to be qualitatively different than water. They clash into the river, with each other, mixing their chemicals to create new ones, purge or form toxins.

The desiring is so strong and novel in its direction that it makes me feel at a loss of my self. As if that self is swallowed in the power of the river, fighting to breathe in the currents carrying it.

But *loss* is not accurate. I have gained and the gaining has replaced. The replacement feels like loss. But the original is still here, working and being worked on. The original was sheltered, is a shelter, a home to go back to, the origin which set the standard.

I remind myself that the rooting of what is internal for the fundamental of the self is a virginial rooting. Confrontation is necessary to break the already fragile defence of inexperience. I have to tell myself these things. They are not habit of mind. And because of that, I suffer them.

My expectations are adapting to new desires, the power of my desiring. There is a natural calculus refiguring itself with every desire captured, won and lost and pursued. Its mechanics are implicit. I don't need to know them for them to work on me.

I can tell someone, as people like to do, that *I have no expectations. I am going with the flow.* But it's false. It's not a lie but it's false. Inside of me is the prefiguration of the world and sometimes it overlaps neatly on the actual world and other times it does not. What is so neutral, so flow-going, is my judgement to its fit.

My equilibrium was at a bottom, the balancing very simple. Like a tight-rope act on a thick beginner's rope two feet above a leisurely river. Gradually, the height increased and the rope narrowed with the increments. Now I feel that my equilibrium is a few dozen feet above a surging river. It is rising as I walk across it trying to solve a Rubik's cube. A new layer is added to the cube with each dozen feet increment. The river surges harder too. The rope is threading down until it is so thin and expert, I'm so high up, my former fallen twin-self struggling for breath in the murderous river, the cube like the psych-ward dilemmas of schizophrenics modelled in a puzzle, and I fall.

Then I feel powerlessness, the tactile hole of it.

"Okay," I say. "Let's do it."

The bartender. She is a big woman, brown and lusty, and she looks good with her weight. Talking to her is like talking to a friend you forgot you have.

"Two tequila shots," says Kelly.

"I got lots of brands," she says condescendingly and temptingly.

"The cheapest one," I say.

Kelly's head turns to me and back to her. "The cheapest," she says.

"Uh uh." Kelly is dancing in her stool. "Uh uh. I need to dance."

"I've never danced."

She says she has attended dance classes since the age of six.

"Even in concerts I bob my head," I say.

"I'd force you to dance."

"I can't even force myself to do it when drunk."

The clear tequila comes. We clink and the tequila disappears.

"I liked that," she says.

"Last time I had tequila I don't want to tell you about it."

"Wasted?"

"Yeah, it's not a good story."

"Later if you want to tell me you can."

"Okay, later."

The bartender sweeps her good big hand on the counter to collect the glasses. "Any food or more drinks?"

"Just drinks please," says friendly Kelly.

"Another tequila or what?"

"Can I get a pornstar?"

"Okay, honey. And you?"

"Sleeve of the sour."

"She called me honey," Kelly tells me.

"Isn't she great?"

"She called me honey."

Past the aisle of the bar is a space of empty tables. They are wooden tops floating in the darkness. Throughout the sides of the bar are dark windowed walls. The cars and people passing. There is a woman looking in the window, shifting her weight to each foot. Her face is dark under her hood.

"I have to go," I say.

"Go," she says.

"Is she looking at her reflection?"

"She's looking at us."

"There's something about her that gets me going."

"Then go."

"I'll leave your ass here."

"Go. I wouldn't blame you."

The drinks come.

A black man behind the dispensable machine has been sitting by himself and talking to the bartender. He has a medium-cut afro. He looks to me like a saxophone player. Then another big woman enters and they hug and talk. This woman does not look good with her weight as our bartender does. The man motions for that bartender and orders the woman a drink. The woman thanks him. They are good to watch and I want to talk to them.

The outdoors woman looks on in the glass window, smoking a cigarette. Kelly waves at her and she does not react.

"It's my mother," I say.

"I don't believe you."

"I have to go."

"Uh uh." And she is dancing.

"You're embarrassing me in front of my mother."

More people in the bar and they are of equal substance to me. Our bartender calls Kelly honey again and Kelly squeals. "No one has ever called me honey."

"He doesn't call you honey?"

"No, he doesn't," says Kelly.

"There's a lot of other guys in this bar tonight, honey."

"There's a woman out there that's been standing, looking at us the entire time."

"Her? She is nothing. Do you want to sit somewhere else?"

"No, we're not bothered. We think it's his mother."

"Is your mother looking for you?"

"Yes, she is."

"Do you want me to bring her in?"

"Call the cops."

Our bartender eyes the woman. She waves and the woman does not react. "I'm sorry about your mother," she tells me. "She is gone."

"You know what," the friendly and good bartender says. "She is freaking me out."

"Please don't do anything," says Kelly. "We don't want to ruin her night."

"For you, honey, I won't. But she is freaking me out."

I worry I will say something that will embarrass myself to our good bartender and so I stay quiet. She is so present in the small aisle going to each person and interacting. She is a beautiful woman heavy with love. In her youth she may have been slimmer but not more attractive. For her attraction is not of skin or form, even though its suited to her, but the constituents of her person which gives essence to the skin and form. To describe her physically is to alienate her from herself. Her greatest gift to others is presence, her gift to herself is ourselves she reveals.

"Anything planned for tonight?" asks our buxom and inalienable bartender.

"We're traveling here so we're open to whatever happens," says Kelly.

"Where are you from?"

"Ontario."

"Oh, not another Ontario," she says. "So many of you visit here."

We both refuse the receipt.

"Can you call me honey one more time?" asks Kelly.

"Yes. Honey," she says. "Have a fun night, honey. Honey is my trademark. When you work like this you need a trademark and the clients remember and love you for it. Bye bye, honey."

After we leave Kelly asks, "Did you notice she said, *client*?"

"Of course, I noticed."

Outside we stand where the smoking woman was and view into the window. We can see a trace of our reflection, the bar totally visible.

We walk in the street with the young people. The street is crowded with them.

"I'm so happy," I tell Kelly.

"Why?"

"I don't know."

"Well, I must be too."

"Oh. You're just stupid."

"No. I'm happy tonight."

"I know all about happiness. You're not happy."

Then Kelly says, "I think we're drunk."

"One time I walked this street by myself on a Friday night. I walked the entire strip and then back and went home."

"Umpfh."

"Yeah. I'm feeling it now."

"Which one?"

I look at the small-time clubs, the lines of people.

"I don't know."

"I need to fucking dance."

"Calm down."

"No. Fuck you. I need to dance. Uh uh."

"You embarrass me."

We walk the packed and fun-sized street for a short time, looking at the small-time eateries.

"What are you in the mood for?"

"I don't know," I tell her. "This isn't a place for food."

"It's for drinking and clubbing," she explains.

"It's for something."

Then we cross the ill-timed street where people are squatting in the sides. A medieval time-warp of morbid myth, forlorn knights and beggar kings.

"This is so sad," says Kelly.

A man dressed for the coldest winter is lying on the ground.

"It's meth," I tell her. "He's okay."

"There's tinfoil by his hand," she tells me. "It's heroin."

"Really?"

"Yeah. They put a smidge on it and light it under and smoke the fumes."

A crowd is stuffed under the overhang of a complex of abandoned storefronts, time-displaced and dirty. It looks like they are sharing a filthy and tattered tarp which is wrapped around so as to hide them. We turn right into a zone with orange pylons blocking off the pavement and we walk in the road. We go into a scaffolded sidewalk with lamps fixed to the plywood-decked ceiling. When we get out a man asks for two-hundred dollars.

"Sorry, I have no cash," I say.

"Sorry," says Kelly.

The man is unconcerned. He says, "I'm trynna buy a phone."

"Sorry."

We cross the street and he watches us. Beyond in the opaque and cobbled streets the lights are greasy. Security guards stand outside closed offices.

"What are you thinking?" I ask.

"I'm up for anything," she says.

"I know what you're thinking," I say.

"It was really, really good."

"I think it was good because we were drunk."

"Maybe."

"Whatever. We're drunk again, anyway."

We sit and the waiter comes with a jar of water and glasses. He switches on a plastic candle.

"Hola again. I remember you," he says.

"The food is so good we had to come back," says Kelly.

"All right amigos, do you know what we're having?"

"Give us some time," I say.

Then, "What's mole?" I ask her.

"No idea. Try it."

The waiter comes back.

"Can I get the chimichangas," says Kelly.

"Absolutely. Which meat?"

"No meat," she says happily.

I wait for the waiter to write in his notepad.

"I'll get the beef enchiladas and can I pay half for one extra enchiladas?"

"You cannot, sir."

"Okay, I'll get two sets of two beef enchiladas. Can I do that?" I ask in happiness.

"Yes, you can but you will be charged for the meal twice. There is no discount."

"Okay, I'll get two beef enchiladas," I say. "They're very good."

Soon the enchiladas come and we eat slowly.

• • • •

THE COFFEE TASTES LIKE the brewed soul of an oak tree and the cream fills my stomach as much as a meal would and the caffeine hits both in energy and mood. I enjoy that all things sensory are enlarged with that maligned pleasure called *hangover*.

Outside I wait for a long time and I regret not walking. But I can't walk one hour swinging a bag of food. I am very hungry.

The driver lowers the window and I say, "Yes, for me." I sit down next to him with the food hot in my lap.

"How are you friend?" he asks. He is an Asian man with Burberry glasses and a fresh fade haircut that smells fresh.

"I'm great today. How about you?"

"Wow, that smells delicious. I'm hungry."

"My favourite."

He drives out and says, "Please make sure no oil spills on the seat."

"I'm concerned about it too."

"Oh, my goodness." An elderly man is at a crosswalk. "My goodness," says the driver. The old man clutches a rolling cart. The driver mouths, *go*. Another car stops on the other side and the man pulls on his cart.

"I know him," the driver says. "He likes walking with nothing in his cart. He buys nothing. Very cheap man."

We drive on and then I ask the driver about the nude beach near the university.

"Yeah. Once. I don't go nude."

"I'm just curious."

"I guess it's a place to see. You don't have to go nude. I only visited once for curiosity too. With my friends. We don't go nude. But we're not going there now?"

"Oh, no," I say. "I was just asking."

"Good. When you do go, don't bring food."

"Certainly."

"And be prepared. Getting there is a leg workout."

"Takes a long time?"

"No," he says shaking his newly done head. "There's so many fucking steps."

We enter a noisy suburb of stucco homes glowing in the post-noon, white specked in the floating summer fluff, ice cream and pizza trucks, with a long-going shoreline facing it.

He parks.

On the white sand there are hunks of twisted trees which look like sculptures. In the far distance is the blue and glassy Canadian city, the horizon of mountain and few cargo ships which are so big as to seem close enough to grab and break.

There are seagulls in the thick-grained sand and seagulls swirling in flight. Chambered shells and cream-coloured whelks. The water spills widely, glittering, and soaks in the sand.

Before the sand is a patch of grass with a circular pebble-stone bench table where on I mix the blood sauce pork and rice. Bees court the blood sauce cup. A bee skims my ear with a chainsaw buzz.

Walking on the grass are crows and there is one which is bigger than the others. Its chest feathers are ruffled and its head looks cowled. It walks widely as if in parody of other birds.

I spill coconut water in the grass and the bees hover it. I clump the other dish into my rice. It is of pork in a watery peanut sauce. It drips on the table. I defend my ears from the bees. I pick a morsel of rice on a plastic spoon and catapult it far on the grass and the crows soar to it like black things shot from cannons. They peck the dirt even after it is gone.

I lid the cups and stuff them in the bag and slap bees from flying in the bag. I leave and a crow jumps on the tabletop. Its beak stabbing into the stone. A few others copy what it's doing and fly off.

About the Author

Sonny Gast began reading books at nineteen years of age. He started with philosophy; going from the ancients to continental to post-modernism. He was not initially interested in stories, theatre, art or drama. He started to read fiction after realizing the reading of philosophy lacked what he was reading it for. Then he discovered that in him were mountains of interest for the arts. A world-shifting book for him is The Myth of Sisyphus by Albert Camus. He rarely enjoys what he reads.

His favourite writers are Ernest Hemingway, Cormac McCarthy, Gerald Murnane and Bruce Chatwin.

His writing strives for simplicity and personal truth. He does not care to entertain or inspire, but to suggest and ponder.